By The Same Author

Grand Openings Can Be Murder

70% Dark Intentions

Free Chocolate

Pure Chocolate

Fake Chocolate

Story Like a Journalist

There Are Herbs in My Chocolate

AMBER ROYER

OUT OF TEMPER

**GOLDEN TIP
PRESS**

GOLDEN TIP PRESS

A Golden Tip Press paperback original 2021

Copyright © Amber Royer 2021

Cover by Jon Bravo

Distributed in the United States by Ingram, Tennessee

ISBN 978-1-952854-12-5

Ebook ISBN 978-1-952854-13-2

Printed in the United States of America

To my dad, who taught me to look for the best in people. He's been there through the hard times and celebrated the good.

Dad, you are AWESOME!

Knightley, my lop-eared rabbit, hops over and sniffs at my suitcase. He knows I'm going somewhere, I think. He looks up at me, all sad eyes, his white fur stark against the geometric rug.

"Don't look at me like that," I tell him. "I'm only going to be gone for three days. They asked me to lecture about chocolate on board a cruise ship, and to do a couple of demos. Do you really expect me to say no?" I pet him. "Though it is nice of you to worry."

Knightley, obviously, doesn't have anything to say about this. He should be used to me traveling by now. I own a bean to bar chocolate business, and I've taken several trips over the summer to visit the farms where some of the cacao beans used in my chocolate are grown.

"You really think he's worried about you?" my best friend Autumn asks. She's sitting in the little chair in the reading nook next to my closet. She has made a nod to the fact we're going on a cruise by using a tropical print band to pull back her afro, and pairing it with matching tropical print sandals. Her look is still elegant, with a cream blouse and palazzo pants, rather than beachy. "Maybe he's just afraid your aunt won't remember he is supposed to get treats."

"Knightley is probably reading anxiety," I say. "It's been a long time since I've been on a boat." Autumn knows I feel ambivalent about going. My late husband had been a marine engineer. He'd died in an accident aboard a boat that he'd designed. The thought of going sailing – something I'd always loved – had soured in me after that. I've pulled myself up out of my overwhelming grief, even started to come to terms with life going on without him. But going out on the ocean feels like a whole new set of challenges.

"You need this." Autumn's phone dings, and she takes it out of her pocket. "Our Uber is here."

"Tell them we will be down in a second." Though it is going to take more than a second. My suite is on the fourth floor of the partially renovated hotel my aunt is in the process of flipping. I zip my suitcase closed, pushing Knightley back to avoid zipping his nose. I right the suitcase, then I fidget with the handle. I haven't been entirely honest with Autumn. "I have to tell you something."

She studies my face. Her voice sounds skeptical when she says, "What?"

"This isn't just a girl's trip." I take a deep breath, and everything comes out in a babbling rush. "Logan's coming. He's part of the business now, and I couldn't exactly tell him no, not when the cruise line was willing to cough up an extra cabin and–"

"Hey," Autumn says, to get me to stop talking. After a beat she says, "So what you're telling me is that you didn't invite me on this last-minute trip because you wanted me to see the Caribbean, but because you wanted someone there to make sure things don't get too crazy between you and Logan? Because if that's what you need, I'm there for you."

"No," I insist. "It's not like that. I just – I don't know where things stand with Logan. He kissed me that one time, and then we never talked about it again. We work together now. And we're becoming friends."

"Then maybe you should bring it up," Autumn says. "Obviously, you want to know how he feels. But he may feel just as awkward as you do, and if you both are afraid, the whole trip could drown in a sea of awkward."

Anxiety ripples through my chest at the mere thought of doing that. I poke Autumn's arm. "Why are you always trying to make me do the difficult stuff?"

"Because I care." She bends down and scratches Knightley between the ears. Then she opens the door out into the hall. "Come on. Before our Uber leaves us."

"Right." I turn back to the lop. "Bye little bun. Don't eat the baseboard while I'm gone."

I leave Knightley sitting on the rug in the living room of my suite. Naomi will take good care of him while I'm gone.

Autumn has already made her way down the hall and pushed the button for the elevator. That was one of the first things Aunt Naomi had had repaired when she had taken over the hotel. Otherwise, I never would have taken the suite up on the fourth floor.

There's still a ton of work to do on this place. It's coming along faster since I had enlisted one of my friends to help. Tiff is in the elevator coming up, while we're trying to get on to go down. She's a real estate agent by trade, and usually dresses like she might be showing a house at any minute, with her relaxed black hair perfectly coiffed and her makeup tastefully done. Today, her face is bare of makeup, and she's wearing sneakers. She's got a measuring tape in one hand, and her tablet in the other.

"Ordering supplies?" I ask.

The elevator doors stay open. It's not like the hotel is open to guests, so no one is calling for it. Aunt Naomi is a house flipper – I guess technically now, she's a hotel flipper. And now Tiff has taken charge of dealing with contractors taking care of tasks beyond the scope of Naomi's skills. Things like getting the wiring up to code.

"I'm thinking custom flooring for the larger suites," Tiff says. "I need to grab some measurements and see if it works with the budget."

"I wish I could stay and help."

Tiff laughs. "No you don't. Not when you're going on a cruise."

I exchange a look with Autumn. I haven't told anyone but her that I'm hesitant about going on the boat, not even Tiff, who is a good friend. I feel stupid, because from the outside it must seem like an ideal little getaway. "It's a work thing," I insist. "I'm going to be up to my elbows in chocolate."

"Like that's a bad thing?" Tiff gestures with her measuring tape. She sighs. "Ken and I took a cruise for our first anniversary. I got a different spa treatment every afternoon. You need to get a hot stone massage."

"Those are the best," Autumn says. She extends a hand with perfectly manicured inch long nails. "I need to get a manicure myself. But you should go for the aromatherapy and hot stones. Soooo relaxing."

I can't see any flaws with Autumn's nails that need manicuring. I could never keep long nails like that with the job I do. But a massage . . . that I could go for.

"If I can find the time," I say. This cruise really is mainly about work. But a massage might be what I need to stave off the anxiety about the boat. I was a physical therapist before I quit to become a chocolate maker. I, of all people, ought to know about the benefits of movement and massage in stressful situations. The mind and the body are connected in complicated ways. "I want to say goodbye to my aunt on our way out. Have you seen Naomi this morning?"

Tiff says, "She popped out for a bit."

"Where'd she go?" I ask.

"I don't know. Just out." Tiff turns to Autumn. "Are you excited to be going on a brand-new cruise line? I've heard only good things. Even if this is only their third sailing."

Well, that was weird – and a little rude. Which is not like Tiff at all.

Autumn doesn't seem to notice. "That means everything on the boat will be brand new too. I–"

Something dings, and the elevator doors unexpectedly start to close. I wave goodbye to Tiff, and then Autumn and I are heading for the ground floor. When we get to the bottom, there's a woman with a toolbox waiting to board. Must be the electrician. I give her a curt nod.

She studies my face for a moment, though there's nothing remarkable about my brown eyes, pale lightly-freckled skin and long brown hair. After a second, she snaps her fingers and says, "Hey, it's the Cajun chocolate maker. Solve any more murders lately?"

I smile politely and pause to make conversation. Autumn gestures that she is going out to the Uber, to make sure the driver doesn't leave us.

I have become somewhat recognizable, after solving two murders, both of which had happened at my shop, which is located on Galveston Island's Historic Strand, not far from the cruise terminal. But I'd rather be known for my chocolate than as a murder magnet, as I had been dubbed by a local blogger. I tell the woman, "I'm done with mysteries. I'm actually headed out on a cruise, to talk about how I make my chocolate."

She laughs – then tries to manage a straight face. "Wait you're serious."

I laugh too – nervously. "Why wouldn't I be?"

She flips back her long hair. "Because there's only one cruise leaving today. My boyfriend's on it – because he's a puzzle junkie." She slows down, like I must not be getting her point. I'm not. What does liking puzzles have to do with cruising? She says, "Because it's a murder mystery cruise."

I blink, a hint of unease rising in me. "What? Liam didn't say anything about that."

But it makes sense now why he was so excited to book me for this particular trip.

"Well, your first problem was listening to a guy named Liam."

I laugh, and this time it's genuine. "Thanks for the heads up."

Only – now I have to go tell Autumn exactly what I've gotten us into. And hope she still wants to go. Because Autumn used to be a mystery writer. Who quit writing. Under mysterious circumstances.

Maybe I just won't tell her until we get there. Because I'm not sure I could handle a stateroom all to myself.

It doesn't take long to get to the cruise terminal, but by the time we arrive, Autumn is already picking up on my nervousness. "What is up with you?" she asks. "Logan isn't even here yet."

"He got here hours ago," I tell her as we get out of the car. "We're supplying our chocolate to one of the on-board boutiques, and we also need supplies for the demos. Logan's taken charge of transporting everything over from the shop."

The ship looks enormous, and there's a festive air to the terminal, with people laughing as they prepare to start vacationing.

Autumn and I trundle our luggage across the pavement. Autumn says, "I haven't been on a cruise in almost a decade. I'm planning to make the most of this one."

"Same," I say. "About the enjoying it part. I'm not going to focus on the past."

We make our way into the building and get in line. We wind up standing behind a couple wearing matching deerstalker hats. Farther up in line, there's a girl in a flapper dress, with elbow-length white gloves and a long strand of pearls. And there are at least five people in this line wearing fedoras.

Autumn turns me toward her, makes me look her in the eyes. She has a round face, the shape emphasized by the band containing her hair. "Tell me what's going on."

"I just found out, right before we left," I babble. "This is a mystery themed cruise. Please. Don't just leave me here."

Autumn looks at the line, which is moving at a reasonable pace. To my relief, she says, "It will be fine. Chances are no one will even recognize me."

"Autumn?" a voice says from behind us.

I recognize that voice, turn towards the guy who owns it.

"Felicity?" he says. "What are you doing here?"

I take in Arlo, my first ex-boyfriend – from back when we'd both been in high school. He's a cop now – only rather than his usual tailored dark suit, which he fills out admirably well, he's wearing a rumpled trench coat and tweed suit, with a hideously out of date beige tie. And he's holding a plastic cigar. I ask, "What are you doing here? Dressed like that?"

"I'm a speaker," he says. "They wanted me to talk about being a real cop."

"And the getup?" Autumn prompts.

"It's for the welcome party. It's full costume, and you know how cruise ships work. It can take hours before your luggage gets to the cabin. So I decided it would be easier to come fully dressed. The idea is to attend the party as your favorite fictional detective."

"You're Columbo," I say. "I should have guessed."

"It's actually nice seeing you here," Arlo says. He smiles at me, and I feel a little zing. Arlo's Cuban, but without a trace of accent. He has intense dark eyes and expressive lips – and he is newly single, since he arrested someone connected to his former girlfriend. "I'd thought I wouldn't know anyone."

"I don't think that's going to be a problem," Autumn says. She waves at someone who has just come in the door. It's her fiancé Drake. As in the guy she'd gotten engaged to after knowing him for like a month.

I am not a spontaneous person, and I've had trouble dealing with change after the loss of my late husband, so I've had trouble accepting the instant engagement. I know a lot of it is me, that I've found myself avoiding Drake because of it. And here I'm about to be in a situation where I can't do that.

Drake's mom comes in after him. Her hair is cut short and curled under, showing off her chunky green hoop earrings. She's wearing a gold blouse and a green and purple floral scarf, slung back over the shoulders. She waves back at Autumn and shouts across the gathering crowd, "Somebody cancelled, and we got tickets after all!"

I arch an eyebrow at Autumn, no longer feeling guilty about not initially telling her that Logan was going to be here. "You weren't going to tell me you invited them?"

She shrugs. "You keep saying you want to spend some time getting to know my beau."

I had said that. It only makes sense, since I'm Autumn's matron of honor, for a wedding that's going to creep up on my calendar far before I'm ready for it. I want her to be happy, but I'm still not sure how to feel about a guy who behaves that impulsively.

At least Drake is cute and always neatly dressed. Even on a cruise he looks put-together, in a soft tee-shirt and jeans, and some high-end basketball shoes. He's clean shaven, with a recent fade haircut and flawless black skin. All points in his favor – unlike Arlo, who usually dresses neat, but currently resembles a rumpled umbrella.

Someone who had been ahead of us in line notices us and starts threading his way back through the people towards us, saying, "Excuse me, excuse me, I'm sorry."

It's Ash Diaz – a local Galveston blogger, and a major pain in my backside. Ash seems to think of me as one of his pet story subjects, and he's had a lot to say about both of the murder cases I'd found myself a part of. He has square glasses and a skinny tie, light skin and dark hair. Ash wheels his ergonomic suitcase up to me and asks, "Koerber, what are you doing here?"

I sigh. "Let me guess. You're also a speaker?" It's starting to feel like Liam has a sick sense of humor, inviting me onto this boat alongside this particular group of people. Ash is a shoddy reporter. I hope he's not going to be leading any panels on ethics or anything.

"Actually," he says, "I'm helping with the on-board mystery LARP. They invited my local group to run it."

I blink at Ash. "You LARP?"

I can't picture it. How could someone so obnoxiously arrogant be into live action roleplaying? Didn't that require team cooperation and stuff?

Ash grins, looking more at ease than I've ever seen him. "You've never bothered to even look at my 'About' page, have you?"

It had never even occurred to me to try to learn more about Ash. Why would I? I never asked to have him in my life, and I would love to get rid of him. But I smile and say, "I'll check it out once I get to my cabin."

Since this cruise is sailing out of Galveston, there will probably be other locals on board. I'm so busy worrying who else might show up that I forget to be anxious about going back onto a ship.

Chapter Two

Autumn and I are sitting at a table with plates of appetizers and cups of rum punch by the time Logan finally catches up to us. He's ditched his usual pilot's jacket and tee combo for a red Hawaiian shirt with pineapples and gold flamingos on it – and shorts.

I snuff back a laugh. It's more startling than funny. I never thought I'd see him wearing shorts. He looks good in them – just different. We changed for the party, so now Autumn is wearing a sparkly dress with a long strand of pearls. Which makes Logan's clothes look doubly casual.

"Nice shirt," Autumn says, gesturing at Logan with her cup.

"Thanks," he says. Logan's green eyes sparkle with good humor. There's a smile on his generous lips that softens his usual demeanor, despite his perfect posture and strong jaw. "It's nice to be on vacation for once."

"We're still here to work," I remind them, even though we're currently in the middle of a party. The atrium is several levels tall, ringed by the balconies of some of the staterooms, and decorated with palm trees and tropical greenery – which I'm almost sure is all fake.

The tables are scattered throughout the space, and more people are standing in random areas, having conversation with strangers, seeming to sort themselves by costume choices. Not everyone here has dressed for the event – but most have.

A guy wearing a white jacket and a bow tie leads the way over to our table, flanked by a girl in a deerstalker hat with pigtail braids peeking out from the flaps and a guy wearing an old-fashioned suit and an obviously fake curly-edged mustache.

Bow Tie Guy gestures at the three of us. "You have to take pictures with us." Then he points at Logan. "Especially you."

Logan looks taken aback. "Me? Why?"

"Because you're supposed to be Magnum P.I., right? I need you to complete my costume."

Logan blinks. "What?"

Autumn says, "It's a costume party. Arlo is here somewhere, dressed as Columbo. This guy is supposed to be one of Humphrey Bogart's characters–"

"Actually," Bow Tie Guy interrupts, "I'm Rick, from Magnum. He was the bar owner – and he went through a Bogart phase. Which is why I need Magnum to complete my photos. I'll be sticking with you for the whole party."

Which is just a little too meta, right? I giggle nervously. "How long is this party?"

The girl points to Autumn, "So obviously you're Miss Fisher."

Autumn hadn't intended to dress in character, but she still looks pleased. "It's the vintage jewelry, right? I do give off a 1920s vibe."

Then the girl points to me. "But I'm not sure who you are."

I start to say I didn't come in costume, but before I can the fake-mustached Hercule Poirot says, "I have deduced it with my little gray cells. Unassuming blouse and plain black pants. Hair pulled up, so it looks short without having to cut it. You, my dear, must be Jessica Fletcher."

My mouth slides open, but no words come out. Logan gets to be Tom Selleck, and Autumn is a scandalous hot-head from the roaring twenties – but I'm everyone's favorite spinster aunt? With fashion sense stuck in the 1980s?

"Come on," Logan holds out a hand to help me up. "It's obvious these guys aren't going to be happy unless we take a picture."

Logan isn't much into TV or books. Does he even know who Jessica Fletcher *is*?

"But I didn't wander out of Murder She Wrote," I insist. "I'm not dressed as anybody."

Logan looks sympathetic. "I guess you don't have to–"

But Autumn is already pulling me up, even though she's the one who'd said she wanted to keep a low profile, lest anyone recognize her.

I pose, and several other partygoers come over to add their own costumes to our group – and then I spot Liam Bosch, the guy I had skyped with to get this gig in the first place. He's wearing a slate gray dress shirt and a black skinny tie. He's a white guy in his late twenties, with carefully styled sandy-blond hair.

I wave at him, and he waves back. He doesn't look embarrassed or anything. I make my way over to him.

"Hey," I say. "You could have told me this whole thing had a murder mystery angle to it."

"Yeah," he says, "but if I did that, you probably wouldn't have come. Ash said you're a bit shy about playing up your notoriety. But you're a real-life amateur sleuth. That makes you one of the biggest draws on board this boat."

"You know Ash?" I should be mad. But I'm not even really surprised anymore. Even though Ash had pretended to be surprised to see me. Ash is probably hoping I'll do something on board this boat that will be embarrassing enough for him to write about me again. He hasn't had much to say since I'd managed to solve a second murder and then stay out of the news for almost a month, and Logan had settled into the rhythm of working at my shop.

"Ash is my cousin," Liam says. "On the Puerto Rican side of the family."

"Bosch is Dutch, isn't it?" I ask.

He looks surprised. "How did you know that?"

I gesture out the window, towards the port we haven't yet left. "There's a Dutch influence in Southeast Texas. There's even a town called Nederland. I've been to their Heritage Festival a couple of times."

"I did not know that," Liam says crisply. "I've never been to Texas before."

Which makes it interesting that Ash and his blog are fixtures on the Gulf Coast. Why didn't Liam ever come visit his cousin?

I ask Liam, "And yet, you signed on with a cruise line sailing out of Galveston?"

Liam nods vigorously. "I'm getting in on the ground floor with a new venture. This is our third sailing, and we've been fully booked every time. If Sunset Cruises takes off, we'll start sailing out of other ports. I could wind up organizing events for an entire fleet of ships."

Autumn comes up to me and says, "Felicity, we should go." She puts a hand on my arm to pull me away from Liam, but then her body language stiffens. "Too late."

I follow her gaze. There's a guy walking this way. He's got salt and pepper hair topped with a cowboy hat, and his clothes remind me of something the Crocodile Hunter might have worn. I assume he's in costume. But something about the arrogance of his posture makes me second-guess that assumption. That, and that his face looks like tanned leather.

He grins at Autumn, and I'm afraid his leathery cheeks might crack. "Autumn Ellis, as I live and breathe."

"Flint." The sharpness in her voice is unmistakable. As is the frown on her face. Autumn pretty much likes everybody, so this tense edge to her puts me on edge.

"I'm surprised to see you here," Flint says. "Given that you'd decided mystery writing was a waste of time. I take it you've started writing again? Planning to make a comeback? You know how hard that can be, after this many years?"

"I'm here to support a friend, who is demoing her business," Autumn says, gesturing at me.

"What kind of business?" Flint asks.

Before I can answer, Autumn crosses her arms over her chest and says, "She does craft chocolate. Probably the best I've ever eaten. And her shop's pastry chef does baked goods."

Flint sneers. "I never cared for chocolate. Or sweets in general, really."

Autumn says, "Try Felicity's dark chocolate. It will change your mind."

This is probably the weirdest fight I've ever witnessed. But I'm smiling. Does Autumn really think my chocolate is that good?

Flint looks at me and says, "Why?"

I say, "Dark chocolate has flavor compounds similar to coffee and wine. Different beans can have a wide variety of flavor notes, from berry to leather." I try not to look at his cheeks when I say that. "And you can have a bar that is eighty percent cacao beans – or higher – so it's not sweet at all."

Flint looks curious. But he says, "If you like that sort of thing."

"Even if I didn't like chocolate, I'd still be here for my friend," Autumn says. "But you wouldn't know anything about having friends, would you?"

Flint's grin fades. "I have friends. Not everyone sided with my wife after the divorce."

Autumn looks surprised. "You and Clove broke up?" She points across the room to where a woman with bright red hair is sitting next to Ash, gesturing with a champagne flute as she tells a story. Ash is taking notes. Autumn doesn't look angry anymore. She says, "I'm so sorry."

Something happens to Flint's face, like the leather has pinched in and taken on a shade of fire. His hands balls into fists. "If you would excuse me."

Flint stalks over to Ash's table. He says loudly, "Take those ridiculous glasses off and stand up."

Autumn pulls me towards the table. "We have to do something, Felicity."

Okay. What does she think we're going to do?

Ash looks up at Flint. "Why do you think I'm going to do that?"

"Because I really don't want to hit a guy with glasses."

Ash rolls his eyes. "You really are living in the stone age, Flint. You can't fight people at events anymore. Remember the code of conduct you had to sign?"

I hadn't been sent anything like that, probably because I'm here with the cruise line, and not whatever mystery conference programming they're both part of.

"You think anyone is going to blame me for punching the guy who broke up my marriage?" Flint shrugs. "If they decide to kick me off programming, it will still be worth it."

Ash stands up, holding out a hand. "All I did was tell the truth. Let's just talk–"

Flint punches him. Ash stumbles backwards, bringing a hand up to his jaw. "That really hurt."

"Good. I'm glad." Flint shakes out his hand. He's probably bruised his knuckles. "You're so quick to tell everybody else's secrets, you think nobody's figured out yours?"

Flint turns on his heel and walks away.

Clove looks wide-eyed up at Ash, who is using the back of his hand to blot his busted lip. Clove asks, "What is he talking about?"

Ash makes a face, but it obviously aggravates his injuries and he winces then takes on a more neutral expression. "No idea. I don't believe in secrets. I'm pretty much an open book."

The girl dressed as Sherlock Holmes with pigtails comes over to Ash. "You okay, sweetie?"

She leans in close to look at his lip.

"Yeah, I'm fine." Ash looks embarrassed. He pats at her back. "Don't make a big deal out of it."

"If you're sure you're okay." She takes a step back.

Clove takes the girl's hand, showing off a ring on her finger. "I finally get to meet the girl who stole Ash's heart. Congratulations."

I feel my eyebrows knitting together. Ash is engaged? Seriously? It feels like everyone I know are about to get married. Even Ash, who is arrogant and unethical enough to repel any potential love interest.

Whereas, I'm a relatively recent widow, still trying to reconcile myself to the idea that I might want love again. Confused emotion sparkles through my chest, a mixture of everything from jealous to hopeful. I look around for Logan, but he seems to have left the room. He must have missed the whole fight.

Arlo, on the other hand, is headed this way. He's got the Columbo raincoat thrown over his arm – and he looks so much better without it. He makes eye contact with me, and for a second it is intense. I keep having these spark moments with him. Which up to this point have felt inappropriate, because he was very taken. Now that he's not – it's just terrifying.

But then he keeps going, and Bow Tie Guy and Fake Poirot move aside to let him approach the scene. Arlo asks Ash, "Are you going to want to make a complaint? We haven't left port, so I'm still within my jurisdiction."

"No," Ash says. "But thanks. I don't want to wind up delaying the cruise."

"Are you sure?" Arlo asks. "Logan just told me he witnessed an assault."

Ash nods. "I've already caused Flint enough trouble for one lifetime. I wrote about him on my blog. I may have insinuated that he killed his wife – only to have her show up like three weeks later – alive."

"Just like Agatha Christie," Arlo says. I'm confused as to what he's talking about, and I quirk an eyebrow at him. Did she have a book where that had happened? I've read most of the well-known Christie novels, and I don't remember anything like that.

But everyone turns to look at Clove – the woman who had done a real-life disappearing act. She drains her glass. "Long story."

"But he said you broke up his marriage," I say. "How does that even make sense, if Clove left before you wrote the article?"

I'm looking at Ash, but Clove responds, "That's an even longer story."

Ash says, "I was digging into Flint's past, and I presented a few facts on my blog that Mrs. Bates didn't know. So when she got home, she confronted Flint."

Autumn says, "Why do I get the feeling that you've known Clove for a while?"

Clove and Ash look at each other and start laughing. Ash says, "Mrs. Bates is my mom's best friend. She babysat me when I was a kid."

I wonder where Logan went off to. It must have been important, for him to miss the fallout of the assault he reported. But I wish he was here to share an incredulous look about Ash having actually been a kid.

A horn sounds, and there's motion, and the boat is leaving the dock. There goes Arlo's jurisdiction.

There's steady gentle rocking as the ship makes its way through the water. I suck in a breath. I'd kind of forgotten I was even on a boat.

Autumn drapes an arm around my shoulders. "You okay?"

"Don't I look okay?" I ask.

But Autumn's known me longer than just about anybody. She turns the draped arm into a hug. "It's okay to think about Kevin. It doesn't mean you're stuck in the past."

I drop my voice to a whisper. "It's more about physically being on a boat. I'm a little sacred."

I look up to catch Arlo looking at me. I think he heard what I just said. I feel heat filling my cheeks. I turn to Autumn. "I think I'm going to go to the room for a little bit."

I go out into the hall. It's a narrow space, and I can definitely feel the boat moving. It's subtle, since this ship is huge. Nothing like the sailboats I used to go on with Kevin. I draw in a deep breath. This is a totally different experience. A chance to really move on.

"Felicity."

I turn to find Arlo standing in the hall, his hands clasped in front of him.

I feel sudden moisture in my eyes, though I'm not entirely sure why. "Yeah?"

"I just – are you not okay?" His warm brown eyes are so full of worry. "These past couple of months. You seem to have things together, and I was so busy with Patsy. I should have thought more about how hard it might be trying to cope."

I put a hand on his arm. His very built arm. "I'm doing a lot better. It's just – Kevin's accident was on a boat. A boat he loved. That he designed."

Arlo says, "You remember that catamaran we went out on that time I fell overboard?"

I snort out a laugh. "And you were wearing those white pants, so when you got back on deck, I could see that you had flying saucers on your boxers."

He blushes. "Forget that part. Think about how much fun we had, after you managed to rescue me, all on your own. You love the ocean. And you love sailing – even if your asthma sometimes got in the way, you'd sit down and recover and then try to help out with the sails. I hate to think you've lost that about yourself."

I can't speak for a few moments, I'm so overcome with memory and youth and hope and loss. Finally, I manage to speak. "I'm trying," I tell him. "I'm here, aren't I?"

He nods. "You're being brave. Let me know if I can help."

And there's that zing of a spark again between us, our eye contact locked and heartbeats racing. Which is confusing, because I think I'm into Logan. I've already asked Logan to be my plus one to Autumn's wedding. Logan and I had shared that brief kiss. Now that he's part owner of the shop, Logan shows up at Greetings and Felicitations a lot now.

And yet, I'm looking at Arlo, and I can't catch my breath. Only not in an asthma symptoms kind of way. I force myself to break eye contact and look down at the floor.

I tell Arlo, "Let me know if I can help *you.* You should get back together with Patsy. Because it still feels like you two belong together."

His generous mouth pinches into a straight line. "That's not likely. She has a lot of family drama going on right now. Her parents have threatened to disown her if she marries the guy who arrested one of their own."

"And you're not interested in a relationship that isn't heading towards marriage. You've always been that kind of guy." Arlo had given me a promise ring, back when we'd been in high school. He'd been a bit unfocused about most of his life at the time – and had gotten into a bit of trouble – but it had been very clear that he'd wanted a family. Which is why the fact that he's never been married puzzles me. What exactly had happened to him in those intervening years?

Arlo shifts his weight, and I see his shoes change positions. "I'm willing to give a relationship time to grow. But I'm not interested in being with someone who is always going to put her family's happiness ahead of mine. I need a partner who's all in."

"Felicity," Logan turns the corner into the hallway. He nods at Arlo, but barely registers that I was in the middle of a conversation. "They need you in the ballroom. There are some questions about the setup for your demos."

I nod, feeling embarrassed, though I haven't done anything wrong. I make eye contact with both guys. "Sure. Okay." As I walk past him, I tell Arlo, "I still think Patsy's the one."

Logan quirks an eyebrow at me as I follow him over to the bank of elevators.

Instead of telling him something about Arlo that's frankly none of his business, I ask Logan, "Where did you disappear off to?"

Logan gestures up. "I followed Flint. I wanted to see where he went after punching a guy in the face." That behavior might seem odd in anyone else, but Logan used to be private security. He can get a little obsessive when something seems suspicious to him. "Flint went out on deck. I'm pretty sure I saw him throw something off of the boat. And then he went to the top of the ship and found himself a deck chair by the pool. He's still sitting there, as far as I know, typing furiously into his phone. I couldn't see who he was texting."

"I hope he knows about data rates on cruise ships," I quip, remembering that I wanted to look up more info on Ash before we leave local waters – and local phone rates. I may not get the chance.

Chapter Three

When we get to the ballroom, Liam is there with a guy and a girl in matching waitstaff uniforms. All three of them are unfurling white tablecloths onto round tables. This room doesn't have any windows. Instead, the walls are segmented by elaborate golden molding, with each segment framing beautiful rococo style-paneling featuring pale 3-D flowers and delicate golden birds.

Liam sees me standing in the middle of the room and makes a *wait there* gesture. He finishes straightening the cloth on the table he's been working on. Then he walks over and says, "We're trying to figure out if you need a heating element for tomorrow's demo. This one is where you're showing how to make a basic truffle, right? And chocolate coated nuts?"

"It's a bit more than that. I want to show them how to balance flavors–" I hesitate, because I hear a dog barking.

The ballroom door opens, and a beagle wearing a yellow vest comes running in, then stops not far from where we're standing and sits, looking expectantly backwards. A woman who's probably in her mid-forties follows him in. She's petite, heavily freckled, her brown hair cut into a bob. She's wearing a purple tee-shirt that says *Must Love Dogs*, paired with sneakers with purple accents.

"I see you've met Satchmo," she says.

"Yeah. He's adorable," Logan says. "Is he some kind of service dog?"

"Retired police dog," the woman says. "But he's in training to become a therapy dog, for a program for women suffering from PTSD. He was a cadaver dog, so being in positive situations is healing for him too."

"I've heard of that kind of thing being used with soldiers," Logan says. "But PTSD can affect a lot of people. Sounds like you're working with a promising program."

The woman grins. "I like to think so."

I bet Logan is thinking of a friend of ours, who has been having a hard time dealing with the emotional fallout of having been threatened by the first killer I'd caught. Miles is finally starting to do better. Maybe getting him to take care of Clive the octopus was a more helpful idea than I'd realized.

"You're not supposed to pet a police dog, right?" I ask. Though, I don't know if it's the same for therapy dogs.

"You can when he's off duty. It's always polite to ask first, though." She makes a hand gesture, and Satchmo, released from his sitting position, trots over to me.

I lean down and scratch his neck, and he leans in against my leg with a happy sigh. I can't help but laugh. "I was a little anxious about being on a boat again, but this cutie is helping already."

"Bea is here to do a presentation on police dogs," Liam says. "You know the mystery crowd. Half of them are writers, wanting to know how to write things accurately. And she's been training police dogs for twenty years. Which makes her a bit of a rock star here."

"If you're dealing with anxiety," Bea says, waving away Liam's compliment, "maybe you should partner with us for the LARP. It would be good practice for Satchmo."

"I wasn't planning to participate," I say.

"Nonsense," Liam insists. "Cruises are really about marketing. If you want to sell out of all that chocolate we stocked for you in the boutique, you want to be visible at all the big events. We're going to do a little Snack and Chat at the end, where we'll introduce all our guests of honor."

"I'm a guest of honor?" I ask.

Liam nods. "Ash wrote your bio. He's writing one for Autumn, too. I'm going to try and talk her into taking Flint's place on our programming panels."

I can just bet how well that's going to go over. Autumn is going to tear that bio into pieces. Still, I force a smile. I had realized this cruise was going to be work. But I hadn't realized how much of it was going to become mandatory. "A Snack and Chat sounds great."

"I already put Logan, Arlo and Autumn on your team card," Liam says. "I suppose you can have five."

"If Autumn is participating in the LARP, she's probably going to want to work with her fiancé and future mom-in-law," I tell him. My limbs feel heavy under the weight of all the upcoming awkwardness. Though the thought of spending the next few hours with both Logan and Arlo together makes me cringe, it would be rude to ask to transfer to Team Drake with Autumn.

Liam, however, looks intrigued. "Oh? We have another happy couple on board? I'll also have to ask her about doing our newlywed game."

I can't help a startled laugh. "You really don't know Autumn."

The door opens again, and Ash is standing there, a little out of breath. "Hey," he says. "Have any of you seen my phone? I've been running all over the ship looking for it."

Logan winces.

"What?" Ash asks, looking troubled.

Logan looks at me. "You know how I said I saw Flint throw something overboard?"

"Yeah," I say slowly.

Logan turns to Ash. "Well, when you think about it, it could have been a phone. Was it green?"

"The case was, yes." Ash's face goes white. I feel a pang of sympathy for him. The thought of Ash without a phone – that has to hurt him a lot worse than his rapidly bruising face.

He looks to Liam. I'd never imagined I'd see such a lost look in Ash's light brown eyes.

Liam puts a hand on Ash's arm. "We'll get you a new phone at one of the boutiques, once we're out in international waters. In the meantime, I can get you a password for the ship's Wi-Fi."

Ash nods, looking miserable. "Flint's going to have to pay for this."

"It's not like you should be using your phone while we're out at sea anyway," Logan tells him. "Don't you know what kind of data rates you'd be racking up."

Ash shakes his head. "This is my first time on a cruise ship."

When Logan tells him the rates, he looks like he's going to faint. After that, Liam is in a hurry to square things away with us so he can help his cousin.

Once we get my demos sorted, and Bea sorts out a few details about Satchmo's travel arrangements, Liam hands up a packet of information on the LARP, and Bea drags us into one of the lounges to make a plan. Apparently, we're supposed to have some kind of team costume. I sigh. This is so not my thing.

Logan takes out his phone and calls Arlo to join us. Apparently, this *is* Arlo's kind of thing. Which makes the whole planning experience worse.

We wind up cutting out ridiculously oversized Sherriff stars out of gold construction paper and pinning them to our shirts with corsage pins. It's about as much of a costume as Logan is willing to go for. And even then, he grumbles and heads for the bar to get us all drinks.

I was right about Autumn. She and Drake immediately partner up for the event and come to join us in the lounge, just as Logan returns with our drinks. Mine's just water, and I take it gratefully, taking a long sip.

Logan asks Drake, "Where's the rest of your team?"

Drake says, "My mom is somewhere on the deck outside, dolphin watching. She's promised to come in in time for the LARP, and Autumn is getting us a fourth as we speak, so we'll have a rounded team."

Autumn sends a text and then shuts off her phone. "Annnd . . . done. No more data charges for me."

Arlo asks Drake, "Have you ever done a game like this before?"

Drake shakes his head. "I'm a big fan of word puzzles, but truly, the whole LARP scene–" He looks around and drops his voice. "It strikes me as a little dorky." He gestures towards Arlo's costume tie. "No offense."

"None taken." Arlo says. "We all have our comfort zones."

Logan snorts out a laugh. I'm not sure what that was about. Probably something that happened when I wasn't there, since Logan and Arlo have become friends and started hanging out, after sharing a near death experience.

Arlo gives Logan a sharp look and continues, "This is my first LARP too. I solve crimes for a living, so it's not like I usually spend my off time hunting for clues for fake ones."

"Yeah," Drake gestures at Arlo with the half-full wine glass he's brought in with him. "How is it fair to have three real cops – and someone like Felicity – all on one team?"

Technically, Arlo's an ex-cop, which means Arlo and Bea are the *real* cops, but no one quibbles.

Besides, I find myself grinning. I know there's not a word for someone who's accidentally gotten involved with solving two murders, but who isn't actually a detective, but it sounds awkward, the way he's not lumping me in with Arlo and Logan and Bea – but not separating me from them either.

Logan says, "Don't forget the dog's a cop too."

Then Arlo says, "I guess it will be embarrassing if we don't win this thing."

Bea says, "Maybe we should mix up the teams. One of us could go with your team, Drake."

"Sorry," Autumn says, "But we already have our fourth. I ran into my friend Rachelle at the party, after you all left. Her husband already got seasick, while we were still in view of the dock. She's taking care of him, then she's going to meet us when the LARP starts."

I know Autumn has other friends, outside our shared friend's group. And since Autumn is the one who never moved away from Galveston, it's not surprising one of those friends would show up here. There's no reason for the tiny spark of jealousy in me, that my best friend is close to someone I've never even met. I quash it – I've been blessed to have so many kind people in my own life that I shouldn't complain. Or begrudge my friend the same.

Bea asks Autumn, "Why are they wanting you to take Flint's place on these events? Are you an expert or a super fan?"

Autumn scrunches up her nose. "I used to be a writer. And I tried to tell Liam I'm not interested. Panels are not exactly something I feel comfortable doing. He's a difficult person to say no to. But I did it."

"I feel a little bad for Flint," Drake says. He threads his fingers through Autumn's. "Autumn told me that since he's no longer part of the entertainment, Flint won't get his stipend, and he's going to have to pay for everything."

Autumn doesn't draw her hand away, but her body language stiffens at Drake's words. "But honey bear–" Her calling Drake honey bear has to be the most un-Autumn-like thing I've ever heard Autumn say. It is a bit disconcerting. "Flint knew the consequences of what he was doing. He's not a nice man."

Liam comes by to collect his crafting supplies. Which obviously came from the Kiddie Corner area of the ship. Not that I've seen any kids on this particular cruise.

He hands all of us who have agreed to be speakers a small paper ticket. "These are for the mystery-theme raffle. All of our special guests get a free entry. The big prize is a signed copy of *Murder on the Orient Express*. Liam turns to Autumn, waves a

ticket at her. Then he pulls out a couple of extras, offering
Autumn four tickets like some kind of special bribe. "There's still
time to get you on that programming list. I know our guests
would love to hear what you have to say."

I expect Autumn to tell him to go throw his bribe tickets
overboard, but instead she looks at Drake – who gives her an
encouraging shrug-nod, like he's saying it's her decision but he
thinks it would be cool – then over at me. Then she turns back to
Liam and takes the tickets. "Fine. But only because my fiancé
loves antique books."

"Awesome!" Liam picks up the basket of craft supplies.
"Enjoy dinner, and I'll have your schedule sent to your room by
the time the LARP starts." He turns to me. "Your two teams are
my two favorite teams to win this thing. Which do you think it
will be? The cops and trained investigators?" Then he turns back
to Autumn. "Or the mystery writer, the rare books expert, the
physics professor and the archeologist?"

Liam leaves us all looking at each other, as he walks
away with the basket full of safety scissors and crayons and
construction paper. Over his shoulder, he glances back and says,
"Did I mention that part of the prize for solving the crime in the
LARP is fifty tickets for the raffle?"

"Why don't I trust that guy?" Logan asks.

"Good instincts," I tell him. "He intentionally omitted the
fact that this was a theme cruise when he offered us this gig."

Arlo makes a tutting noise. "Just because the guy is trying
to line up the best entertainment for his guests doesn't make him
untrustworthy. I've seen a lot worse than him over the years."
Arlo shudders and I wonder what, in fact he has seen. There were
a lot of years between when he'd left Galveston and when he'd
walked back into my life.

Logan says, "I know Autumn's the writer, and Drake,
you're the books guy."

Drake grins. "My mamma is a geophysicist, recently
retired from field work and teaching in Galveston. It was a bit of a

disappointment to her that I preferred books and basketball – like my dad – to numbers and staring at dirt."

Which means Autumn's friend Rachelle must be the archeologist.

Autumn says, "I think it is fair to warn you that my boo has a competitive streak."

I glance at Logan and Arlo. I say, "I'm pretty sure my whole team has a competitive streak."

Bea says, "You bet your boots I'm competitive."

Given the looks on all three of their faces, this whole thing just got a lot more interesting.

Chapter Four

I'm still thinking about Arlo's missing years hours later, when we all assemble in the ballroom to get our team instructions. What am I missing that would help me understand the guy? And why does that suddenly seem so important?

The teams have assigned places at round tables that seat eight, with two teams to a table. We're sharing a table with the two guys who had been at the party as Rick and Poirot – only they're now wearing tee-shirts that resemble the outfits worn by Shaggy and Fred from Scooby Doo. There are two girls with them, in Daphne and Velma tees.

Logan gestures at Fred's – Formerly Rick's – shirt. "What happened to needing me for pictures, Craig?" Interesting. Logan had gotten Bow Tie Guy's real name. He does really pay attention to details. "I've still got on the Hawaiian shirt."

Craig says, "We're part of the LARP group hosting this event. We can't ask everyone else to do team costumes, without leading by example. You can't get more classic than Scooby."

"Don't be modest," the girl wearing the Daphne shirt says. She looks directly at Logan and bats her lashes. I sigh. Yes, we all know Logan is hot. She tells him, "Craig is the president of the LARP league. He and Ash basically organized this event."

"That we did," Craig says. "But I didn't want to make unilateral decisions. I couldn't get my team to commit to the Magnum PI look, so here we are. But we can totally do Magnum again all day tomorrow if you want."

Logan cringes back a little. "Actually, I'm probably going to be busy tomorrow."

Daphne says, "I've never seen Magnum PI."

Arlo says, "You're missing out. The classic detective shows have a lot of heart."

She scrunches up her nose. "I'm more into anime. Have you ever seen Detective Conan?"

"Detective who?" Arlo asks.

This whole generation gap thing is just embarrassing. And we aren't even that old.

I look for Autumn and spot her and Drake just coming in, with Drake's mom following a bit behind talking to Rachelle. I recognize Rachelle. She's an older black lady who comes into my shop a lot in the mornings, for a plain black coffee and whatever Carmen has baked. Carmen always calls her Dr. Watters, so I'd assumed she was either a medical doctor or a professor, and I never thought to ask her first name. More than once, I've watched her do the crosswords in pen.

I think Autumn's team had just a good a shot of winning this as we do.

Autumn's team have on matching blue tee-shirts for their costume, with *Galveston* stenciled across the fronts, above images of cartoon sharks. Where had they gotten those? The shops on the ship haven't opened yet. And it's not the kind of shirt a group of people actually from Galveston would wear.

Ash's fiancé Imogen takes the stage, looking flustered. She's still dressed like Sherlock Holmes. Liam follows her up there, studying something on his phone as he walks. The stage has been decorated with props to make it look like an office, with poster board cutouts on the walls to give the impression of a window and a jail cell, along with images from various mysteries.

Imogen asks, "Where is Ash?" before she realizes the microphone is already on.

Liam shrugs and covers the microphone with his hand before answering. I still get the gist: Ash is late, and Liam is going to cover for him.

Pasting a fake-looking smile on her face, Imogen scans the audience, then says into the mic, "Acclaimed investigators of the world, we need your help. Somewhere on this ship, a jewel thief has hidden the Egg of Zeld, a diamond the size of a man's fist. To win the reward, you must be the first team to uncover the identity of the thief and recover the diamond and bring it here, to this satellite office of Scotland Yard."

"That's right," Liam says, reading stiffly off his phone. "The thief is somewhere among you – or among the staff in the boutiques and shops on board. You should speak with everyone, including other teams – and make sure to get the clues from each shop. And if that means taking a break for a little shopping – there will be special discounts for LARPers that won't be lower at any other time during the cruise."

Imogen adds, "Use the form on your table to collect clues and make your guess as to the thief's identity. If you get stamps from all the shops, even if you aren't the first team back, you will still get a collector's mug commemorating the experience, and one of these lovely question-mark shaped keychains." She holds up a purple keychain. "They're made of material that changes color in the sun. Each team can approach myself, the great detective, Sherlock Holmes, and Chief Inspector Liam twice to ask for help during the game. Have fun, but be safe. There won't be any clues in hard-to-reach places, and there is no need to run." She raises her hand in the air. "The game shall now commence!" She drops her hand with a swish, and the room erupts into conversation as the different teams reach for forms and start planning a strategy.

Bea suggests, "I say we head down the promenade and start with the shops. We can each take a store, collect the clues and have a better idea what to ask the other teams."

"Good idea," Logan says. "We definitely need to get a head start on Drake's team."

"Why?" I ask. I knew Logan was competitive, but this seems excessive.

"We may have made a little wager. If he and Autumn win, I have to scrape the barnacles off his houseboat. Since he found out I dive, he thought that would be hilarious."

"Drake has a houseboat?" I ask.

At the same time, Arlo asks, "So what does he have to do if you win."

"Change the oil in one of my planes." Logan pinches his lips together. "I'm not sure if I should really let him, though. Does he seem mechanically inclined to you?"

Arlo shrugs, "Drake said he's good at sports, but that's not the same thing."

Bea says, "I see now why you're so keen to win. Your life may literally depend on it."

At the sound of her voice, Satchmo raises his head, which had been resting on my shoe. The beagle has really taken a shine to me since Bea gave me permission to give the dog a few bites of my filet mignon.

Imogen hands out walkie talkies and tells each team how to set them to a unique channel, so that if we decide to split up, we can still keep in touch across the ship. Since we'll be more or less together, I drop mine into the bag I'm carrying.

As she takes a walkie talkie, Bea asks Imogen, "How did you get interested in LARPing?"

Imogen says, "One of my close friends was starting a group. I've always loved games and puzzles, so it just seemed natural." Imogen lays a reassuring hand on Bea's forearm. "You'll have fun tonight, I promise. We tried to make it interesting, even if you're not super into games."

Bea says, "That's sweet, but I intend to win."

Without need of a leash, Satchmo walks at my side as we head up to the promenade where the shops are located. I can still feel the boat moving, but the rocking is gentle. If I don't think about it, maybe I can forget the anxiety.

The spa and the gym are at the promenade's far end, so everyone has to walk past the enticingly decorated shop windows to get there. Despite my team's urgency to solve the game's jewelry heist, I can't help but being drawn towards the displays, especially one featuring opal jewelry. I adore opals – so much that my dad bought me an opal pendant necklace when I was thirteen. I still have it. And this shop has a seashell pendant with a large opal set in the center of it.

I look down at Satchmo. "Let's go talk to them. Where better to ask about a jewel heist than a jewelry store? Am I right?" And if I happen to buy something – Liam did say the price would never be lower.

Satchmo isn't paying attention to me, though. He's focused on something right at the edge of the shop's doorway. Which is fuzzy. And moving.

At first I think it's a rat, and I flinch back, bringing a hand to my mouth with a soft squeak – but then the fuzzball lets out a plaintive meow, and I realize it is a skinny, scrawny kitten. Which must have somehow snuck on board.

Satchmo barks and the kitten makes a run for it down the promenade.

Satchmo gives chase. His tail is wagging like he thinks it is a game.

"Wait! Stop!" I take off after the dog, though running isn't my thing, even though the treatments I took worked, and I haven't had an asthma attack in over a month – and that one was in extreme circumstances. I'm still not a strong runner, or fast, but all my fellow detectives have gone into shops farther up the promenade, and they obviously aren't coming to help. I completely forget about the walkie talkie buried in my bag. I should have had it out in my hand once I lost track of the others, but I can't hesitate to look for it now. Satchmo's a nice dog, but he still has dog instincts. I need to make sure he doesn't hurt that kitten.

The two disappear from view on the other side of a pillar that has been plastered with an electronic map of the ship. I try to run faster. When I catch up, it looks like Satchmo has the kitten pinned.

"Drop it, Satchmo!" I command.

But then Satchmo looks at me with a pained expression, and I realize it's the kitten that's clinging to Satchmo's leg. The beagle makes a point of licking the kitten's face with wet slobber, as though to emphasize to me how wrong I was in impugning his character.

He really had been chasing the kitten because to him it was a game. And now it looks like he isn't sure whether he won or lost.

"I'm sorry I doubted you." I get the kitten detached from the dog – it seems more than happy to cling to my shirt instead, wiping the dog slobber onto my shoulder as it tries to chew on my paper sheriff star. Which is gross and adorable at the same time.

We've made it all the way down to the open area outside the spa and the gym. In the center of the space, there's a giant ice sculpture, of a setting sun with sheets of tinted ice forming the "sky" behind it and a whale leaping up out of glistening ice waves. It's the cruise line logo, done seven feet tall, still breathtakingly beautiful even if the sun's rays are dripping a little water off their points.

Satchmo wants to explore the sculpture, but this time when I tell him no, he sits down. Good. Apparently, he can remember his training, as long as there are no running kittens involved.

I examine the ice whale more closely. Whoever sculpted it paid extra attention to the eyes and mouth, giving the creature an expression that seems softer than ice should allow, making the whale seem perfectly content and at peace. I know this image is a corporate logo. But at the same time – there's something about those curling waves, about the bulk of the whale itself, that captures the power of the ocean. And for me, the ocean is both love and loss, some of my best memories, one of life's crushing blows. And yet, the ice whale seems to be saying that acknowledging that s okay. That I can be here, on this boat, and maybe find a sense of closure and a little peace. Except for the pinpricks of kitten claws digging into my shoulder. The kitten starts squirming, but I can't let it go. It can't just wander around the ship, without getting hurt. And it needs food, soon.

I need to figure out who to give the kitten to, so that I can get back to my friends, and to this game they are so intent on winning. I don't want to be the one to let everyone down— especially not since I've been paired with a group of real-life detectives. There's part of me that wants to prove I have just as logical of a mind as they do. All that we'd figured out before I lost track of the group is that the game's jewel thief probably wasn't anyone who works in the kitchen or as a lifeguard. The game hasn't been going on for that long, so I'm not sure whether we are behind or ahead of the other teams.

"Hey, little one," I tell the kitten. "Settle down, okay. I need to wear this shirt again."

Some guy comes out of the boutique attached to the spa, pushing the door so hard it hits the point where it stays propped open. Satchmo suddenly goes from sitting there, tongue lolling, watching the kitten climbing my shoulder, to on his feet, alert, ears at attention. He lets out several short barks then takes off for the open doorway.

I follow, using both hands to keep the kitten from jumping off.

"Satchmo!" I shout as the dog disappears behind one of the displays. There's no one in the boutique to help me catch him. Bea is not going to be happy with me if I lose track of her dog.

"Hey!" a girl says, coming out from the spa. She's carrying a box of plush whales – the ones featured in the Sunset Cruise logo – obviously to replenish the shelves. "You can't bring a cat in here."

"Yeah, well what about the dog?" I move deeper into the shop, stepping into an alcove to look for the beagle. Instead, I see a familiar bunny outline on the labels of some of the products. This boutique is where the ship has chosen to display my chocolate, on a tiered display. The tallest shelf is just above my eye level, and the boxes are neatly arranged. It looks really nice, actually.

"What dog?" the girl asks.

As if in response, Satchmo barks. Somehow, he's gotten into the tiny space between the tiered chocolate display and the wall. The girl follows me over to it. "You certainly can't bring a dog in here."

I hand the girl the kitten. "Hold this."

She squeaks out a protest but takes the meowing ball of fluff. I lean forward to try and pull Satchmo out of the space where he's wedged himself – only to realize that something else has been shoved in between the display unit and the wall. No, not something else. Someone.

My heart goes cold, and the strength goes out of my arms, which just dangle in front of me, as I stay leaned over, unable to look away. Bea had said that Satchmo had worked for the police as a cadaver dog. The beagle must have alerted to the presence of a body when the boutique door got left open. And not just any body. I'm looking at the crumpled form of Flint Bates. And given the amount of blood on his shirt, and the grimace on his face, it is a good guess that he's been murdered.

I groan. In the past few months, *Greetings and Felicitations* has been the scene of two murders. We're not even near my shop anymore – but somehow Bates wound up behind a display of my chocolate. Out of all the other shops and products on this floating shopping mall. My. Chocolate. "Seriously. Not again."

"What?" The horrified girl backs away, still staring at the bit of Flint's hair that's visible around the display.

I sigh. "There's security on this ship, right? You should probably call them." I dig in my bag for my walkie and hold down the button to talk to my team. "Hey, guys?"

Over his walkie, Arlo asks, "What's up, Lis? Did you find any clues?"

I grimace. "Not for the LARP. But there's a big clue to a real-life crime. I think y'all need to join me here at the spa."

"Is it something serious?" Bea asks.

I just stare at my walkie. I really don't want to have to say out loud that I've found another body. This makes three, after all. After two, I'd been called a murder magnet. Now what will people say?

Finally Logan says, "Either she hung up or . . ."

"You really think she's found another body?" Arlo asks.

"She what?" Bea squeaks.

But it doesn't matter. They'll all be here in a minute, more prepared than I am to deal with this.

Chapter Five

"You didn't touch anything did you?" Arlo asks. He's peering across the room at the display, dispassionately taking in the scene of Flint's death, watching Logan examine the body.

"You think by now you still need to ask me that?" I reply. I have my arms crossed because I feel cold. I'm sure it's just the shock of finding Flint, but I rub my hands against my forearms, trying to warm myself.

Logan says, "He hasn't been dead long. This happened shortly before he was found."

Liam comes into the room, along with Imogen. Sherlock Holmes and someone who is quickly turning into my own personal Moriarty. Liam looks at Logan, who is over near the chocolate display taking video of the body with his phone. "What on earth are you doing?"

"Trying to preserve the evidence before we move the display," Logan says. "We've been in contact with the ship's captain and the Coast Guard. Since we're in international waters, this is FBI jurisdiction. The captain has contacted them. There's a storm coming in, and it's going to be tomorrow at the earliest before anyone else gets here. We can't just leave the guy there."

Liam's face goes white as he asks, "Is it really Flint?"

"I'm afraid so," Logan replies. He starts panning his phone to get a record of the room, from the perspective of someone standing at the display.

Arlo asks, "Who had access to this room, from this morning on?" He has his phone out too, making notes.

Liam says, "The spa staff could have come in here, if they wanted to. They have keys that open the sliding doors between the spa and the boutique."

Wendy – the girl I had handed the kitten to – says, "Sometimes they come in here if they run short of product." She gestures to a wall stocked with high-end shampoo and massage oil and body lotion.

"Who was in here today?" Arlo asks her.

Wendy raises her hand in a *who-knows* gesture. "I was here this morning, when some of the valets helped bring that chocolate in for the special display. They needed my key to let them in. But I locked up, and after that, there shouldn't have been anyone in here, until I came back and opened up at 6:30."

The LARP had started then, so Liam and Imogen would have been heading for the stage at that point.

Arlo asks, "Did anything look disturbed or out of place when you got back?"

"No," Wendy says.

I ask, "Did you have any reason to go look in the alcove?"

Arlo gives me a look. With both of the previous murders I'd been involved in, he'd told me repeatedly to leave the investigating to the professionals. He'd proved his point when I had nearly been killed – both times. This time, I guess he thinks he's doing me enough of a favor to let me stay here while he gets the basic facts of the case, without me trying to ask questions.

Wendy shakes her head. "No. I have no idea how long that guy was lying there. I mean, he could have been alive when I got here. What if I could have helped him? I feel horrible."

Arlo says, "You had no reason to know anything was wrong. Don't take on guilt that isn't yours. Just try to think if there was anything you saw or heard that could help us now. It doesn't matter how small of a detail."

Wendy takes a deep breath, lets it out slowly. "Okay. I was trying to fill in some of the empty-looking stock, so I went into the back like four times while we were open to grab more boxes. I was trying to pay attention to what was going on out here, but obviously I missed something huge."

If Flint was killed shortly before I found him, it had to have happened while Wendy had the boutique open. Which means Flint must have been killed basically right in front of her. It is really hard to believe she was in the back long enough for someone to kill a guy, without her hearing anything. But Wendy looks shaky and in shock, like tapping her could make her collapse. I really doubt she's the killer. Even if circumstances give her the greatest opportunity.

"You're sure you didn't hear anything?" Arlo asks.

Wendy shakes her head. "Not anything suspicious. There were a couple of the LARP teams who came through for the clues and the coupons. I heard and saw them come and go, so no one would have been hanging out here while I was in the back. One of the teams all bought plush whales as souvenirs."

Which explains why she had needed to restock them. Everything she's said so far seems logical – except that it makes it impossible for the murder to have happened.

"Other than you and the staff of the spa, who had keys to this store?" Arlo asks.

"I'm the manager, so me, and Nigel, who covers some of the shifts. I don't think anyone else." Her voice sounds a lot stronger now, since she's had to recover herself enough to talk. Now, she taps a finger to her chin, thinking. "Probably security?"

Arlo turns to Liam. "What about you?"

Liam says, "I only have keys to the cruise line gift shop, because my office is in there. I'm in charge of events and guest satisfaction. If you need a party, I'm your guy. But I have surprisingly few keys."

Arlo turns back to Wendy. "Is it possible that someone could have stayed in here all day, from the time the new display was stocked this morning?"

"I don't think so," Wendy says. "At least, all the valets who came in with Mr. Hanlon left before I locked the door,"

Logan nods. "We all left together. I walked with them as far as the elevator."

Liam is still near the doorway, and most everyone is looking at Wendy. Quietly, Liam takes out his phone and tries calling someone. Whoever it is doesn't pick up.

"Who are you trying to reach?" I ask.

Liam jerks the phone away from his ear. Though really – if he'd wanted privacy all he had to do was leave the room. Sometimes people don't think straight when they're in shock. "Nobody," Liam says, earning him skeptical looks from all the cops and ex-cops in the room.

Arlo steps over to Liam. "Spill it."

Liam sighs. "I still can't get ahold of Ash. I'm afraid something might have happened to him too."

Arlo shakes his head and gives Liam an intense look. "What you mean is you're afraid Ash might have done something, since nobody seems to be able to account for his whereabouts during the murder."

"How would you know exactly when that was?" Liam asks.

Logan says, "The body's temperature. Flint has to have been killed within the last half hour."

"I'm sorry I asked." Liam looks even paler.

Imogen says, "Ash wouldn't hurt anybody. I'm worried he's in trouble too. We need to find him."

That gives me a light feeling of déjà vu. It hadn't been that long ago when one of my shop employees, Mateo, had gone missing, and I'd been convinced of the need to find him.

"Somebody already checked his room?" I ask.

"Yep," Imogen and Liam say at the same time. Imogen adds, "He's not in there. I popped the lock to check."

"If I didn't know better, I'd say Sherlock Holmes is the jewel thief," I quip.

Imogen's face goes pink. "How did you figure it out so fast?"

"I was right?" I ask, startled.

"Apparently," Logan says. He sounds pleased as he moves over to put a hand on my shoulder. Which is the closest he's gotten to me since our kiss. A little thrill of excitement bubbles through me as Logan squeezes my shoulder before letting go. "Though we still haven't found the missing jewel."

"I bet it's in her hat," Arlo says, laughing.

"Really?" Imogen looks at Liam and raises both hands in an *I-can't-right-now* gesture. Then she takes off the hat, removes a giant plastic jewel and hands it to Arlo. "Do you know how long we spent planning this?"

"Long enough to actually learn lock picking?" Bea guesses.

"True," Imogen says. "But it doesn't matter, because somebody died for real and my fiancé is missing. I'm not about to do the re-enactment of the crime skit now, am I?" She looks like the reality of that is just now hitting her. This isn't a game. Flint isn't just going to get back up and dust himself off.

I look down at Satchmo, who is leaning against my leg again, hoping that maybe more meat will fall from the sky since he's done his job and now the humans are taking over. And he wants attention, since the kitten is gone. The guy who runs the check-in desk at the spa took it to find it some food and maybe a bath. The way he was cradling the little ball of fluff, I think the tiny stowaway is in good hands.

Satchmo makes a hopeful noise. He deserves a treat, but I don't have one. What I do have is an idea. I gesture towards Imogen's backpack, which looks like the kind that holds a laptop – plus everything you need for a day away from home. I ask, "You don't happen to have anything in there that belongs to Ash, do you?"

She nods. "I have his sweater. You know how he's always getting cold in those large auditoriums."

I did not know that, but I'm not going to point out how little I pay attention to Ash, unless he is writing about me.

"Satchmo here used to be a–" I don't want to say cadaver dog. Imogen looks freaked out enough already. "A search and rescue dog. Since we have Ash's sweater, maybe he can smell it and then try to do his thing."

"Good idea," Bea says. She reaches into her pocket and gives Satchmo a treat that looks like dehydrated bacon. I swear the beagle gives me a look that means, *See? That's how you do this.*

While Imogen is pulling the sweater out of the backpack, I ask Liam, "What happens now? To everything you had planned? Are we still doing lectures and demos and raffles?"

Liam purses his lips, then says, "According to the captain, we are likely to still be at sea for several days, while the authorities conduct their investigation. We'll want to keep people as calm as possible, especially since we will not be making landfall for shore excursions. As I understand it right now, we'll still be doing the classes and events, as scheduled."

Which means I'm still doing a demo in the morning, and Autumn is still going to be on the mystery author programming – despite the fact that the guy she's replacing died a violent death. At least Autumn has a solid alibi. If Flint died some time after the LARP started, she'd been with all of us in the ballroom, and then since then with her team.

"Can we get back to finding my missing fiancé?" Imogen hands me Ash's sweater. It's thin, high-quality wool, in a plum color so deep it is almost black.

I'm not sure exactly what I'm doing, but Bea gestures at me encouragingly. "Tell him to seek."

I lean down and let Satchmo get a good sniff of the sweater. "Seek." Then feeling silly, I add, "Please."

Satchmo's tail wags and his nose hits the floor, and he starts sniffing. Then he heads through the opening between the boutique and the spa, confidently making his way up to the reception desk and then down the hallway leading towards the changing areas. The whole area smells of lavender and eucalyptus, but that doesn't seem to bother his sensitive nose. This is meant to be a calming space, with light gray walls and heavy glass vases filled with peony-heavy flower arrangements and minimalist sofas and water coolers with cucumber slices floating inside. But that doesn't stop the anxiety rising in me. After all, why would Ash be here, instead of at the event he helped plan?

Bea, Logan and I follow Satchmo, leaving Arlo to finish securing the crime scene. He insists that Imogen stay behind. I'm not sure if he's worried about her helping Ash, or if he's afraid something might have happened to the blogger after all.

In the men's side of the changing area, there are a number of individual changing cubicles, with floor to ceiling doors. Satchmo makes his way over to one of them. The door is closed, and everything is quiet and still. The room feels *too* silent, and I feel tension telegraphing off both Logan and Bea.

My heart drops. The dog is telling us that Ash is on the other side of that door. Could there have been two murders here tonight? As much as Ash and I hadn't gotten along, the thought of him dead is horrifying.

The beagle whines and scratches on the door. There's an immediate banging from inside.

"Hey!" It's definitely Ash's voice, though muffled. Relief floods through me. He shouts, "Is somebody out there? Help! The door's jammed!"

It doesn't take Logan long to get the door open, and Ash is so grateful to get out, he hugs Logan, who makes a grumbling noise and then pushes Ash away.

Logan asks, "What were you doing in there?"

Ash says, "I got a message saying I'd won a free manicure and shoulder massage, but I had to get down here right away. When I got here, nobody knew what I was talking about, but the guy at the desk said that they could fit me in before they closed and he'd sort it with management later. Only, once I came in to change, I heard somebody do something to the door. I

screamed to be let out, but this space must have been
soundproofed. I've been in here for hours."

It seems odd that the staff wouldn't have come looking
for him. Maybe they had, and by that point, he'd given up
shouting. After all, someone had decided he must have left.

Logan looks at me. "He could be telling the truth. Or it's
possible he could have jammed that lock himself, from the inside."

Ash blinks at us from behind his glasses. "Hey. Why does
it sound like I'm the one who's in trouble? I got locked in a
glorified locker. What am I missing here?"

"A lot," Logan says. Turning to me, he adds, "Don't tell
Ash anything. Let Arlo question him before he gets his story
straight."

"My story about what?" Ash looks genuinely confused.
Logan turns and starts walking back towards the front of the spa.
Ash repeats, louder this time, "My story about what?"

Giving Ash an apologetic smile, I turn to follow Logan.
Bea and Satchmo follow me.

And Ash follows the rest of us.

When we get to the reception desk, the guy in charge of it
is back. He now has on a name tag reading *Renato*. He's got the
kitten in a wire cage behind the desk, with a bowl of water,
another bowl of something that looks suspiciously like lobster,
and a stuffed whale for company.

Logan leans on the desk and nods back towards Ash. He
asks, "Do you remember this guy?"

Renato nods. "Of course. He's the guest who didn't have
an appointment. I sent him back anyway, but Paola said he never
showed up. She gave up waiting and went to go eat dinner. I
thought it was odd, but I glanced into all our main spaces and
didn't see him, so I assumed he changed his mind and left."

Well that's no help. I ask, "There aren't any cameras in
this area, are there?"

Renato looks offended. "I should say not! We respect the
privacy of our guests."

That makes sense. Even if it is disappointing that there's no way to confirm Ash's story.

Logan asks, "Was the spa open before the LARP started? I know the shops were closed until we reached international waters."

Renato says, "We were open, but my shift was split because of the extra late-night hours, so I asked the therapists to keep an eye on reception. They would have come up here if someone rang the bell."

"But they probably wouldn't have noticed someone walking quietly by?" I ask.

Renato replies. "Probably not. I'm sorry. I wish I could be more help."

Logan asks, "Was this door closed or open?" He gestures to the open area connecting the spa and the boutique. There's a sliding door recessed into the wall. Each space also has its own front door.

Renato says, "The door between the spa and the boutique is always kept locked if no one is on the boutique side to staff it. Only a few of us have keys to open it."

Ash says nervously, "Isn't anyone going to tell me what this is about?"

Arlo sees Ash through the opening and tells Logan, "Take him out to that bench past the ice sculpture. Don't let him talk to Imogen until I've gotten to question her."

For this not being Arlo's jurisdiction, he sure is taking charge.

Chapter Six

Liam is standing alone inside the boutique, and he doesn't look happy. Not that he looked happy before, but now his body language has gotten defensive, with his shoulders up near his ears, and the dismay on his face is unmistakable.

Arlo is out in the hallway now, talking to Imogen, and Wendy is sitting on a bench by the wall not far away from them, staring off into space. Logan takes Ash over to wait his turn to be questioned, then stations himself to keep anyone else from coming this far.

I ask Liam, "What happened to you?"

Liam says, "We just got done talking with security. Apparently, somebody forgot to turn the camera system on to record. This is our third voyage, and we've recorded nothing, since day one."

I wince. "That's a big oversight."

But it isn't likely something that we can chalk up to this particular killer's actions. Because how would anyone outside of ship security even have had access during both of the previous voyages?

"Tell me about it," Liam says. "Security isn't even my department, but the captain is acting like it is my fault. I could get fired."

"I'm sure that's not true," I tell him. "He's probably just frustrated and taking it out on whoever happens to be in front of him."

"Maybe," Liam says. But his shoulders don't leave the vicinity of his ears.

This feels like everything is spooling out of control. I need to take back control of whatever I can. I move out into the hallway, to find a quiet spot of my own. I pull out my phone and turn it on. There are the dings of incoming texts, and I flinch, thinking about how much each one of those must be costing me, now that we're at sea.

Logan asks, "What are you doing?"

I click on Carmen's contact. "Calling the shop. I need to give Carmen a heads up that there's been another murder. That way, she will be prepared if the press – or the gawkers – descend on the shop again."

Logan says, "I don't see why that would happen. The biggest media leak has always been Ash, and he's right here."

"Still." I move a little farther from the spa doorway, then I make my call.

Carmen is the pastry chef at Greetings and Felicitations. She's a gifted chef, and in her off time, a hobbyist surfer. I trust her to keep everything running when I can't be at the shop. She's proven her abilities to handle even busy days.

Once I've explained what happened to Flint and how I'd been the one to find the body, Carmen says, "I'll get to the shop extra early. As soon as the news breaks that you're involved, I'm sure people will be coming out of the woodwork to see the murder books."

She's referring to the copies of *Emma* and *The Invisible Man*, which are in a glass case, along with a card detailing how each text had helped solve a specific murder. The card had been Carmen's idea, to embrace the fact that a lot of the shop's business comes from those who are curious about how a chocolate maker got caught up in two murder cases.

"Come on," Liam tells me. "Arlo says he's done with us for now. I need to get you and Imogen back to the ballroom, so we can announce your team as the winners of the LARP. Otherwise, people will be all over this boat all night."

"He already questioned Imogen," I ask.

Liam nods. "Apparently, she didn't have much to say." Liam pulls out his phone and pulls up an app, from which he makes a shipwide announcement that the game is over, and all the players should return to the ballroom.

"Where's Bea?" I ask. "She should come with us too. People would love to see Satchmo on stage."

"She and Satchmo are already looking for clues in the ballroom," Liam says. "Which is actually rather convenient."

A lot has happened while I was on the phone.

I go with Liam and Imogen, though secretly I'd rather stay with Arlo and Logan and try to help with the case. Which is silly, I know. After all, as I keep telling people, I'm not a detective, amateur or otherwise. I got drawn into two cases because people I cared about were involved. But it's not something I'm really planning to make a habit of. And I never met Flint Bates before today. So why do I feel like I am abandoning him, as I walk away down the promenade?

Imogen seems a little out of it, so I just let her be. She drops behind us, walking slowly.

I try to make conversation with Liam as we walk. I ask, "Have you and Imogen done a lot of acting together? You looked so natural as Sherlock and the Inspector."

Liam gestures down at his clothes. "Chalk that up to the costuming. Lucy from the LARP group handled that. I've never met Imogen before."

"Really?" I ask, glancing back at Imogen, who manages a small smile in response. "But she's your cousin's fiancé."

"I've seen pictures of her before," Liam admits. He takes out his phone and starts scrolling through his saved photos. "Ash's engagement photo is really cute." He holds up the phone, showing me a picture of Ash and Imogen on the Sea Wall, with Pleasure Pier in the background, the images of Galveston's coast providing a riotously colorful backdrop. In the picture, Ash is holding up a puff of cotton candy, and Imogen has her mouth open to take it. It looks natural, like a snapshot – but my guess is it was carefully posed by a professional photographer.

Well, the fact that they've never met makes the possibility that Imogen and Liam had gotten together to kill Flint a lot less likely. Though not impossible, since they both had a reason to want to protect Ash, and Flint had threatened to reveal some damaging secret about him. Sometimes people meet and immediately decide to do stupid things together.

This whole murder mystery theme for the cruise had brought together an interesting mix of people. Without it, it is unlikely that either Flint or Clove would be here – let alone together. And neither would Autumn. I ask Liam, "Who recommended making it a mystery conference in the first place, and that you invite authors? Or was this whole thing your idea?"

"No," Liam says. "I can't take credit for that. It was one of the LARPers. It sounded like a great idea, and the cruise sold out very quickly. I did put a lot of work into the planning, though, so if anyone asks, I'm taking full credit."

I laugh. "As you do."

When we arrive back at the ballroom, Bea is standing near the door, and Satchmo is snuffling around somewhat aimlessly.

Imogen walks past her, heading for a little seating area off to the side of the room. Liam goes with Imogen.

I ask Bea, "What's Satchmo doing?"

Bea says, "I have him scenting off a sample of Flint's blood. Just in case the killer came in here with it still on them. I figured having the place cards saying which team was sitting where could come in handy."

"And has it?" I ask.

"Not really. Satchmo hasn't found anything." Bea calls Satchmo over to her. She says, "I'm going to see if he might be of more help to Imogen right now."

Liam lets Bea take over comforting Imogen. I sit down at the spot where my team is supposed to be. Liam comes over to stand near me.

I ask him, "Who all would have known that Flint was going to be on this cruise?"

Liam pulls up an image on his phone. It's a flyer for the mystery cruise, and across the bottom there are six headshots, each with the caption *Award Winning Author*. The picture on the far right is of Flint Bates, award winning author of the *Read me a Clue Mystery* series, among other works.

I say, "So everybody would have known."

Clove is on the flier too, though her last name is listed as Dunn. Her latest claim to fame is *The Roberta Flats* mysteries.

The list is rounded out with Aarti Andrews, who writes the *A Little Spice is Nice* mystery series, Tucker McDougal who does the *Lost to the Dark* books, Leo Ruiz who writes *Detective Vargas* and Greta Gray who does *Dead in Alaska*. They all look friendly in their headshots. If these are the headliners, maybe Autumn will actually have fun on the panels.

Liam says, "Whatever you do, don't tell anyone there's been a murder. I've asked the other staff who have knowledge of the incident to also keep it quiet. The news is going to get out soon enough, and then people are going to demand to be let off the boat. If we can delay that until the morning, we can have a more coherent idea of what to tell them."

"So you want me to get up on the stage and pretend nothing is wrong?" My heart starts beating faster. "I've never been a good liar."

"You won't have to lie," Liam says. "Just answer what I ask. It's not likely to come up."

I look at the faces of people coming in, who are still happy, still on vacation. I wish I was one of them. The Scooby Doo team of LARPers makes it back, looking dejected, especially Craig, who keeps getting these disappointed looks from the girls. I guess since he's the guy in charge of the LARP league, they figured that being on his team meant they were a shoe-in to win. But Craig must have been playing fair, not asking for any extra clues. Is that because he's an honorable guy? Or because he didn't expect anyone to be able to out-think him?

I guess it doesn't matter, now that the game is over.

Waitstaff start coming around to each table with trays of snacks.

Bea comes to sit next to me, so we can be ready to go together to accept our prize. Not all of the contestants come back, but a goodly number of them do. After all, they've been promised fancy snacks and prizes.

Eventually, Liam and Imogen take the stage and go into their Sherlock Holmes and the Inspector routine. As soon as she's "on," her entire demeanor changes, and you would never guess she had been upset over her fiancé being a murder suspect just a few minutes earlier. They make it comic, and it isn't long before they have the whole room laughing when Imogen pretends to fall on the floor with shock that someone has solved the mystery before her.

Imogen shades her eyes with her hand. "Who of all these detectives has dared to upstage Sherlock Holmes and Inspector Liam?"

"It was us!" Bea waves our clue sheet in the air – never mind that most of it isn't filled out – and Satchmo barks at the motion, wagging his thin beagle tail so hard it looks like he's going to fall over. We make our way up onto the stage – which is really only three steps higher than the main floor and barely big enough for the band I imagine usually occupies this space.

Imogen, in an exaggerated British accent, says, "My goodness, if it isn't the Felicitations Finders. How did you find your way back to Scotland Yard?"

"We took a two-decker buss and a taxi, Ms. Holmes," Bea says, getting an even bigger laugh.

"And have you solved the case?" Liam asks. "You and that wee hound of the Baskervilles?"

"He's a retired police dog," I point out. Then I add, "He solved the case all by himself."

That gets *me* a laugh, which I have to say feels good. Not as good as the relief of having found Ash unharmed. But still, it's a relief from all the stress. I look out at the audience, and then it hits me. Someone out there in the audience, who is laughing along with us, is probably a murderer. And I can't warn anyone that someone they're sitting next to, someone they trust, could be dangerous.

Imogen asks, "So what was the vital clue, Mrs. Koerber, that led you to unraveling this heinous crime?"

I know she's talking about the fake jewel heist, but the image that pops into my head at the words *heinous crime* is of Flint's face, lying still against the floor. I shake the thought away, try to put the smile back on my face, but my voice sounds forced when I say, "The case was finally cracked when we uncovered that you, Ms. Holmes are very good at picking locks."

"Me?" Imogen sounds genuinely outraged. She is a very good actress. "How dare you accuse me?"

Liam says, "If it is Ms. Holmes, then where is the Egg of Zeld?"

Bea points at Imogen and gives Satchmo a cue with her other hand, and the beagle barks three times. Bea says gravely, "It is underneath her hat."

Imogen's mouth drops open overdramatically, and she brings both hands to pull the deerstalker farther down onto her head – leaving the outline of the fake diamond clear to be seen through the hat. She hops forward, like she's going to run away, and Liam chases her across the stage, where they both pick up rapiers and pretend to have a duel that somehow leaves Imogen sitting on the stage with her hands cuffed together. I'm pretty sure she slipped the cuffs on herself.

Then Liam pulls a giant basket from behind the prop desk and hands it to Bea. It's full of Texas-themed food items, a couple of boxes of my chocolates, mystery-themed tee-shirts, paperback mystery novels – and an envelope that probably contains the raffle tickets.

Liam then gives a rundown of the events for the next few days – if the cruise even continues that long. But he was right – it's easier to just not say anything about what might be going on than to actively lie. Or to deal with the chaos of telling these people their vacations are ruined.

Sometime during the duel, Logan and Arlo show up and go sit at our table, with Ash in tow. Ash makes eye contact with me, still up on the stage, and I can tell he knows now just how much trouble he's in.

Liam does the Snack and Greet portion of the presentation quickly, just giving a brief bio of each presenter and listing out a couple of our accomplishments. When he introduces Autumn, there are a few murmurs of surprise.

The ballroom clears out quickly after that, as the disappointed teams sign their walkies back in, then head for the stations outside the doors where the consolation prizes are being handed out.

Autumn comes over towards me, moving against the stream of traffic.

I ask Bea, "Do you mind if I give her the raffle tickets? I think she and Drake are a lot more interested in winning that book than we are."

Bea says, "I don't mind. I never win anything anyway." She yawns. "Satchmo and I are going to bed. I'll be in the main dining room for breakfast, if you want to spend some more time with him."

"You'd let me borrow your dog?" I ask.

She leans down and pats the beagle between the ears. "He seems to like you. And you seem calmer since you've been hanging out with him. I just need him for my demo at two o'clock."

Autumn gets to us and says, "If someone else had to win the game, I'm glad it was you."

"Nice shirt," I tell her. "How did you come up with matching ones, if you didn't know about the game ahead of time?"

She gestures over towards Liam, who is helping take down the decorations from the stage. The whole Scooby Doo crew are helping too, rolling up the giant poster of the jail cell. Autumn says, "As soon as we realized the shops were closed, I told Liam we weren't participating unless he helped us out. He seems really eager about having me participate this weekend. I wish I knew why. I'm terrified he's going to embarrass me, to try and create drama."

"He doesn't strike me as that kind of guy." I gesture at her shirt. "So the sharks were Liam's choice?"

Autumn nods. "Apparently he could only access the ship's main gift shop, so there wasn't much to choose from."

Bea says, "Goodnight," and then taps the basket. "Let me know tomorrow how we're splitting all of that up." Then without waiting for a response, she leaves.

I make sure no one else is close to us, then I ask Autumn, "Has Arlo tried to talk to you yet?"

"Arlo?" Autumn looks confused. "No, why?"

That's good. He must not consider Autumn a suspect – despite the very public fight she had with Flint. But the FBI guys might not be so considerate. I say, "Please tell me you didn't leave your group at any time during the LARP. Not to go to the bathroom, not anything."

"No, I didn't." Autumn's eyes go wide, filling with anxiety. "Felicity, what's going on?"

I lean in close to her and whisper, "Flint got murdered."

Autumn gasps. She starts to say something, but I hold out a hand to shush her.

"Liam asked me not to tell anybody."

She nods, slowly. "I think I should head back to the room. There's no way I can pretend not to know that, not in front of Drake, two guys with cop instincts and my future mother-in-law."

"That sounds reasonable." I check the envelope. I was right – it's full of raffle tickets. I give the envelope to Autumn, who doesn't even try to fake being excited about the raffle anymore.

After she leaves, Drake and his mom Charlene come over to our table. I reach into the basket and take out a box of my chocolates. "Check these out. I won some of my own chocolates." I open the box to show off the designs, protected behind the plastic seal. She makes appropriate oohing and ahhing noises over all the work that went into them, then asks if she can taste one.

I put the lid back on and hand her the whole box, saying, "I hope you had fun with the game."

Charlene replies, "I did, but this is way past my bedtime. I just wanted to tell everyone goodnight."

Drake asks, "Where's Autumn?"

I tell him, "She went back to our room, to go check out her schedule for tomorrow. She said she might need to make notes."

Drake seems a bit disappointed that Autumn left without telling him goodbye, but he lets it go, and he and his mother head back to their room.

Chapter Seven

So it's just me, Logan, Arlo, Ash, and Imogen left in the ballroom. I join them at the large round table.

"I didn't do it," Ash insists, looking straight at me. "You know I wouldn't kill another human being."

I look at Arlo. "You aren't arresting him, are you?"

Arlo shakes his head. "No. I just questioned him, to get his statement while it was still fresh – but as the one person who disliked Flint and doesn't have an alibi, Ash is going to be in real trouble when the folks who have the jurisdiction needed to arrest him get here."

Imogen lets out a squeak. "He really might get arrested?"

"Isn't that what you were so worried about earlier?" I ask. "You were practically catatonic."

She shakes her head. "I was just thinking. About mortality. Out out, brief candle and all of that. If anyone seemed like he could take care of himself, it was Flint. And there he was. Dead." She looks at Arlo. "Please, you have to prove Ash innocent. He can't get arrested."

Ash grimaces. "Even if that happens, don't worry. They don't have any evidence. Because I didn't do anything."

I still don't know whether to trust Ash or not. He is smart enough to have locked himself into that cubicle, so that there's no clear proof of where he was, at what time. But while Ash doesn't really care about other people's feelings – he's never struck me as capable of murder.

Arlo sighs. "Then just tell me your secret, Ash. That waitress claims you swore in front of everyone that Flint would pay for threatening to reveal whatever it was. The agents that are coming to investigate this don't know you. They're going to take that accusation very seriously."

Ash sighs right back. "The problem is, I don't have any secrets. I'm pretty much what you see. Handsome? Definitely. Conceited? Maybe. Secretive? Definitely not."

"Then why–" Arlo starts, but Ash interrupts.

"Remember how I told you earlier that Flint took my phone and threw it overboard? That's what I was talking about. I was going to demand he buy me a new phone. The one that I had cost almost a thousand bucks." Ash looks across the table to me. "Please, Koerber. You've got to help me here. You're good at finding the real killer instead of the obvious one. Because you care about people."

"And you expect me to care about you, after everything you've done to me?" The words are out of my mouth before I can stop them. But I only half regret being so harsh. Ash has insinuated on his blog that he thought I was a murderer, that he believed I was trying to break up Arlo and Patsy, that now he thinks I am a personal murder magnet – though after tonight, I'm beginning to believe that that last one might be true.

Ash winces. "I do, actually. After that interview I did with you, I realized that that's what you are at your core – someone who cares. I thought we were finally becoming friends."

I'm ready to keep throwing the past at him – but that last bit makes me stop. Are we on our way to becoming friends? It's hard to say. I ask, "You really think you understand me?"

Ash grins. "Remember what I said about not letting people in? You might not let them in, but you'd do anything to keep them safe. And me going to prison is definitely not safe. Look at me. Do you think I'd last two days in there?"

He does have a point. And it's interesting – maybe he has gotten to know me a lot better than I've gotten to know him. I hesitate. Then I say, "I need to know that your secret wasn't something horrible before I try to help you."

"Lis," Arlo says, "this isn't any of your business."

"We're in international waters," Ash points out. "Technically, it isn't any of yours either."

Arlo crosses his arms and harrumphs back in his chair. "It might be. I'm still sorting that out with the Feds."

"Think, Ash," I tell him. "Flint thought he had something on you, even if you didn't realize it. What could you have done?"

"I buy a ton of pictures. Maybe I bought something and didn't realize what it was?" He throws both hands up in the air, obviously frustrated. "I don't know! I'm not cheating on my fiancé, I haven't stolen anything, I'm not blackmailing anybody – I even pay my taxes. To the penny. It makes sense why Flint would have wanted me dead – but not why I would have killed him. Sure he punched me and took my phone, but even I have to admit I kind of deserved it."

"So you honestly don't know your own secret?" Arlo sounds skeptical.

"But I do." Clove walks into the room. She's holding a manila envelope. "I just got this faxed to me. It was in a folder on Flint's desk. Luckily his housekeeper still likes me better than him."

Ash says, "You think Mr. Bates knew I was going to be here?"

Clove shrugs. "Hard to tell. But listen, sweetie. Your mother loves you, and what I'm about to tell you doesn't change anything."

At Clove's words, Ash's cheeks go chalky. "What doesn't change anything?"

Clove comes over to the table and takes a seat next to Ash. She puts a comforting hand over his. "Sweetie, you're adopted. Flint and I always knew. We were friends with your adoptive parents, even before you were born. I guess Flint thought you knew. He was never very good at worrying about other people's feelings, so it might not have occurred to him that this fact had been hidden from you."

Ash says weakly, "And so the thing in your envelope?"

"It's your birth certificate. And newspaper articles about your birth parents, and when they were sent to jail."

"Jail?" Ash repeats, even more weakly. His hands are trembling as he opens the envelope.

"That's probably what Flint thought you were hiding. That you were spilling everyone else's secrets, when your own parents had been convicted of multiple murder."

This time, Ash just manages a wordless squeak. He pulls out the newspaper articles and spreads them across the table. He just blinks at them for a long time, then he pulls his hand away from Clove's. "You really expect me to believe my real name is Ashley Brewster? I'm a Diaz." He gestures at his own face. "Do I look like a Brewster to you?"

Logan gestures right back. "Well, yeah. Maybe."

Ash's mouth drops open. I watch as everything inside him shatters, about what he thought he knew about himself, his culture, his place in the world. "I need to find a phone," he says urgently. "I need to call my mom."

My heart squeezes with empathy. Before Kevin had died, I'd thought I knew my place in the world. I'd been living in Seattle, a married physical therapist with fellow professionals as friends, a nice house, and a pet bunny. After I'd become a widow, and given up my practice to open my own craft chocolate business, I'd moved in with my aunt. The only thing I still have of my former life is the rabbit.

I'm sure the day they'd called me to the hospital after Kevin's accident, my face must have looked much like Ash's does right now. It was a different kind of loss, a different feel to the grief – but there's no way that this Ash, so raw and vulnerable, just cold-bloodedly killed someone.

"You can use my phone," Imogen says. She stands for a moment behind Ash's chair and gives him a hug from behind. He kind of crumples into it. Then she helps him up and leads him out of the room.

I gesture in the direction the two just went. "Well, that nixes any motivation Ash would have had for killing Flint. He obviously didn't know."

"Maybe," Arlo says. "It is possible Diaz is just that good of an actor." Arlo sounds like he's trying to convince himself. "Or that he has some other motive we don't know about. He's still the only suspect with a history of animosity with the victim who is without an alibi."

Logan looks at Clove. "Are you sure that you never left the group you were with during the LARP?"

"I don't LARP," Clove says. "I was with a group of fellow authors, down in one of the bars, right up until Detective Romero had me paged, so he could notify me of the death. I was a couple of glasses of prosecco in at the time. And now that I've had to hurt Ash so badly, I think I'm going to go and finish the bottle. I settled my grievances with Flint when we split up. If you're looking for someone who might still be harboring grievances about the past, you should try Imogen."

She leaves. Which puts me there alone with the two guys I have feelings for. And the silence between the three of us is suddenly awkward.

I break it, asking, "So, how exactly did Flint die?"

"We're not really sure," Logan says. "Either he was stabbed with something thin and round, or he was shot. There's nobody on board who can do a proper autopsy, but the docs downstairs can tell us they weren't able to find a bullet."

Arlo stands up from the table. "I really shouldn't be discussing the details of the case with a civilian."

"Don't tell me you don't want to talk about it with someone," Logan says. "It really is intriguing."

Arlo huffs. "Lis, I can't stop Logan from getting you involved in this. Just promise me you won't do anything stupid this time."

Logan says, "It's usually the other way around. Felicity's the one getting me involved, because she wants someone to help her, instead of push her out of the way."

Arlo's mouth opens, but he thinks better of whatever he was about to say. Finally he says, "But if she listened to me, at least she'd be safe. Because that's all I've ever wanted."

Arlo turns on his heel and leaves.

Logan looks at me levelly. "He's still got a thing for you, you know?"

"I know." Because what else am I going to say?

"You going to do anything about it?" Logan asks.

I study Logan's face. Logan and I had shared that kiss – and then we hadn't shared another since. We're both so tentative with each other, because we both have bruised pasts. And we haven't been able to figure out how we fit into each other's lives. After all, I hate violence and Logan carries a gun. Well, he usually does, when he's not on a cruise ship that doesn't allow it. But we're trying to make our connection into something bigger, and we've been getting closer to achieving something meaningful.

I should say no, I'm not going to listen to whatever Arlo has to say. I kissed Logan. I asked him to be my plus one to Autumn's wedding. I told him I wasn't looking for a rebound guy – when he's been devastated by being the rebound guy in the past.

I should say no. But what I actually say is, "I don't know."

And the pain on Logan's face tells me that maybe I'm not the only one who has been thinking about that kiss and what it might mean. But he just nods and changes the subject.

He clears his throat. "The reason I said it's intriguing is that it looks like Flint was shot, but if so, they should have been able to retrieve the bullet. And there should have been more bruising. So maybe he was stabbed with something that left a hole in the shape of a bullet. It's almost like the whole ice bullet thing."

"You mean where someone gets shot with a chunk of ice and the evidence just melts away? That's been done in so many mystery shows now that it is practically its own trope."

Logan nods. "Yeah. I didn't mean the melting, exactly. Just that this wound doesn't seem to make sense, but there's got to be a perfectly logical explanation."

"Not that you think he was literally shot with a chunk of ice?"

Logan shakes his head. "I don't think so. I mean, it's possible, but it seems unlikely."

There's something nagging at my brain. What have I seen recently that would make a round hole, and go deeper than an icepick but not bruise like a gun? And then it hits me. I think about that stage duel between Imogen and Liam. "Could you actually stab someone with a fencing foil?"

Logan considers this. "You're not supposed to be able to, since the blades are flexible. But I suppose someone angry enough could find a way to hold it to do damage. What exactly are you thinking here?"

I gesture towards the now-empty stage. "Liam is Ash's cousin, and Imogen is his fiancé. And those two are each other's alibis. I know it sounds crazy, but what if the two of them killed Flint, to protect Ash? And then they were using the murder weapon like toys, on stage."

"That sounds a bit far-fetched," Logan says. But he sits for a moment thinking about it. "But it couldn't hurt to check those foils for blood residue. In the morning, obviously. It's a bit much of a long-shot to drag everybody out of bed."

"Then let's go down to the bar," I suggest. "We can at least verify Clove's story."

Chapter Eight

The bartender is polishing glasses. She's probably barely old enough to drink, let alone serve alcohol. She has a goth punk look going on, with a black top and metallic purple skirt, and purple streaks in her black hair. She greets us with, "Just letting you know, last call is in about thirty minutes."

"Thanks," Logan says. "But we're not drinking tonight. We just came for some information."

This bar is small, with dark wood and brass, the opposite of most spaces on this ship.

There's a soft noise from a table in the corner, a tinkling of ice in a glass. I turn, and there's a woman sitting there, trying to get the last dregs out of her drink. She's in her late twenties and has long dark hair and Latina features, and long fingernails with tiny palm trees painted on each one. It is obvious she's been crying.

I ask the bartender, "Who's that?"

She shrugs, though she looks guarded. "I dunno." She turns to Logan. "What kind of information?"

Logan takes out his phone and shows her a picture he snapped of Clove. I hadn't even noticed him take it. "Was this woman in here earlier? She claims to have been here with a bunch of friends."

The bartender's face relaxes visibly, now that it's clear the information we want isn't about her. "She was, yeah." The bartender really looks at me. "Hey, you're the chocolate detective, right?"

I nod. That sounds better than murder magnet.

"Cool!" She moves over to the fridge and takes out a carton of half and half. As she answers Logan's questions, she squirts club soda into a couple of glasses, adds the half and half then drizzles in chocolate syrup down a long spoon. She says, "No, I don't think any of the writers left until after the redhead got the message from the staff." She puts the two glasses on the bar. "Here. A couple of egg creams on the house. Unless you get tired of chocolate. Geeze. You said you weren't drinking booze, but I didn't even think. Maybe you're not thirsty at all."

"Who can get tired of chocolate?" I say, taking one of the glasses. I mean, yes, it is possible to test too many truffles and think you will never want chocolate again, and I definitely don't eat it every day. But am I going to turn down something special that someone made for me? I take a sip. The beverage is creamy and fizzy, and has a nice hit of chocolate flavor. I take a couple of more sips. I tell her, "It's nice to have something simple and sweet after such a stressful day."

"Sorry I couldn't have been more help," the bartender says.

Logan and I take our egg creams to a table. I tell him, "I haven't had one of these since I was a kid. I would visit my grandfather in New York."

"I thought your family was from Texas and Louisiana," Logan says.

"My grandpa on my dad's side," I tell him. "The Italian side of the family, that I rarely get to see. There was a deli in my grandpa's neighborhood that had an old-fashioned soda fountain. I'd go up there for a week in the summer, and he'd take me to the art museums and we'd eat all the good food."

"It can be hard to remember that people have more than one side to them," Logan says. "Especially when they've embraced something whole-heartedly, like you with your Cajun flavors."

"Hey," I tell him. "I make a mean lasagna too."

There's movement near our table. "Excellent. I'll come over for dinner," the woman who had been drinking alone says sarcastically as plops her empty ice glass on our table and plops herself into an empty chair.

"Can we help you?" Logan asks.

"Probably not." She wipes at her eyes with the back of her hand. "But I just want to warn you. Don't listen to a word Clove says. She's the bitter ex-wife. With the emphasis on bitter."

"And you are?" I ask.

"I'm the new girlfriend. Or at least I was. Somebody killed my Flint, and I don't intend to let them get away with it."

There's the clink of a fumbled glass hitting the bar. I look up and the bartender is staring at our table, open mouthed. Liam was right – news about this murder is going to make its way around the ship, whether we want it to or not.

Still, I exchange pointed looks with Logan. Why is this the first time we're hearing about a girlfriend?

"How did you meet Flint?" I ask.

"I work at a dry-cleaning store. Flint's been a customer for years." She gestures with her hand, and those tiny palm trees are captivating as her fingers move. "I'm Lupe, by the way."

We introduce ourselves, and then Logan prompts, "Go on."

"It's not much of a story. He had a button come off the cuff of his shirt, and I fixed it for him, without him having to come back for it. We started talking, and he took me out for coffee and pie. We just . . . clicked."

It must be nice, having love come that simply. It had been that easy for me and Kevin too – though we'd met in one of those undergrad classes everybody has to take no matter what their major. But with Logan – there's been all kinds of complications, not the least of which is his past. And with Arlo, there's history between us, not all of it good. Can I really overcome all of that baggage to belong together with either of these guys? At least I've admitted to myself that I want to move on. I still miss Kevin, and sometimes the grief comes at me sharp – like my initial response to being on this boat – but I think I've finally accepted that I've got to live life without him.

It's like that whale sculpture – I've finally made my peace with the ocean for taking him.

But Lupe – her pain is sharp all over, like the edges on a caltrop. I've been there. I mean it when I tell her, "We'll do our best to find out what happened."

"Like I said," Lupe says. "Don't pay attention to what Clove told you. Flint had a sweet side. He could be generous. I wanted to go back to school, so he gave me the money to get my business degree. He called it an investment in our future."

Logan asks, "Where were you during the same hours Clove was here?"

My breath catches. He can't ask her that. Not that bluntly. Not when her boyfriend is lying dead somewhere in the lower decks of this ship. I kick him under the table. He ignores me and looks steadily at Lupe.

Lupe gets a sad little smile on her face and says, "I was in my room. Alone." She stands up, leaving her glass on the table. "The irony is, Flint wanted me to go with him to dinner and to explore the ship, but I was too embarrassed, after he hit that kid. If I'd gone with him – maybe he'd still be alive. And I wouldn't need an alibi."

With that, she leaves.

I tell Logan, "That was rude. You shouldn't be so blunt when she's grieving."

He says, "There's no such thing as rude in a murder investigation." He drinks the last of his egg cream, then adds, "Besides, don't you think there's something odd about her story?"

I consider it. "Autumn did say that Flint isn't a nice guy. It does seem odd that Lupe thinks he's this great person, when he hit a guy in front of everyone."

"That too," Logan says, "But I'm talking about the pie. Three of the people Arlo and I have spoken to told us that Flint hated desserts. And anything frivolous. Like those fake nails."

"That's right," I say. "I even heard him say he didn't like sweets. But why would Lupe make up something like that?"

"I don't know," Logan says. "But tomorrow, I think we should talk to Clove. If anyone here knows about this supposed girlfriend, it will be the ex-wife."

"I think we should talk to the LARPers," I tell Logan. "That whole group that Ash is a part of. Maybe they know something about what Clove was saying about Imogen."

Logan is grinning at me in a way that seems far too light for the circumstances.

"What?" I ask.

He looks down at the table. "I just – I've missed this. The part of you that comes alive when you're trying to solve a puzzle. Even when you're doing it for a person you claim to dislike."

I feel a blush spreading across my cheeks. "Just because Ash is annoying doesn't mean I want him to go to jail when he's innocent. And the more I think about it – I think he might have actually been trying to help me, that day he came to do the interview. He certainly gave me a lot to think about."

Logan's grin turns bittersweet. "I love how you are always willing to give people a second chance. Even when it has been far past the time when they should have taken it."

He's talking about Arlo, isn't he? I owe Logan something here, even if we've never made any promises to each other.

"You're not mad?" I ask. "About whatever this is with Arlo?"

Logan sets his glass on the table. "I'd be lying if I said I'm not disappointed. I thought lately – at work at the chocolate shop – you and I had a rapport that's been building towards something. But I'm not going to be that guy. You know, the one who pushes you to make a decision because I'm feeling possessive. If you settle for me, while daydreaming that you might have something better with somebody else, you'll wind up resenting me. And that's not fair to either of us."

I stare into the last inch of egg cream at the bottom of my glass. And despite everything, I feel a little smile creeping onto my face. Logan feels something between us.

But then he says, "If you think your history with Arlo means there's something there, you should pursue it, until either you realize it's what you want, or until you find closure."

"You really want that?"

He nods, solemnly.

The boat starts rocking more noticeably. I put my hand on my glass to keep it from sliding on the table.

Logan says, "Arlo did say there was a storm rolling in."

"Then why don't we go back to the dock?" I ask.

"If we do that, there's a chance that the killer will get away, if we get close enough for them to swim to shore." Logan puts a hand on mine. "This is a big ship, and it's just a storm, not a hurricane. We'll be fine."

"Right," I say, but inside I'm quavering. I came out here intending to make peace with the ocean, and with the past. But what if it doesn't want to make peace with me? "I need to try and get some sleep. Our event is the first thing on the schedule in the morning."

Logan takes his hand away. I may be imagining it, but I think I've disappointed him even more. "Yeah," he says. "Well, goodnight."

By the time I get back to the room, Autumn is already asleep. I try to move quietly, finding clothes to change into, heading for the dime-sized bathroom. But I wake her up anyway.

She pulls the white satin sleep mask off her face. "Did you have fun talking to Logan?"

"I guess," I say. "It got complicated."

She sits up. "Did he kiss you again? Because I have to say, it's about time."

I sit down on my bed, which given the size of this cabin is only about three feet from hers. "I wish it was that simple."

"Go on." The reading lights above each bed come on. Autumn must have found a switch.

"Logan said that Arlo still has a thing for me."

Autumn points the sleep mask at me. "Please tell me that isn't news to you."

I shrug. "We've had a couple of moments. But Arlo was taken. And now he's not, and I have two viable love interests. I've never been the kind of girl to wind up in this kind of situation. Usually that's girls who don't care about leading people on."

"We all know that's not what happened," Autumn says. "But when I was writing, multiple love interests were always more about opportunity for growth and change. Close your eyes and picture your life five years from now. It will help you see what you really want."

"That's silly."

"Come on. Do you want to wake up in the morning and have café con leche while you talk about family and watch the waves with Arlo? Or do you want a travel mug of espresso while you hop into a plane and fly away with Logan?"

"Both those images are appealing," I say. I close my eyes, but all I see is my old life, having soy milk lattes on the sailboat with Kevin, while he reads to me. If he was still alive, there's be no question of who I'd choose, or what life I'd want for myself. We had been deeply in love. I'd had this all figured out. I open my eyes and say, "It's no use. What I want in five years is what I wanted fifteen years ago – a smart guy with a great sense of humor, who I can talk about books with and travel with and discuss each other's work without getting bored."

Autumn laughs. "Well except for the books part, I think you could have that with either Logan or Arlo."

My response is more somber. "But both of them come with so much baggage. And I do too. What I don't want is to hurt either of them. It was so much easier when it was just me and Knightley and my memories of Kevin. Maybe the reason I'm so hesitant is that what I really want is to be alone."

"Nobody wants that for you," Autumn says, even as she stifles a yawn. "You're too much of a people person for isolation to make you happy. Picture yourself alone with a cup of strong dark coffee and a piece of toast for company."

"People pay for that at spas and retreats," I point out. "Sometimes you just need a little alone time."

Autumn starts putting the sleep mask back on. She gets cranky without a full night's sleep, so I'm probably lucky to have gotten this much conversation out of her at this hour. "But every day for the rest of your life?"

I picture that, and even with Knightley in the image, it seems a little bleak. "You do have a point. But I'm not ready to make those kinds of decisions about my life yet. It wasn't that long ago that I was trying to live life for Kevin, since he can't anymore."

"Then don't choose yet. If either Arlo or Logan really is what's going to be good for you, then he will understand you're still figuring things out."

Chapter Nine
Friday

I will say one thing for cruise ships: the breakfast options are always decadent. I've opted for eggs benedict, because hollandaise is something I'm not prepared to make for myself that early in the morning. It requires too much time, and you have to pay attention to it so it doesn't break.

A lot of the food on board this cruise line has a Texas bent to it, so there is also a chicken fried steak benedict, which Autumn seems to be enjoying just as much.

She edges her plate towards me. "You have to try this."

I cut off a bite. The steak is crisp, and the yolk from the perfectly poached egg oozes gloriously on top of it. There's creamy gravy, and a flaky biscuit instead of the English muffin. I tell her, "This may be even better than mine."

We're at the same table with Logan, Arlo, Drake and Charlene. This room is huge, and the tall, arched ceiling only emphasizes the effect. There's still a lot of gold in the décor, but it has a more modern feel than the ballroom, with blown glass bubbles for light fixtures and geometric edges to the pillars highlighting that around the edges of the space, there's the railing of a balcony that winds its way around a second floor. We're up near the top of the ship, so the movement of the boat is more pronounced up here.

I ask Drake, "You have any experience changing oil on a plane?"

Drake sets his coffee up in its saucer. "Not planes, but cars. I've changed the oil in a '69 Chevy and a 1975 VW Bug.

But that was back when my grandpa was alive, and I'd help out with his hobby cars. So it's been a while."

Logan clears his throat. "Maybe we'll change the oil together."

Arlo elbows Logan. "More mechanically inclined than you thought though, right?"

"What?" Drake asks. He looks from Arlo to Logan and back again, like he's not sure whether he's the punch line of a joke.

Logan says, "We were just talking about how we didn't know you that well yet."

Drake laughs, for longer than I would have thought. He elbows his mother, who pushes said elbow away in an attempt to look dignified. Drake says, "We were talking about how little we know about you as well. Mamma still thinks I should have gotten to know all of Autumn's friends before I proposed." He points at Logan. "She asked me if I thought you'd be able to name the last book you read."

Logan's lips narrow into a line. "I read books. Occasionally."

I ask him, "So what is it then? The last book you read?"

Logan shrugs. "Tactical Theory and the Applied Examples."

Drake says, "You're joking."

Arlo replies, "He's probably not."

There's a moment of stunned silence, which Arlo fills by asking, "So how did you propose, anyway?"

Drake grins. "I have a couple of friends in a band, and we went down to Autumn's brother's coffee bar for them to play a gig. I got them to play her a song, and throw all these rose petals, while putting the two of us in a spotlight. It would have been terribly embarrassing if she had said no."

"I wasn't about to give you the chance to change your mind." Autumn pulls his face towards her and kisses his cheek.

"On that note," he says, "I did promise you a romantic walk before you have to go entertain the masses."

The two of them get up and, with linked hands, thread their way out of the dining room.

"We've actually got a meeting," Arlo says. "Logan and I are supposed to talk to the captain about . . . about an incident that happened yesterday."

"It's okay," Charlene says. "Autumn told us what happened. That poor man."

"Then you understand why it is important that this gets handled delicately," Logan says. Then he turns to me and says, "Don't worry – I'll be there in time to help out with the demo."

Logan and Arlo have been so at odds in the past that it is strange seeing them working together like this. But I guess I shouldn't be too surprised – they are both on the side of justice, after all. And Arlo is alone on this boat, without any of his usual backup. But I can't help but feel a little left out, seeing Logan going off to work on the case without me. Even if it only makes sense. After all, I keep protesting that I'm not really a detective. And this time, the only real reason I have to get involved is Ash's request that I help him.

Last night it had really felt like Logan wanted to work with me on solving this. But it's obvious I haven't been invited to meet the captain, and Logan has.

Which means Charlene and I wind up the last two still sitting at the table. I've never had a conversation alone with her before, and I have no idea what she likes to talk about.

The boat is still rocking from the storm. Charlene says, "I hope Drake and Autumn aren't planning on going up on the main deck. It was so windy out there, earlier I saw a deck chair blow into the pool. They said the pool was likely to be closed for most of the day."

"I'm sure they'll find somewhere inside to walk." We sit quietly for a moment before I tell her, "It is such a relief to know someone else is as overwhelmed by how quickly this engagement happened as I am."

Charlene takes my hand and squeezes it. "I heard a bit about how you told Autumn she's rushing things. But she said you've come around. Is that not true?"

Charlene's gaze is intense. I'd hate to be a student in one of her classes who came up with a wrong answer. Not that there is a right or wrong answer to that particular question.

"I'm starting to," I tell her. "I would never make a decision that important that quickly, but Autumn seems to know what she's doing. And Drake seems to really care about her. So who am I to judge?"

Charlene lets go of my hand. "I understand what you are saying. And on one level I agree. But my Drake has never done anything impulsive before. Never. Not that Autumn doesn't seem like a perfectly nice girl. I do hope they're as good of a match as they seem to be."

I take the last sip of my coffee. "I think I'm becoming more of an optimist in general."

A hand waves in my general direction. "Oh hello!"

I look up from my coffee cup to see Bea approaching our table. She has an apple in one hand and a yogurt container in the other. Satchmo is trotting along at her side.

I peel the breading off the small piece of chicken fried steak Autumn left on her plate and offer it to the beagle, who takes it from me, then lies down under the empty chair next to me, his tail thumping against my foot. A few moments later, he's back to sitting up and watching me, seeing if there are any more treats forthcoming.

"Now you're not going to convince me Bea didn't already feed you some quality dog food this morning."

Bea says, "You'd never tell it from those eyes he's giving you right now. Do you still want him for the morning?"

I drop a hand down to pet Satchmo. "Sure! I'll get Logan to watch him during the demo."

"You shouldn't need to. Just find him a quiet corner and tell him to stay put."

"You mean stay," I say.

"No, specifically say *stay put*." As she says this, she looks down at Satchmo, who flops down and stops giving me those eyes that stay he's starving. Bea puts her breakfast down on our table and takes out her phone. It's been powered off, but she switches it on. "Actually, let me text you his whole list of commands."

We exchange contact info, and she sends me a cute graphic. Some of the commands have uncommon phrasing – possibly so they won't be used accidentally. But some are for tricks. I tell Satchmo, "Pass the teacup."

Satchmo stands up and goes to Bea, who hands him a napkin from the table. Satchmo takes it in his mouth and carries it the few feet back to me, where he pushes the napkin into my hand. "Nice!" I tell him. "Good dog."

Now he looks like he wants a treat again. He's going to have to settle for a pat between the ears.

Then I get him to pass the napkin on to Charlene, who says, "What a delightful dog. We used to have a beagle when Drake was little."

Finally! Something to talk with Charlene about. We both like animals.

I start to tell Charlene about Knightley, but I spot Imogen standing up from her table, across the dining room. It's not surprising that she's there with her friends from the LARP group. Ash is with them, but while they are laughing about something, he looks miserable. Imogene leaves the table by herself. I may not get a better chance to ask her what Clove meant last night.

"Excuse me," I tell Bea and Charlene, "but I have to go do something." I tell Satchmo, "Stay on my left."

He trots beside me as I make my way towards the same door Imogen is heading for. She sees me coming and smiles a tight smile. "Hey."

"Did you sleep at all last night?" I ask.

There are dark circles under her eyes, and she looks like the paper coffee cup in her hand is the only thing holding her up.

"A little," she says.

"Can we talk?" I ask.

"Why?" She looks wary.

"Because I really would like to help Ash. But I can't do that if I don't know what's really going on."

Imogen gestures with her cup. "Let's find somewhere quiet."

I follow her into a small observatory. Three of the walls and the ceiling are made entirely of glass, because this space projects out from the main body of the ship. Rain is falling onto the flat roof, matching the angular setting. Inside, there are opulent overstuffed leather sofas and chairs, with black tables inlaid with gold and silver patterns, some of which make up stylized images of whales.

Imogen sits in one of the chairs and draws her legs up underneath her. Today her hair is down, and she's wearing a simple dress. "What is it you want to know?"

I sit down at an angle to her. I'm watching the rain pounding angry and sad against the deck. How could I have thought I would find peace here, on this boat? Suddenly, Satchmo is trying to climb into my lap. I think his therapy dog training is kicking in. He's really big for a lap dog, but this chair is huge, so I let him join me in it.

"I said, what is it you want to know?" Imogen repeats.

I draw myself back to the conversation. Imogen has enough problems right now, without me adding in my past, which I've been working so hard to overcome. "Last night, Clove told us you might have had a motive for killing Flint. How did you even know him?"

Imogen's lips start trembling. "That isn't fair. It had nothing to do with me."

"What didn't?" I ask. She's not making any sense.

"How would Clove have even known? I never met her before yesterday."

"Known what?" I ask.

"Flint knew my father, back when I was really little. They were friends, and had even talked about writing a book series together. One day, the two of them went out on a boat together. Flint had some kind of Hemmingway complex, and he wanted to shoot at sharks. My father ran fishing charters down in Kemah. Supposedly, he had volunteered to drive the boat for Flint to get into federal waters, where that kind of fishing would be legal. But everyone who knew my dad said that wasn't the kind of thing he would do. He loved sea life, promoted humane, responsible fishing. Still. They went out on the boat together . . . but Flint came back alone. He claimed there was an accident, that my dad went overboard trying to land one of the sharks. It didn't make any sense, but they couldn't find evidence of foul play, so whatever happened out there, Flint got away with it."

I shift forward, forcing Satchmo to find a better position on the chair. "I don't understand. That would have been a huge scandal. Why wouldn't Clove know who you are?"

Imogen says, "My mother remarried, and both of us took Henry's last name. And when I was little, I went by Genie, not Imogen. So there was no reason she'd know me, and I had no intention of bringing it up."

I shake my head. "Clove obviously knows more about you than she was letting on. Maybe she had some reason for not bringing up the past – until Flint's death forced her hand."

"Maybe." Imogen considers this. "I wish she could have just kept whatever she knows to herself. Henry's my dad now, and all that loss and pain from so long ago – it's not something I ever want to think about."

"But that's what had you contemplating the void yesterday," I say. "Flint's death bringing back your father's."

"Yeah." She looks so sad now, framed by the rain. It feels like this moment itself has been taken out of a Hemmingway story.

"You had to know Flint was going to be on this cruise. Were you planning to tell him who you are?"

Imogen shifts backwards in her seat. "I was planning to avoid him."

That at least sounds plausible, though the two of them both being on board still seems a bit of a coincidence. I can't help but ask, "Does Ash know?"

"No." Imogen takes a long drink of her coffee before saying, "I didn't even realize he knew Clove before he introduced me to her yesterday. I don't think he really keeps up with his mom's friends much."

"But you're engaged," I insist. "Don't you think he deserves to know about your past?"

She laughs. "He doesn't even know about his own past. Mine is probably the least of his worries. I don't think it would be healthy to drag everything that happened when I was a kid into an adult relationship."

I'm not sure I can agree with that, but saying so would only derail the conversation. Instead, I ask, "Was there ever a time when you and Liam were separated last night during the LARP?"

"Is that your way of asking if I killed Mr. Bates?"

I say, "Or if Liam might have." I do still have my theory about those fencing foils.

Imogen says, "Liam is basically a big teddy bear. He couldn't even catch that mouse we found when we first came on board."

"Are you sure it wasn't a kitten? Like the stowaway one they're keeping in the spa?"

She smiles, for the first time since we've come into this rain-room. "I mean, it could have been. We only saw it for a second before he jumped back and let it run past us."

"But that doesn't answer the question," I prompt. "Was there ever a time when you or Liam were alone during the LARP."

"He did go to the bathroom, but he was only gone for three or four minutes. I doubt he would have had time to get all the way down to the other end of the promenade to murder someone."

I have to agree with her there. I get a text from Logan. He's heading to the Blue Note, a lounge on the other side of the ship, for last minute preparations for my demo. Which means that's probably where I should be headed, too. I start to stand up, and Satchmo jumps out of my lap.

Imogen says, "Please. If Ash has to know about my dad, let me be the one to tell him."

I nod. "You should probably do that soon. It's relevant to the murder investigation, so it's going to come out one way or another."

"I understand." Imogen stands up. "Have fun with your demo."

Chapter Ten

After Imogen and I both leave the observatory, I make a quick stop to wash my hands, and by the time I get to the Blue Note, Logan has everything set up perfectly. Similar to the lounge I'd been in with Imogen, this space has glass walls, though the ceiling in here is opaque. The chairs and sofas in here are covered with plush blue velvet. Many of them have been pushed up against the wall so that a phalanx of folding chairs could be set up in front of a curved bar.

There are already a couple of people in the audience, waiting – including my Aunt Naomi and Uncle Greg. I rush over to where they are sitting. "What are you two doing here?"

Satchmo barks once, as he trots along behind me.

"We wanted to surprise you," Naomi says. She leans forward, holding out a hand to encourage Satchmo to come over to her. She ruffles Satchmo's ears, then looks up at me. "I figured you could use a couple more friendly faces in the audience."

"Heck, I just wanted the vacation," Greg says. He works offshore, so he doesn't always get to spend as much time as he likes with my aunt. "We stayed in our cabin last night, and ordered room service."

"That explains why Tiff was being so awkward before we left. I asked her where you were. She must have been trying not to ruin the surprise," I say, shaking my head at the silliness of it all. "Let's get together later. They do afternoon tea here in the library at four o-clock. Liam says they do a Victoria sponge that's to die for."

I regret the choice of words, but obviously Aunt Naomi hasn't heard yet that there's been a murder aboard the boat. She beams at me. "I do love a good afternoon tea."

Uncle Greg makes an exaggerated grimace. Then he grins. "And I love doing things that make your aunt happy."

The thing is, he's not just saying that. They spend so much time apart that when they are together, they both go out of their way to plan things the other will like to do. I love the relationship that they have, and for some reason, I'm not jealous of their happiness, despite my loss. Maybe it is because I see how hard they work at it.

Aunt Naomi leans up against Uncle Greg, a hug that really isn't a hug. "He's not kidding. He also agreed to get facials and pedicures later."

I try to imagine what would happen if I asked Logan to do that. Or Arlo. And honestly – I don't know either of them well enough to guess how they'd respond.

"Felicity," Logan says. He's holding up an extension cord, and the look on his face says there's trouble. "This doesn't seem to be working."

I get Satchmo settled in the corner, then I go over to the bar, and we sort things with the staff. Fortunately, they find a replacement cord, which also has multiple outlets, so I can get the chocolate melting in the tempering machine and set up the mini panner at the same time.

There's something about working with tabletop-sized machines that makes me happy. The machines themselves are just cute. They aren't practical for anything except demonstrations, but investing in the set means I have small machines to work with if I want to experiment with making tiny batches of new products.

Logan also has a table-top sized melanger on the bar, but I tell him, "That's for the other demo."

He asks, "We're not showing the bean to bar part of it first? Since that would be what happens in chronological order."

I tell him, "Liam thought starting with how to use chocolate would excite people, and then they would want to learn more in-depth stuff later."

"Fine." Logan takes the melanger off the bar, but he still looks uncomfortable with the idea.

I fill the spot with a mixing bowl and a piece of marble, so I can show how to table temper chocolate as well.

Arlo comes in too, taking a seat a few rows behind my aunt and uncle. I guess he's got a few minutes to spare, despite trying to solve this murder before the FBI guys show up.

I wind up with a packed crowd, standing room only five minutes before I'm supposed to start speaking. I am glad Naomi and Greg are here. I always get nervous before I give a presentation – though I'm usually fine once I start talking – and this is by far the biggest crowd I've ever addressed. Somehow, this is more intimidating than the demos and events I've been doing at the chocolate shop.

Plus I am going to have to be extra careful working with all of this equipment, considering how badly the boat is rocking. If we're still at sea tomorrow, and I do the demo with the table-top chocolate making equipment, it will be even more of an issue.

But I carry on as best I can, talking about choosing flavors, and how working with single origin chocolate is like working with fine wine. There are so many flavor notes, and even when blending in other ingredients, or when baking with it, you want to work to highlight the qualities of the chocolate you have chosen. I say, "Many bakers prefer to work with a more standardized product, and there are excellent chocolates for doing that, if what you want is a chocolate cake that tastes a neutral form of chocolaty. But at our shop, we prefer to make each chocolate's uniqueness stand out. Which is why our pastry chef, Carmen, sent along some basil-infused brownies that show off our Peru chocolate."

I cue Logan, and he circulates through the audience with a plastic container full of wrapped samples. There is a mixed reaction in the audience – some people are really taken aback when chocolate tastes like something they don't expect, but most of the audience seems to really like Carmen's creation. I anticipated this response, so afterwards, Logan goes back through the audience.

I tell everyone, "This time Logan is sharing one of our most popular truffles, which is inspired by the flavors of bread pudding. You're getting milk chocolate and nuts, with a hint of booze. While you're enjoying them, I'll be demoing making a batch of chocolate covered nuts using our panner and many of the same flavors."

A panner looks like a globe with a hole in one side that, when running, rotates like a clothes drier. I pour some almonds into the bottom. "Basically you're making a snowball." I turn on the machine, and the almonds rattle inside. "But you can't coat the nuts directly with chocolate, because chocolate sticks to chocolate. So first we add honey, and then cocoa powder to prepare the surfaces." I add these ingredients. "After that, it's all about temperature. We're going to add some very hot chocolate. If you ever try panning – be very careful. The chocolate needs to be around 160 degrees." I hit the squirt bottle of chocolate Logan has prepared for me with the temperature gun. 161 degrees. Perfect.

I use mitts to protect my hands, and I wait for a moment when the waves seem to have subsided, then I squeeze the heated chocolate onto the surface of the almonds. I let the whole thing rotate for as long as I can. I have the audience file past the machine so they can look inside. Getting a good thick coat on a panned product can take around six hours. But all I need is a thin shell to demonstrate the process. So before the audience gets bored with my chatter about all the things you can coat with a panner, I blast the coated nuts with supercooled air to finish them.

From the audience response it seems like between the two treats, everyone has found at least one that they like. We also let them try the nuts we just made. It can be expensive giving away samples, but since the cruise line is letting us sell in the boutique, I'm sure that we will make up the cost quite quickly, especially after this demo. There's a table set up at the back of the room where we have boxes stacked to hand sell after getting everyone hungry for cacao.

I start in on the part of the demo about handling chocolate. First, I want to show two ways of tempering.

I pour some melted chocolate out onto the marble slab and hold up my infrared thermometer gun. "When working with chocolate, the most important thing to keep in mind is temperature. When you break a chocolate bar, what do you hear?"

Logan helpfully demonstrates, breaking one of our Ecuador bars for the audience.

"There's a snap," someone says.

"Exactly," I say. "That snap is a sign that the chocolate is in temper. This means that the crystalline structure is correct for an enjoyable eating experience. There are six different forms that the crystals can take when chocolate cools, and what we want today is called Form V. Most of the others will give you a mushy finish. Form VI is close, and you do get something that hardens – it's just not quite right." I gesture at the bar Logan is still holding. As previously noted, he is hot, so some members of the audience are more focused on him than on me anyway. I say, "When you buy a chocolate bar, or chocolate wafers for baking, the chocolate is already tempered. So long as you don't go above 94 degrees, that crystalline structure stays intact, and you can carefully melt your chocolate to coat berries or pretzels, or something simple without having to re-temper it. But I think it is actually easier to temper the chocolate for your projects instead of worrying if you've passed 94 degrees."

A woman in the middle of the audience raises her hand. When I nod at her, she says, "But when chocolate gets hotter, won't it just burn?"

"That's a good point. When you melt chocolate, you always want to do it gently. If you're working with a lot of chocolate, like we do at the shop, you may want to invest in a tempering machine like the one I'm about to demo. Otherwise, if you're melting it on the stovetop, make sure to use a double boiler.

If you try to melt it directly, you'll probably wind up with a pot full of carbon."

"I just melt it in the microwave," some guy shouts out. "You're making it more difficult than it needs to be!"

I keep the smile plastered on my face. This is my presentation, and I'm not going to let some random heckler get to me. I say, "You can melt chocolate in the microwave, if that's what you prefer. Just keep a very close eye on it, microwaving at no more than ten or fifteen second intervals. Otherwise it can burn from the inside out, and you won't be able to see it happening."

"Yeah," a woman on the front row says. "I watch a lot of cooking shows, and I've seen people try to microwave chocolate, but they forget about it, and when they open the door, smoke comes out."

I nod. "Usually those are the shows where people are just learning to cook, right?"

I'm back on track now, and my audience is with me. I measure the temperature of the chocolate on the marble, then start working it with a pallet knife in one hand and a bench scraper in the other. The boat's excessive rocking makes coordination difficult, and when we hit a wave off rhythm, I stumble and wind up flinging chocolate up at my own face. The audience laughs, but it is kindly laughter.

Logan hands me a towel, and I wipe up my face. I ask the audience, "Better?"

The same lady who made the comment about the microwave disasters points at her own nose and says, "You still have a spot there, love."

I wipe at it. Everyone seems satisfied that I'm reasonably chocolate free, and I resume working the chocolate, until it develops peaks when I let it drop from the scraper.

The rest of the presentation goes as planned. I get a "surprise" video call from Carmen, who takes the audience on a virtual tour of the shop, showing off the areas where we make chocolate, the kitchen, where she has a tray of cookies coming out of the oven, the coffee bar, and the seating area with the pink and gray color scheme and our small selection of books.

"Speaking of books," I say, "Carmen, how it the cookbook coming?"

Carmen holds up her tablet and shows a picture of a chocolate souffle. "I've been testing recipes like crazy." She looks past me, out at the audience. "In case you haven't heard yet, we have a publisher for the *Greetings and Felicitations Cookbook*, and there's a release date. In a little over a year, you'll be able to sample some of my culinary genius at home."

"Why so long?" someone from the audience calls out.

"We have to double test every one of the recipes," Carmen says. "First, I make it, then I get someone else to test if they can replicate the results. Then it all has to be photographed. In the meantime, come into the shop when the ship docks, and I'll have lots of samples."

There's a murmur of happy noises throughout the crowd. Which I translate to even more potential sales.

Carmen says, "There's one more special guest here today."

Tiff walks into the camera's view, standing next to Carmen. Tiff is holding Knightley, who usually isn't big on being picked up, but today he's looking all cuddly. He's always liked Tiff, and she's extra patient with him. Knightley's picture is on most of our products. He's always been my little mascot. There are a few *awwwws* in the crowd as my bunny eats a piece of parsley, and I tell everyone how I got him as a rescue, letting everyone know that it is much better to take a bunny to a rescue center than to try setting one free, as domesticated rabbits don't do well in the wild.

When the presentation is over, and most of the chocolate has been sold, Arlo comes up to me and says, "That was fascinating."

I gently push his shoulder. "Since when did you like lectures? About cooking, no less?"

Arlo says, "You're a good speaker."

I feel unexpected heat in my cheeks. Why would him saying that make me blush? "Thanks."

"Would you come out on the deck with me? The rain has let up for a while, and I'd like to ask you something." Arlo has always been so self-confident, but right now he looks shy, his head tilted down, his shoulders raised, looking hopeful through his thick eyelashes. He hasn't looked at me like that since all those years ago, when we first started dating.

I can't help but glance over at Logan, and Arlo sees me do it. He winces. Logan, however, is too busy trying to get the leftover chocolate out of the tempering machine to notice.

"Sure, okay," I tell Arlo.

I call Satchmo to come with me, and we head outside, where the deck is wet, with water still dripping on it from the higher decks. The air feels clean and fresh, a calm in the middle of the storm.

I move towards the railing, watching the waves, which are still high, smacking against the boat. It is a little thrilling, a little scary. I'm beginning to get used to the ocean again.

Arlo asks, "Do you ever wonder what might have been, if we'd just talked once after that blow-up back at prom?"

I keep my eyes on the water. "So much has happened since then. I don't regret my life with Kevin, and that never would have happened if you and I had still been together."

"I know that, Lis," Arlo says. "And I would never want to take those memories away from you. Do you – we've never really talked about him. Do you want to tell me what Kevin was like?"

I realize that Arlo and I haven't seriously talked about much of anything since I came back to the island. I mean, we have had conversations, even resolved a few things about our breakup, but we were discussing the kids we used to be. But our lives as adults? A lot of that is blank to each other. "Okay." What about Kevin was most important? What would Arlo want to know? "Kevin was the kind of guy who would stop at a gas station on a road trip and come back with flowers. One time we drove from Seattle down to Joshua Tree, and when we stopped overnight, he pulled out this giant basket with chocolate covered strawberries and prosecco and a whole picnic. And these ridiculous daisies. I don't know where he got it all, but it wasn't there when we packed the car. He must have stopped while I was sleeping and put together this huge romantic gesture."

"That's not something I would have done," Arlo says. "I'd have come back with taquitos and coffee, and considered myself being thoughtful. You really would have missed out if you'd stayed with me."

I finally look at him. "But Arlo, that *is* thoughtful. You're a very different person. For me to expect for you to have done the same things Kevin did would just be weird."

"I can be romantic," Arlo says. "I know I wasn't very good at that when we were together before. But I was a kid, and I didn't really understand what romance was."

"I don't think I did either," I say. "Kevin was certainly better at it than me, and he shaped my views of what romance could be. He had such a practical job, but when he got home, he could just turn work off and be fully present. Even when it was something little, like him noticing that my coffee cup was empty or that I had a headache and he'd come rub my temples. I – I miss that."

There's heat at the back of my eyes, and I blink away the desire to cry. Not that Arlo would think any less of me for it. He'd asked me to talk about something he knows is deeply painful.

"I'm sorry," Arlo says. "I should have said something after the accident. Sent flowers then, or a card at least."

I shake my head. "Why would you? It had been so long. And the way things ended–"

"That's just it," Arlo says. "I never got closure. I always assumed that there was something wrong with me, something that made me unlovable. You know my dad left when I was a kid, and then you –" He stops, blinks back moisture that is glistening in his eyes. "There was always this little voice in the back of my head telling me that if I wasn't perfect enough people would leave." He shrugs. "Not that I'm trying to make you feel bad about it. You were that important to me. And I should have handled things differently. Zeke told me about your wedding, and when you moved to Seattle – and when you came back to Galveston. And why."

Zeke was one of our mutual friends, back in high school. He's one of those people I've kept in touch with over social media, in that vague occasionally liking their posts kind of way. I hadn't realized he'd been paying that much attention to my own status updates. Not that I'd ever talked much about Kevin's death on social media. I know a lot of people share every triumph and tragedy in their lives online, but I personally don't feel comfortable with that.

"How *is* Zeke?" I ask.

"Fine," Arlo says. But I can see he's not getting drawn off topic.

"I hadn't realized that you two are still friends." Why hadn't it occurred to me that just because Arlo had left the island, he hadn't cut all ties with it? After all, his mother was still here. And there was some reason he had come back.

"I would be surprised if you knew much about my life at all, Lis."

His words sting. I swallow back heat that floods my throat and chest. "That's fair."

Satchmo puts a paw on my leg and starts whining. He wants to bring me comfort with his warmth and his presence. I wish it was that simple.

After all, how do I deal with this gaping lack in myself? I'd started getting to know Arlo again while he was still with Patsy. And apparently, I hadn't bothered to really learn anything substantial about who he is now. Just like with Ash. Who else haven't I bothered to really know?

I say, "Then tell me. What happened after you left? And all those years in between."

Arlo turns around and leans against the wet railing. "I found my way. It wasn't easy. I needed a sense of purpose, and I didn't get it at any of the first jobs I took. Can you picture me as an assistant beekeeper?"

I look at Arlo's strong hands. "Yeah, I can see it. How did that happen?"

"When I left Texas, I went to New Mexico. I took a joyride through an apple orchard and damaged some of the hives when I crashed into them. Once I recovered from the bee stings, the guy who owned the farm offered me a job. He decided I needed to learn patience. He was right, but harvesting honey wasn't something I wanted to do for the rest of my life."

"They have apple orchards in New Mexico?" I ask.

Arlo gives me an amused look. "That's not the point, Lis. The point is it was a turning point. And I started looking for what might give me meaning."

"So you became a cop, the same way I turned to chocolate making when I was looking to find my own way, after Kevin died."

"Yeah. I suppose so." He looks at me for a long time, then finally says, "I found my purpose, but living up to it wasn't easy. I've thought about throwing in the towel more than once. I've seen how horrible people can be to each other, seen some things I wish I could unsee."

I nod. "Me too, recently." I, for one, would like to unsee Flint, lying dead with his face smashed up against my chocolate display.

Arlo leans closer to me and puts a hand on my arm. "I am sorry for that. Statistically, most people aren't going to encounter one murderer, let alone three."

"I hope you didn't bring me out here to tell me to stay out of it this time. Again."

Arlo gently squeezes my arm. "I'm hoping this time I'm not going to have to. We already have a solid suspect."

I start to pull away. "Arlo, Ash didn't do it."

"I didn't say he did."

"Then who?"

Arlo drops his voice. "Possibly Liam. I'm only telling you this because I want you to stay away from him."

"So my guess about the fencing foils panned out?" I can't help but feel a bit of elation that my idea may have helped crack another case.

Arlo moves his hand off my arm. "Actually, no. Logan used hydrogen peroxide as a home-made blood residue test, and the foils came back clean."

My smile fades. "Oh. So I didn't help then,"

Arlo shrugs. "You got me to look into Liam's past. Which is helpful. He's got an arrest on his record for assault."

"But how could he have gotten all the way to where Flint was killed and back? If he was only gone for a couple of minutes."

Arlo laughs. "So you've been talking to Imogen?"

I don't know if that laugh means he's not surprised that I'm trying to help Ash, or if he thinks it's cute that I'm trying to help or... or what. I repeat, "So how could he have gotten all the way there and back?"

Arlo says, "Imogen had a couple of glasses of rum punch at the party. So we're not sure how sound her judgement was on how long Liam was actually gone."

"That seems–" I start, but Arlo interrupts.

"I really shouldn't be talking about the case," Arlo says. "I probably shouldn't have said as much as I already have. Not that you wouldn't just hear everything from Logan." He sounds jealous about that last bit.

Fine. He doesn't want to talk about the case. Instead, I ask, "Why stay a cop, if there's so much you want to unsee?"

"Because I get to help people who need it. Because otherwise, the people doing bad things win." There's an intensity in his brown eyes that matches his words. An intensity I find attractive. "I'd rather fight the darkness in human nature than succumb to it."

"That's poetic," I say, trying to keep my voice even, despite the way his sincerity has taken me off guard.

Arlo hesitates, then he says, "Are you and Logan together. Because if you are, I just – you know."

I know what he's trying to say. I just don't know how to answer. "Arlo, it's complicated. Logan and I – maybe we've been trying to get to something. But with Kevin and everything I haven't been able–"

Arlo interrupts. "Let me uncomplicate it."

He pushes away from the railing, takes my face gently in his hands and kisses me. Intensely. It's such a familiar kiss. Something we've done a hundred times before, yet not in so long. It's like the years fall away between us, and we're right where we are supposed to be. And everything would shatter if I moved away to come up for air.

Arlo's the one who finally breaks the kiss. He says, "You do still feel something for me."

I'd be lying if I said no. Instead I say, "That just makes things even more complicated."

Arlo leans down and pets the beagle, who is still sitting where we left him. Arlo says, "I just want a chance to get to know you again. Is that too much to ask?"

"I don't know." And I mean it. Because if I'm already the little voice in Arlo's head telling him he's not good enough to be loved, then what happens if he feels like I've led him on? Especially after everything that has just happened with Patsy.

It is starting to rain again, so I use that as an excuse to run back inside, Satchmo racing beside me, nipping at the rain.

I'm looking down, flipping water out of my hair – when I run into Logan in the hallway. Just last night Logan said he wasn't going to be upset if I needed time deciding what I want out of life – and who I want to share it with. But I doubt he intended for me to go out and immediately kiss Arlo.

"Hey, are you okay?" Logan says.

"Yeah, I'm fine," I tell him, though I feel completely off kilter.

"You've got a little–" Logan runs a thumb across my cheek, and it comes away smeared with chocolate from the demo. And Logan's touch feels right, too.

I am so not the girl cut out for this situation. Everyone keeps telling me I don't have to make any permanent or immediate decisions about my future. But if I don't, how can I talk to either of these guys – who are both very much a part of my life – without feeling guilty?

Chapter Eleven

Back in my room, I'm hoping for a little time to be alone and think. I'm not good with change. I've only recently decided that I'm even open to the idea of trying to love again, and that's because Logan pulled me out of my grief. I haven't made any real promises to him, but I owe him something for that. And Arlo – I wouldn't have kissed him back like that if I didn't want to. I can't do things like that if I don't mean it.

I tell Satchmo, who is busily lapping water out of a decorative bowl I moved from the tiny coffee table to the floor, "There's only one thing for it. Forget love. Focus on the case."

I pat the tablet computer on my lap.

He tilts his head at me, one of those oversized ears flopping, like he's not sure if he's heard me right.

"What do you know?" I say. "You're in love with bacon treats."

I definitely have the dog's attention now. Not that I want it.

"I need to get this research done in time to make Autumn's first panel. How am I going to do that with you drooling at me for food I don't have?"

Satchmo is still stuck in the idea of bacon, and seems disappointed that there is none forthcoming.

"We all get disappointed from time to time. We should be half way to Saint Thomas by now." The captain had made an announcement this morning that the delay was because of the storm. A quick check of the weather confirms that the bad weather is supposed to finish blowing through tonight, or early in the morning. Which means that tomorrow, the FBI will be here to take over the case."

I meant to check out Ash's website before we'd left Texas and the roaming charges kicked in, but here we are now, hanging out in international waters, and I'm finally getting around to it. Since I'm already sure that Ash isn't the killer, paying the data fees to look at his site is probably a waste of funds. But I'm curious, and I need context on Ash's family to understand Liam – and if Liam really is guilty, to help solidify Arlo's case.

I access Ash's blog. There aren't any new posts up, not since the one where he announced the sailing of a murder mystery cruise out of Galveston, timestamped a few hours before we left. The post doesn't say that he's on board. A lot of people don't post when they're going somewhere until after the fact, because they don't want to get burglarized while they are away. But Ash doesn't strike me as that type of person.

I'm not sure what has halted Ash's little news engine – the lack of a phone or devastation over either being accused of murder or finding out he's adopted. Possibly all three. I never thought I'd feel sorry for the guy – or miss his news updates – but well, here we are.

I navigate to the 'About' page on the blog. There, Ash talks about himself more openly than I would have expected, sharing the story of how his grandfather inspired him to go into journalism, and admitting that –despite his admiration for his grandfather – Ash never finished his journalism degree. There's a list of links at the bottom of the page. I'm surprised to find that Ash also has a food blog, where he talks about Puerto Rican cooking. And that his home, a recently remodeled property in Galveston's Historic District, was featured last year in an interior design magazine. I click over to the article.

There are a couple of pictures of Ash at home. In one of them, he's sitting on an uncomfortable-looking green sofa with a huge long-haired white cat beside him. In the other, he's in a kitchen that's all white marble and stainless steel, and in the background, through the open doorway, I can just make out Liam shooting pool in the other room.

Wait a minute. Yesterday, Liam told me he had never been to Texas before. And yet, there he is, in the middle of Ash's photo shoot. Why would Liam lie about something like that?

I go back to the main page of the blog, and I realize there's more information here than I have time to digest. Ash has been blogging for years. And it hits me. At one point, Ash had done an exposé on Flint – the whole reason the cantankerous writer had punched him in the face in the first place. I wonder if that article is still up. The blog has a search function. I type in *Flint Bates* and get a hit with a picture of Flint with a cup of coffee in his hand and a black lab at his side. They're both sitting on a stone wall with woods in the background. It looks like a posed author headshot. But once you start reading the article, and get to the part where Ash talks about how Flint and Clove went into those very woods together, to a cabin the couple owned, but Flint came back alone – I look back up to the headshot, and a chill crawls down my spine, even though I know Clove is fine. I can't decide if it is because Ash has spun a compelling yarn with vivid word pictures – or if it is because the wording so strongly mirrors what Imogen said when describing what happened to her father, out on the boat with Flint.

Two went out . . . but Flint returned alone. It's all too ominous.

In the article, Ash lays out a lot of information about Flint – including the fact that Flint had a criminal record. And Ash ends with a plea for anyone with information on Clove's whereabouts in the days before her disappearance to come forward. The whole thing is odd. It draws a vague sense of anxiety into my core.

Autumn comes into the room to grab a lipstick and touch up her hair before heading out. I'm so glad for the interruption, for the sense of normalcy she brings with her. I just want to dish girl talk and think about something lighter than this murder.

Which brings me right back to the relationship drama I'd tried to avoid by focusing on the case. Autumn makes eye contact with me in the mirror. "Why are you blushing?"

"I kissed Arlo," I blurt out.

Autumn slowly puts her comb down on the counter and turns to face me. "You serious?"

"Well, he kissed me. But I kissed him back."

"Girl, you cannot tell me that five minutes before I have to go speak."

"Sorry." I disconnect the tablet from the internet. "Are you really okay with being on these panels?"

"Sure." She pats at her hair. "In the mystery world, apparently I'm still a star."

"You didn't realize that already?" I ask.

"I didn't expect people to recognize me. Or to still be reading my books. But I've talked to people who are."

"Well, I've always thought your books were amazing." Autumn has a way with characters, especially the protagonist of her main series, Melody Blues. There were parts of Melody that I connected with so hard, I would almost have thought Autumn had based her psychologically on me – despite Melody having grown up as a black orphan from the Bronx.

"You've read them?" Autumn looks surprised.

"I'm your best friend. Of course I read them." I hop up off the bed, and Satchmo stands up too. "Didn't I post about how awesome they were all over your social media."

Autumn shrugs. "Lots of people do that kind of thing, to be supportive. It doesn't mean that they actually read the books."

"How have we never talked about this?" I take Autumn's hand. "My favorite is *The Glass by Moonlight*. It has the most poetic, bluesy feel out of all of them."

Autumn looks like she is about to cry. And smeared mascara is certainly not what she needs right before her talk. "You know," she says, "There's a lot of you in Melody. When I started writing her, my best friend had moved away, and I was missing you something fierce."

"We should have stayed in touch better," I tell her. "I know we tried, but there was always so much distance. And a phone call just isn't the same."

"But you're home now. And you're going to be there when I get married. Let's not worry about lost time." Autumn lets my hand go and moves to the door.

"Just one question," I say.

She still has her hand on the door handle. "What?"

"You said you quit writing because something happened in real life, just like you wrote it in one of your books. A hit and run. But I don't remember reading that book."

Autumn's hand starts quivering. "It was never published. I've always thought – there was no way to prove it – but I believe Flint may have had something to do with that death."

There's a soft noise as a sheet of paper gets slipped under the door. Autumn bends over to pick it up. She glances at the text, then says, "This is obviously for you."

I hop up and take the piece of paper from her. I read over it. "This is from Wendy, the girl at the boutique. I think. She just signed it W. But I haven't met anyone else with the initial W aboard this boat."

"Are you going to meet her?" Autumn asks.

In the note, Wendy says she figured something out and wants to talk to me at 2 p.m. at the back of the boat, on the same deck as the ballroom. My guess is that she's going to be on a break from the boutique and wants to meet somewhere private – but at the same time not too far for her to get back to work.

"Yes," I say, after spending a few minutes thinking about it. "She probably feels more comfortable talking to me than to Arlo – and Ash hasn't made it a secret that he expects me to be the one who proves his innocence."

"So you're going to meet someone alone, at the back of the boat, on the strength of a hand-written note? I mean, why didn't she just knock on the door and tell you whatever she wanted right here? That note – it feels like a setup." Autumn takes the paper back from me and flips it over, examining it more closely. "And I don't think that's just mystery writer brain talking."

"Which is why I'm not going alone. I don't want to ignore the chance to get first-hand information – but I also don't want to ignore basic safety measures." I give her my most winning smile. "How about it? Want to be my plus one to this mysterious meetup?"

Autumn frowns at me. "Uh, no. I can help you with sleuthing theory, but I'm not about to jump in front of a bullet for you. Ask Logan to go."

Because we both know he's the kind of guy who totally would. I text Logan the details, plus a picture of the note, on the off chance his phone is on. Otherwise I'm going to have to track him down somewhere on a boat that suddenly feels very large.

There's a knock on the door.

"See," I say. "Wendy must have felt silly and come back to just talk."

Autumn opens the door, but it isn't Wendy. It's Imogen. Which sends a jolt of nerves through me. After all, Imogen's high on my personal list of suspects. Suddenly, Satchmo is leaning against my leg, one paw planted on top of my foot. He must have caught a whiff of my anxiety. Which says a lot about me, and nothing about Imogen's guilt or innocence.

Imogen smiles broadly at us. "Hey," she says to Autumn. "Liam wanted me to double-check that you got your schedule, and that you know that your first panel is starting soon."

"Hey yourself," Autumn says. "We were just heading that way."

I ask, "Why is it so important to Liam that Autumn be on programming? It's almost like he thinks she might bolt."

Imogen shrugs. "You'd have to ask him that yourself. He strikes me as the kind of guy who likes to overplan and micromanage, but I don't know him very well. Ash has talked about Liam, but I never met him before this cruise." She hesitates. "I passed Wendy in the hall. It almost looked like she was coming from here. What's that about?"

I force myself not to hide the note that is still in my hand, or bring attention to it. Satchmo whines and presses his paw harder on my foot.

Autumn says, quite truthfully, "Nobody knocked on our door until you just did."

My phone dings with an incoming text. I've almost stopped caring about how much onboard communication is costing me. Logan has texted back a thumbs up emoji.

I tell Imogen, "We're heading down to the panel in just a moment."

"Good." She hesitates like she wants to say something else, but then she turns and leaves.

After the door has closed, Autumn says, "I know I promised to stop doing this after my guess was so far off last time, but if this murder was a book, and I was writing it, it *wouldn't* be Imogen. She's too obvious."

"But in real cases, Logan says the most obvious solution is usually the right one," I counter. "Which means it could be her, because of what happened with her father's boat." I run my hands across my face. "Or it could have been Liam, trying to protect Ash, before he knew what Ash's secret was. Or Clove, bitter about the new girlfriend or the divorce. Or Lupe, disappointed about something in the relationship. Or even Wendy, because she had the best opportunity to hide Flint's body in the boutique. There's no shortage of suspects in this one."

"Don't forget me and Ash," Autumn says. "We each had a fight with Flint shortly before he died. I know I'm innocent, but are you sure Ash didn't do it? He's smart enough to have framed himself, to draw away serious suspicion."

"I'm positive," I tell her. "It just feels like nobody else could have done it, because of the time frame. Maybe Wendy's information is what we need to figure all of this out."

I take my tablet with me as we go out into the hall. You never know. I might want to take notes.

I tell Satchmo to heel. Then Autumn, the beagle and I head towards the ballroom. Along the way, we meet Drake and his mom, who are also going to watch the panel.

Drake takes Autumn's hand and says, "Hey, beautiful."

The soft smile Autumn gives him – like he's the only thing that matters – no matter what's about to happen – makes me happy. And a little jealous. I'd had that. I'd lost it. I keep thinking that I'm recovering from the loss, that I'm ready to move forward with other people in my life. So when do I stop feeling jealous that other people have what I've lost?

Drake gives Autumn a brief kiss, and says, "You got this."

We all start heading to the ballroom together. Charlene leans in close to me and whispers, "I still think they're rushing things, but when they look at each other like that, you can't argue with it."

"I agree," I whisper back. "What are we going to do?"

We're a few steps outside the ballroom when Clove marches up to Autumn and demands, "Are you even still writing?"

"Excuse me?" Autumn says, looking clearly confused.

"I said, are you even still writing?" She crosses her arms over her chest. "You're taking Flint's place on the programming. Given how you felt about him . . . now that he's . . . it's just tacky. You're not even writing, so why do you need the marketing op?"

Autumn says simply, "The organizers asked me to do this – not the other way around."

Clove rolls her eyes. "Whatever."

Drake steps forward. "I need you to be a little bit nicer to my fiancé. She deserves as much respect as you would want people to give to you if you decided to go back into public speaking after a hiatus."

Clove's teeth click shut, audibly. Then she makes a huffing noise and stalks into the ballroom. We all go in too, and I notice that Drake is walking protectively next to Autumn, keeping himself between her and Clove. I have to say, the more I get to know about Drake, the more he seems like an honestly good guy.

Charlene and I find seats near the front, and the beagle promptly falls asleep under my chair. Drake helps Autumn get settled in at her spot – which is next to Clove at the long table set up on the stage. He looks like he wants to get the panelist to trade out seats, but he can't exactly ask that. He mutters something frustrated under his breath when he comes back to join us.

Though she's keeping her face carefully neutral now that she's on stage, under the more intense lights, Clove looks like she's been crying. Clove tries to hide a sniffle. Autumn reaches into her bag and hands Clove a tissue, looking sympathetic despite Clove's harsh words to her earlier.

Clove says something, but the only word that echoes back over the microphone is, "Dead,"

I flinch. Satchmo raises his head up off my shoe.

Drake leans towards me and whispers, "I have a feeling everyone is about to find out what happened last night."

He's not wrong. The panel starts with nice, easy questions. Where did the writers get the inspiration for their series? How do you write a series without it being repetitive or getting bored as a writer? What is it about each series' protagonist that makes this person a good sleuth?

Autumn has excellent answers for all of these questions. I'm proud of her up there, talking about work I know she put so much of herself into.

The moderator mentions that many authors still have day jobs and asks, "What's your day job or other side gig?"

When it's Autumn's turn to answer that one, she says, "I haven't published in a while, but I still get royalties from my previous works. But mainly I sell jewelry on Etsy."

"You can live off that?" Tucker asks incredulously.

I've wondered that myself. But Autumn always has money when we go for lunch or for drinks, and she prides herself on never being late with bills or holding a balance on her single credit card. So who am I to judge?

Autumn says, "Mostly." She looks out at the audience, as though evaluating whether she can trust them with what she is about to say. "I really don't like the term independently wealthy. But my great-aunt died the year I turned twenty-eight. I was shocked to find out she'd left me her entire estate. Apparently, I was the only one who let her teach me how to crochet as a kid, and how to bake, and kept in touch, even after she was in a nursing home."

What? How do I not know this? We've been friends all this time, albeit long distance ones. I find myself leaning forward, having to fight the urge to jump up out of my chair.

Autumn says, "I didn't tell anybody about it, because I didn't want it to change the way I live, or how people view me."

There's a pause, and a couple of hands go up in the audience. The moderator calls on one of them.

The guy says, "This question is for Miss Ellis. I've read all the *Melody Blues Mysteries*, and I heard that there was supposed to be one more. I even found an image for the book cover in an archive, though apparently the publisher pulled it. Whatever happened to *Write Me a Melody*?"

Autumn's lips form a solid line. Finally she says, "I never finished it. I'd outlined an ending, but it didn't feel right."

"Apparently, Autumn was going through a lot of things at the time," Clove says coldly. "Maybe don't ask her about it."

Yikes! I'm not sure exactly where that icy tone is coming from. Is she mad at the guy in the audience? Or at Autumn?

Autumn looks like Clove just punched her. "I wasn't the only one."

The audience looks riveted, like some of them are hoping for a cat fight on stage. Satchmo climbs into my lap, despite the small chair, hanging half way off the front of my knees. He is determined to quell my anxiety, but I'm not sure anything can do that.

Someone shouts out, "Does this have anything to do with Mr. Bates's murder?"

And there it is. People are craning their necks, trying to figure out who said that.

Clove says, "Possibly," at the same time Autumn says, "Absolutely not."

The other two writers on the stage, Aarti Andrews and Tucker McDougal, look at each other and shrug. The moderator blurts out, "Flint's dead?"

The same guy who just dropped the bombshell about the murder says, "I overheard a couple of crew members talking about it when I went to the spa. And one of them said Flint had had a fight with Miss Ellis right before."

Autumn's body language goes rigid, and her lips form a narrower line. "Flint and I did have a difference of opinion in the past, which was never settled. We used to be in the same critique group. We had a falling out."

"Falling out?" Clove splutters. "You sent dead roses to our house. I'm the one who answered the door, you know? It was the creepiest thing that's ever happened to me."

Drake whispers to me, "Would Autumn really do that?"

The look on his face reads pure panic, like he's realizing that maybe he doesn't know Autumn that well after all.

I tell him, "She would have to have a really good reason."

From the stage, Autumn says, "That was after he slammed *The Glass in Moonlight* all over social media. It was my best book, and he was busy telling everyone I was a hack. All because he was convinced that I had taken his precious pen."

"Well, somebody took it," Clove says. "It could have been you."

"So now you're calling me a thief?" Autumn asks.

"And possibly a murderer," Clove says.

Someone from the audience shouts, "What pen?" but everyone on the stage ignores her.

"What about you?" Autumn asks. "You did divorce Flint, after all. What caused trouble in paradise?"

Clove's face flushes almost as red as her hair. "Flint wasn't good with money. He sank everything we had into another investment scheme."

Autumn looks skeptical. "You sure it wasn't over creative differences? I did a little research this morning. I found out he'd gotten a contract for a new series – with characters I know darn well you two created together, years ago."

Clove snaps, "That happened after the divorce. I was planning to sue him over the creative rights. Which I can't exactly do, now that he's dead."

"But you could write the series yourself," the moderator points out.

Both Autumn and Clove glare at him. At the same time, they both say, "That's not likely to happen."

There's a beat of silence, and the same woman from the audience shouts, "What pen?"

Clove says, "It was a Mont Blanc that Flint received as a gift from John le Carré. It was engraved, and therefore irreplaceable. It was on the table at the beginning of our critique group meeting. But by the end, it was gone."

"Which means you have a one in seven chance of being right assuming I took it," Autumn says. "I don't get Flint's reasoning."

Clove shrugs. "You were the only spy novel fan in the group. Other than Flint himself."

Autumn says, "Did you ever think someone might have stolen it to sell it? To a fan?"

Clove clearly hasn't considered this. She just blinks at Autumn.

The moderator takes a stab at getting the panel back on track, saying, "We haven't heard from Aarti or Tucker in a while. How about a question for one of them?"

It's a valiant effort. I have to admire him for it.

Chapter Twelve

Drake gets up and heads for the door, looking gun-shy. Autumn is still sitting at the table on the stage, distress in her eyes as she watches him go. They're still trying to salvage the panel, so she can't exactly stand up and follow him. So I do instead.

Satchmo isn't excited about getting dumped off my lap onto the floor, but he still follows me as I leave the ballroom. I find Drake in the open area outside, leaning back against the wall.

"You okay?" I ask.

He shrugs. "Do you think she might have stolen that guy's fancy pen?"

I shake my head a definite no. "You know her better than that."

"That's just it," Drake says. "Watching her fighting with that other author up on stage. I don't think I know her at all."

I feel a weight growing in the pit of my stomach. "What are you saying?"

He tenses his lips in a way that looks like he's holding back emotion. "Maybe my friends were right. Maybe my mamma's right. Who gets engaged after a month?"

"You do." I poke him in the chest. "Because in your heart, you know that Autumn is a good person. And that she's the one for you." I can't believe I'm saying this, after all my protests that they are rushing things. But if he pulls away from Autumn now, when she needs him the most, their relationship might not recover. And I've slowly come to see just how much she needs Drake.

Drake huffs out a breath. "You're right. I shouldn't do anything hasty."

Alarm spikes through me. "Like what?"

Drake makes intense eye contact with me. "Like call off the wedding."

A panicked half laugh escapes my throat. "Because she might have stolen a pen ten years ago?"

"Because she's the kind of person who would send somebody dead flowers. I've never seen Autumn hurt anyone before. On our first real date, she paid the bill at dinner for a couple whose credit card got declined. Once I realized what she was doing, I tried to take care of it, but she was way ahead of me – because she saw someone in distress and she acted. So which one is the real Autumn?

"Both." I gesture with my hands, palms up. "People are complicated, and we all have our bad days. Can you honestly tell me you've never done something stupid or mean?"

Drake splutters out a choked half laugh. "One time, I gave a guy a black eye for insulting my favorite basketball team. Sometimes library conferences really can get out of hand. It was not my finest hour."

"Does Autumn know about that?" I ask.

Drake says, "Maybe I should have told her. It didn't seem relevant to our current relationship."

"See." I put a hand on his arm. "Yes, you impulsively got engaged. But now, you've got to put in the work to get to know each other. So what if you're doing it backwards?"

Drake makes eye contact again, and this time it is hesitant. "I know Autumn saw me walk out. What do you suggest I do?"

"Go to the bar and get a couple of drinks and meet Autumn with them when she comes out of the ballroom. Then go somewhere and just talk."

Drake pushes away from the wall. "Thanks," he says, then he hesitates. "You were married for a long time before your husband passed."

"Yeah," I say, trying to keep emotion from welling into my voice.

Drake asks, "Was the work worth it?"

I nod, unable to find words. After a long moment of just staring at Drake, who is looking so naïve and hopeful, I manage to say, "Completely. And that's how I know, if love is real, you don't want to let it go. You never know how much time you really have."

Drake puts a hand on my shoulder. "I'm glad you're starting to find love again, too."

Wait a minute. Is he talking about Arlo? Did Autumn already tell him about that kiss? Or was he referring to Logan, and the amount of time I've been spending with him?

But before I can ask, Drake has already walked away. Satchmo is sitting there, head cocked to one side, that ear flopped up, waiting for me to tell him what we're going to do next. I wish I knew. I peek back into the ballroom, where Aarti is talking about how she tests the recipes that she includes at the back of her books. The audience seems to be paying a reasonable amount of attention. I don't want to disturb everyone by going all the way back up to the front, so I start scanning for a seat at the back.

"Felicity!" Arlo stage whispers from somewhere behind me.

I turn away from the door and spot both Arlo and Logan heading across the open area towards me.

Arlo asks, "Were you watching the panel?"

"When everything self-destructed?" I ask. "Yeah. But it's under control now."

"Good," Arlo says. "You can tell me what happened. I need to get your official statement, anyway, before the FBI shows up. I want to hand them everything as complete as I can."

Logan says, "I'll check out the rest of the panel, then, and see what the vibe is like when people start leaving the room." He gives me a nod that tells me he hasn't forgotten our appointment with Wendy later. But he doesn't bring it up in front of Arlo. Which is good, because Arlo would probably try to nix the meetup as being too dangerous. Or against police procedure. Or both.

I look longingly in the direction Logan is going, because I'd wanted to be there when Autumn got to leave the stage, but honestly, Drake has that covered. I hope. He probably hasn't even had time to make it to the closest bar yet, so I shouldn't be worried about him making it back. But what if he gets down there and loses his nerve? It's not like he could leave the ship – but it is possible he could call off the wedding after all.

I follow Arlo to a seating area near a set of windows. Whoever built this ship was obsessed with glass. The storm is clearing, so there's only occasional spattering of rain.

Arlo asks, "We okay, Lis?"

I nod. "Whatever we are, it's going to be okay. I haven't much had time to process what happened this morning."

"And I'm not planning to push anything," Arlo says, as Satchmo makes his way over to us. Arlo scratches the beagle behind the ears, and Satchmo settles down next to Arlo's chair. "Let's talk about what happened when you found the body."

I go back through everything that happened, from spotting the stowaway kitten, to what was said after Liam and Imogen joined us. Which gives me a natural opening. "It's the weirdest thing. When we were at the opening party yesterday, Liam specifically told me he'd never been to Texas before. But then I saw pictures of him in Ash's house on Galveston. Why would he lie?" I show him the pictures, still up on my tablet.

Arlo has been taking notes. He pauses. "That's a good question. We should probably ask him." Arlo gestures to where Liam is heading for the ballroom.

Liam sees us and waves. Arlo gestures him over.

Liam says, "We're going to have to make a shipwide announcement about Flint's death. After the debacle in there–" He gestures towards the room, where the panel is still in progress. "There's going to be no keeping it quiet."

"That was inevitable," Arlo says. "But before you do that, I've got a couple of questions."

"Shoot," Liam says.

"Felicity tells me that you told her you've never been to Texas before. So how did you like Galveston?"

Liam shoots a look at me that I can't quite read. "It wasn't the bluest water in the world, but I still enjoyed the beach. I didn't see a lot of the rest of the island."

Arlo takes my tablet from me and holds it out to Liam. "But here's the thing. Here's this picture of you, at Ash's place on the island. Can you explain that?"

Liam frowns. "That's what I hate about dealing with the police. If you know the answer to a question, why not just ask it directly?"

Arlo stands up, seems to be re-evaluating Liam. "These dealings with the police. Are they part of why you just lied to me?"

Liam glances off to the side, as though considering running away. But this is a boat, so obviously there's nowhere for him to go. "Okay, look. There's a warrant out for my arrest in Texas. Over a couple of speeding tickets. You know how it is. You get out on those forever stretches of highway, and you lose track of how fast you're going."

Arlo says, "I've been there. Back when I was younger, of course." He gestures at Liam. "You can accidentally get lost in the rhythm of the road. But you can't just accidentally not pay a ticket. That's a choice."

Liam asks, "So am I in trouble?"

Arlo says, "I'd recommend just paying the tickets. This cruise line is going to keep sailing out of Galveston, so if they remain unpaid, we're going to know just where to find you."

"Gotcha." Liam straightens the collar of his shirt. "Give me a couple of months at my current paycheck, and I might just be able to afford to do that."

Arlo shrugs. "I'm homicide. Not my priority."

There's the noise of chatter from inside the ballroom, and people start streaming out of the door. I scan the crowd. Drake is making his way back through in the opposite direction, carrying two glasses garnished with pineapple chunks and strawberries.

Just the kind of thing Autumn will like. Good for him. Maybe he does know her a little better than he thinks.

Arlo gestures out the windows. "The storm is clearing up. Which means the FBI agents will be on their way soon. I hope I don't have to point out that having them think you're interfering with their investigation is a much bigger deal than you asking a few questions of folks suspected by the Galveston PD, Lis." He looks me straight in the eye. "You think I keep telling you to stay out of these things because I'm holding you back. But that's not it. Investigating is my job, and a risk I'm trained for – but not a risk any civilian should take. If sleuthing thing is something you really want to do, go to the police academy and learn how to do it right. You'd have to learn how to handle a gun – and I know how much you hate those – but I could definitely give you a letter of recommendation."

It's endearing. Behind the gruffness he keeps throwing at me, he really does care.

Looking at the concern in his brown eyes, framed by those thick eyelashes, I almost tell him about the meetup with Wendy. Almost. Instead, I take back my tablet and show him the clock on it, saying, "I didn't realize it was getting so late. I need to get the dog back to Bea in time for her event."

I turn to go.

"Lis," Arlo says. "I'm not trying to make you uncomfortable."

If I look back at him, I'll cave. I'll get sidelined from helping investigate. And he'll never get the same information out of Wendy.

I clear my throat. "I gotta go." I bring Satchmo back to heel and head off to look for Bea.

I meet her in the hallway halfway to the elevator, coming back to look for me. Satchmo breaks from heeling and trots over to Bea, who tells the beagle, "No treats for you yet. You're going to have to go through your paces on stage. Then you can have one. Just one."

She's talking to Satchmo like she expects him to understand fluent English. And he seems to pout, like he understands. Which brings a moment of lightness to such a bleak day.

Chapter Thirteen

Bea's presentation is in the auditorium, a much larger space that the ballroom. It reminds me of the historic opera house in Galveston. In fact – I think this room may have been designed after the Grand, with similar tiers of balcony seating and the same rounded boxes with red upholstered vintage chairs. The big difference is that at either side of the stage, there's a dark wooden ramp allowing performers to walk down to the same level as the audience.

This kind of space is usually reserved for musical performances or magic acts, or whatever the biggest headliners a cruise has to offer. Liam wasn't exaggerating when he called Bea a rockstar. I'm there early enough to get a seat on the front row, but the space starts filling up around me.

Imogen sits down a few seats away from me, and soon she is joined by Craig and her other LARPer friends. Liam sits down at the end of the row.

I'm saving the seat right next to me in case Logan shows up to strategize what we are going to do when the demo is over and we go to meet Wendy. She hadn't exactly said come alone, but I'm hoping she won't freak if Logan hangs back and lets us talk. Assuming the note really was from Wendy, and not Imogen.

Imogen had seemed genuinely confused. If she had left the note – let's just say she's an excellent actress. Which may be the case, with her LARP experience and all. I'd seen her change her emotions on a dime last night. So let's just say I'm glad I asked Logan to accompany me to this mystery meet.

I glance down the row at Imogen now. She doesn't seem to be paying any extra attention to me.

Logan comes in and sits down in the chair I'd saved. "Hey," he says, putting his hand over mine.

"Hey," I say, frozen by this touch. I like having Logan's hand on mine. But only a couple of hours ago, I had kissed Arlo.

Logan pulls his hand away, giving me a look that is more puzzled than hurt. He says, "I scoped out the area at the back of the boat. There's a staircase coming down to it. The railing's open, but it wraps around to areas with lifeboats on both sides. As long as you stay out in the middle of the space, there's nowhere to hide to ambush you. I'll get there early and check out those stairs again, and wait on them in case you need me."

"Okay." I glance at the stage, where Bea is adjusting a microphone attached to her shirt. She's traded yesterday's tee-shirt for a black silk blouse and added long, sparkly earrings. I say, "I'll be careful. Though I wish I knew why she wants to meet in such a random spot."

"You won't know until you get there. It's the nature of the gig." He hesitates. "Felicity, there was no way I could bring a weapon on board this ship. So my ability to protect you is limited."

I nod. "I know. They won't even let you bring the pepper spray."

He squeezes my hand. "So be careful. If you get even a hint that you might be in danger, abandon the whole thing."

"I will. I promise." I pull my hand away and turn to watch Bea on the stage. There's a giant screen behind her, showing a close-up of her, making the demo much easier to see.

But Bea has a remote in her hand, and she starts by switching the screen over to a pre-recorded presentation on police dogs. There are video clips of German Shepherds and Doberman Pinschers in action, subduing criminals and finding lost children. There's still shots of airports, schools, even the port. After showing off photos of heroic dogs she's trained over the years, Bea switches the screen back to her closeup and asks, "Are you all ready to meet a real-life police dog with one of the most distinguished service records in the history of Baltimore PD?"

She gets a round of applause.

"All right!" She continues the buildup. "He's one of the toughest cops I've ever met, and he's dealt with murder, theft and kidnapping. Say hello to Satchmo."

She makes a hand gesture and Satchmo trots out onto the stage. When the audience realizes this fierce police dog is a beagle instead of a bruiser, they all start laughing. Satchmo seems to intentionally play this for comic effect, shaking his head and holding out a paw, like he wants to shake hands with every one of us.

Bea says, "I know what you're thinking. But don't let the fact that he's adorable fool you. This doggo's keen nose has been responsible for solving more than 130 crimes. To let you see his capabilities, I'm going to need a couple of volunteers from the audience to join me on stage."

She pulls six random people – including my aunt, LARP-er Craig, and Clove – and has them come up the ramp on the right side and onto the stage. At Bea's direction, each volunteer picks up a different colored three-pound sandbag. Bea says, "I need each of you to place your bag on a different part of the stage."

The volunteers all do as asked.

"Now I need a personal item from each of you. Don't worry—they'll all be returned intact."

When the volunteers each hand her a hat or a scarf for Satchmo to scent on, I realize she hadn't picked these people quite so randomly after all. The objects match the colors of the sandbags. The volunteers all move back onto the ramp, behind Bea.

Bea says, "Despite the presence of all of these scents, Satchmo should be able to pick out the one we're looking for and alert on it."

She bends down and holds out Aunt Naomi's scarf. Bea accidentally drops the rest of the items on the stage. Satchmo sniffs it, at the pile. Bea scoops the items up, and holds out Aunt Naomi's scarf again. Satchmo snuffles around the stage, and heads off roughly in the direction of the purple sandbag. He's almost reached it when he takes a hard right and heads for the wings, soon disappearing from sight.

"Satchmo," Bea calls. She sounds confused.

There's a crashing sound as something falls backstage, then Satchmo comes trotting back with a rolled-up cloth object in his mouth. He ignores Bea and brings the object down the left ramp, right to Liam in the audience.

Liam takes the cloth from the dog, a bemused smile on his face, like he assumes this must be part of the demo. "What's this, little guy?" he asks, standing up and turning to face the audience. He shakes out the fabric. It's a tee-shirt with a shark on it, just like the ones Autumn and her group were wearing during the LARP last night. Only this one has dark bloodstains on it. My insides feel a bit queasy. From the size of those stains, it had been more than just a surface injury.

Logan points out the obvious. "That has to be Flint's blood splashed across that shark."

Which seems even more macabre, considering what Imogen had told us about her father and the boating accident. Flint and Imogen's dad had been out hunting sharks, after all. And hadn't it been Liam who had chosen the shark tees for Autumn's team? Had it been some kind of message? That he knew more than he was letting on? Or even if it hadn't been intentional, even if he really hadn't met Imogen before, could Liam have taken the chance when he'd gotten the shirts for Autumn and her friends to grab an extra one to cover his clothes?

Before I can even think of how to ask that out loud, Liam says, "Now wait a minute." He looks down at the tee and then glances around like he's not sure whether to drop it or run up on stage and give it to Bea. Arlo, who had been towards the back of the audience, starts making his way towards Liam, who looks relieved to have someone wanting to take charge of the shirt. Liam says, "We sell these in the shop, and I hand out a lot of them. Even if my scent is on here, that doesn't make me a murderer."

"I didn't say it did," Arlo says. "But it sure does make for some interesting questions I need to ask." Before the FBI gets here, of course, and it's no longer his case. Not that Arlo is going to let me hear the answers to those questions. As if to echo my thoughts, he adds, "We should talk somewhere a little less public, of course."

"Of course," Liam say. "I have nothing to hide, but I don't want to make this any more tawdry than it has become."

Arlo looks sadly at Logan. "While I'm talking to Liam, can you track down Autumn Ellis, and everyone who was on her LARP team last night?"

"I can probably help with that," I whisper to Logan.

Maybe Arlo reads lips, because he gives me a dirty look. Nonetheless, I follow Logan out of the auditorium.

Once we're back at the elevator bank, Logan says, "I'm sure Autumn's phone is off. So this could be quite a task. We might be able to get the ship staff to page her."

I say, "We can if it comes to that, but maybe this won't be as complicated as you think. She and Drake are probably still pretty close to the ballroom, somewhere sipping cocktails and stopping all of this from putting a rift in their relationship."

Logan arches an eyebrow. "And whose idea was that?"

I run my hand along the railing, as we take a ramp up to a different deck level. "Mine. Drake freaked that he didn't know all this stuff about Autumn's past."

"And you talked him out of postponing the wedding." Logan puts a hand on my shoulder, gently turning me so I have to look at him. "Why? I thought that was what you wanted. For Autumn to take her time and make sure this is the right fit for her future."

"Not since I've gotten to know Drake better. I got to see him stand up for Autumn, and show her nothing but respect. If he pulls away now – she'll be devastated, and it won't be fair. I was worried about her getting engaged so fast because it seemed impulsive." I feel heat flame into my face as I speak candidly. "But a lot of this has been about me. Because if Autumn gets married, that's a whole set of wedding photos without Kevin in them. I'll be there with someone else."

"You mean me," Logan says. "We're still going together, right?"

I had been sincere when I had invited him to be my plus one. No matter what happens, I'm not going to back out of that.

"Of course," I say. But I have to be honest. "If that's still what you want. You should know that Arlo kissed me earlier."

"I already knew that," Logan says. "I told you, I'm not pushing you to make any decisions right now."

"Right." I start walking again. How can he be so calm, knowing I'm trapped between him and some other guy, not knowing what I want? And I don't even want to think about how Logan had found out about that kiss. So much of this ship is made of glass, and I'd run into Logan not long after walking away from Arlo. Had Logan actually seen me kiss someone else? Heat flames into my face. I renew my resolve to focus on the case, though it's difficult to keep myself from just staring at Logan, hoping he'll say something to make this easier. I say, "I don't understand what just happened in the auditorium. Why did Satchmo bring that shirt to Liam instead of Bea?"

"You know why," Logan says. "It's a good chance he's guilty."

I shake my head. "Actually, I think that tee-shirt makes it less likely that Liam did it. He would have to have somehow killed Flint in those few minutes when Imogen said he went to the bathroom. So why not just throw the shirt overboard? Or hide it somewhere closer to the place where Flint was murdered?"

Logan says, "This whole case is starting to feel similar to that book that's on auction. *Murder on the Orient Express*. Do you remember the scarlet kimono?"

"I thought you didn't read much," I tease him.

He shrugs. "I saw the movie."

I pause, thinking about the scarlet kimono in *Murder on the Orient Express*. The whole plot of that book revolved around a group of murderers who planned to kill someone on a train, then get rid of the evidence and exit the train before being found out. They had invented a woman wearing a scarlet kimono as a mystery suspect for Christie's detective to find. "You think that the killer first stashed that shirt somewhere closer to the murder, anticipating being able to go back and get it before the body was discovered, only I stumbled over Flint sooner than expected."

Logan says, "The boat basically stopped moving after that, so it would be easier for divers to find things thrown off of it than it would have been had we continued on to Saint Thomas, so then the killer had to figure out what else to do with the shirt."

I think about it. "Everyone knew about the dog demo. Which makes putting that shirt where Satchmo would scent on it a perfect red herring."

"I wouldn't say perfect," Logan grumbles. "It is possible the killer's DNA is still on that shirt." He hesitates. "Maybe. And there's no guarantee the dog would find it. Which makes the ploy just plain weird."

"It feels like everybody on board this boat had a reason for hating Flint," I tell him.

"Maybe they all did it," Logan quips. "Like in the book."

"That's not even funny," I tell him.

It doesn't take us long to track down Autumn and Drake, who are sitting at a table by yet more windows, holding hands and looking out at the water. Somehow, they've secured a plate piled high with chocolate covered strawberries. Logan and I walk over to them.

Logan gestures to the strawberries. "Can I snag one of those?"

"Sure," Drake says, gesturing at the plate with his free hand.

"I take it everything worked out," I say.

Autumn says, "It feels good to get the past out in the open. We had the ex-es talk while we were at it."

Another thing I think they should have done *before* getting engaged, but I'm going to hold my tongue on that one.

Logan slowly eats the strawberry. Which I have to say is pretty sexy to watch. But then he gets a serious look on his face, and I can tell he's about to kill the blissful vibe.

Logan says, "I hate to ask you both this, but I need you to show that you still have your team tee-shirts from last night's LARP. Drake, your mother's too."

Autumn lets go of Drake's hand. "Why?"

"It just – it has to do with the case. Not that I'm trying to accuse you of anything. This time." Logan gives her a wry grin. At one point in a different case, he had indeed been convinced that she was a murderer. "But we don't want to leave any questions for the investigators who are going to take over."

"We need to hurry," I say with urgency. "It's almost time for that meeting." Both Autumn and Logan should know what I'm talking about. Autumn probably already told Drake, but I'm still trying to be discreet.

"It will be fine," Logan says. "Ship security is going to meet us at your room, so we can have impartial witnesses that what they are presenting are their shirts."

His phone is in his hand, but how had he even had time to contact security? But sure enough, by the time we get back to the cabin, there's a thin guy wearing a uniform that somehow seems too big for him, waiting at the door. Autumn uses her key to open it, and steps over to the closet. She takes out the small mesh bag she's brought for dirty clothes and proceeds to produce a tee-shirt, which the security guy photographs her holding.

Then we go up a couple of decks, to Drake and his mother's room. When he opens it, I can't help but let out an appreciative gasp. Compared to the tiny stateroom I'm sharing with Autumn, this suite is a palace. The living room alone is bigger than our entire stateroom, and there's enough seating between the leather sofa, teal loveseat and small chairs for eight people.

Drake says, "A bit extravagant, I know. It was the only thing they had for a last-minute booking. And that was a call-back, because someone had cancelled."

He sounds embarrassed, though he must be good with money if he could afford this last-minute splurge on a librarian's salary.

We follow him into the suite's shared bathroom, which is still small, but feels about four times the size of the one Autumn and I have. There's even a built-in hamper recessed into the wall. Drake opens it. He looks startled to find it empty.

"Maybe it's in my room," he stammers. We follow him into one of the bedrooms, where the bed is neatly made, but there's a pair of striped boxers on the floor. Drake surreptitiously kicks them into a corner. He opens the closet and flips through the hanging clothes. There's a suit, a couple of dress shirts, a couple of plain tee-shirts, but no graphic tees at all.

"I don't know what happened."

I try to telegraph to Logan with a very intense look that this doesn't feel right. Drake doesn't even have a motive for killing Flint. So why on Earth should his clothes go missing?

There's a rattle of the door handle turning. Both Logan and the security guy step between me and Drake and the door.

When the door opens, Drake's mother is standing there, her mouth open at finding us all in her room. She has her shoes in her hand, and looks very much like she just wants to sit down.

"Mamma," Drake says. "Where have you been?"

"I just took a ballroom dancing lesson," she says. "It's one form of dancing I've never tried. Why? What happened?"

"Mamma." Drake moves over to her and takes both her hands in his. "Do you have any idea what happened to the dirty clothes that were in the hamper?"

Drake's mother looks at him like he is a little dim. "I sent them out with the laundry service. I needed that slip to wear again, and they charge a set price for everything you can fit in the bag."

She opens the drawer of the desk in the corner of the sitting area and pulls out a receipt that lists what was in the laundry bag – which includes two graphic tees.

The security guard takes a picture of the receipt. Then he and Logan both leave. I know Logan is hurrying down to scope out the location for my meet with Wendy.

I, on the other hand, take a few minutes explaining to Autumn, Drake and Charlene why the cartoony tee-shirts are that important. They all look a little stunned.

Eventually Autumn says, "I hope you weren't offended by what I said on stage."

I assume she must be talking to Drake's mom, but the way she's looking at me, she's expecting an answer. After a few beats I say, "Why would I be? You didn't send me dead flowers."

"I mean about the money." The way she says it, Drake and his mother must already know. "You're my closest friend – and I was too embarrassed by it all even to tell you. Nobody knew, except my family, until after Drake and I got engaged. And now, I'm afraid that the police are going to look at that as me being a secretive person."

"Especially because of what happened to her great-aunt," Drake says.

"What happened?" I ask.

Autumn wrinkles her nose, like sharing the story is distasteful. "Great-Aunt Edna was 92 years old and in a nursing home – but her death still came under mysterious circumstances. She was given the wrong medication. It was finally ruled an accident, but the nurse who was handing out the cups claimed the cart had been tampered with."

"I'm sure no one thinks you had anything to do with that." I tell her.

"I hope not." Autumn looks so sad. "I really thought Great-Aunt Edna was going to make it to 100."

I draw Autumn into a hug. "I just hope you realize now that you can tell me anything, and it won't change how I think about you."

Autumn releases the hug and really looks at me. "I had a hard time telling you about the rough spots in my life while you were in Seattle. Your life was going so well. You'd worked hard to get good grades and start your practice. You'd put in the work to make a long-term relationship work. And here I was, quitting the only career I'd ever wanted, never having had a relationship longer than a couple of months. So I gave you the highlights reel. You were too far away to accidentally find out anything else."

There's a pang in my chest. "I'm sorry I made you feel that way. I certainly never intended–"

Autumn interrupts me. "I know that's not what you intended. You were always there for me, those rare times when I really needed to talk. But this inheritance – I didn't want you to feel like I was bragging. That's really stupid, right?"

Suddenly, she's crying and I'm crying too. And though he's on the other side of the room, Drake's wiping at his eyes. Charlene is looking at all of us like we're a little crazy. But her bemused smile makes the moment perfect.

Chapter Fourteen

I get a text from Logan. *It really is Wendy. It looks like she's alone. I'm going up a few more steps, just out of sight. If you get in trouble, work the word, "sunrise," into the conversation, and I'll be there in a matter of seconds.*

Thank you! I text back. *I really don't know how I could do this without you.*

Because, honestly, a clandestine meeting has never been my kind of thing. It feels like I'm taking a step into Logan's world, which is something I've repeatedly insisted I didn't want to do. Logan has been a cop, a bodyguard, whatever he was during his years in Europe. This is so intimidating. I have to remind myself that I'm meeting a girl who runs a boutique on a cruise ship – not a hardened spy.

Logan sends back a hug emoji. I never really thought of Logan as an emoji kind of guy, but it doesn't feel out of place.

I can do this. I take a deep calming breath, then I force myself to open the door leading out onto the deck that runs the length of the boat. I'm just a chocolate maker wearing flip-flops taking a stroll to the back of the ship. A stroll which seems to take forever before I finally reach the area with the lifeboats, and I see Wendy. She's holding something in a bag with the logo from the boutique. She looks tense, literally pacing the open space. She catches sight of me and breaks into a relieved smile. I give her a little wave. Because honestly, I don't know the protocol for this kind of thing.

Wendy says, "I'm glad you actually showed."

Still approaching, I ask her, "Why the clandestine meetup? We could have just talked when you stopped by my room."

She clutches the handle of the bag in both hands. "I'm not sure I can trust your roommate. You shouldn't either. Because what I found – did you read her Melody Blues books? This murder could be something like the one in the first book. I just started reading it after I met her yesterday."

"When did you meet Autumn?" I ask. Because if I have my timeline correct, Autumn's team never made it to that end of the promenade that houses the spa and boutique.

Wendy takes a few steps closer to me and then stops. She says, "I snuck into the costume party. I'm a sucker for those mini quiches and the free prosecco. The shop wasn't open, so I didn't see any harm in it."

I say, "I might well have done the same thing. Did you get one of those cream puffs?"

"Yeah." Suddenly, her eyes go wide. "Felicity, look out!"

I turn to look behind me, at the life boat, and I catch just the impression of a blur of motion before I get pulled off balance, banging my shoulder painfully as I fall into the lifeboat, and hitting my knee on a spar in that way that makes pain echo through my entire body – which means that for a few moments, I can't get up.

There's a scream and a bang, and by the time I'm up again, Wendy's gone and Logan is bleeding. He's standing on the deck, holding his arm.

"What happened?" I ask.

"I was about to ask you the same thing," Logan says. "I heard Wendy tell you to look out, and by the time I got down the stairs, I caught a glimpse of someone pushing her overboard. The person who pushed her turned around and shot me – and then jumped off. I think they somehow swung onto the deck below, because there's a dangling rope, but nothing in the water."

"Not even Wendy?" I ask.

Logan looks troubled. "I'm sorry, Fee. I didn't see any sign of her."

I rush over to the railing and look for myself. "Where could she have gone?"

"I don't know. Like I said, I didn't see anything in the water." He gestures to my pocket. "Use your phone to report someone gone overboard."

I take out my phone. "Who attacked us?" I feel like I'm asking the obvious question here.

"I don't know. His – or her – face was covered."

Some people go into shock from the pain of a gunshot wound, even if it doesn't hit anything important. Logan seems more or less okay – there's a strained note in his voice, and a look of pain on his face, and he's gone a little pale. But he seems perfectly functional.

I call Arlo, who is with the captain. I explain what happened.

There's a brief discussion on the other end of the phone, then Arlo says, "They're going to get rescue divers into the water immediately."

I wait for him to berate me for doing something so dangerous, but he doesn't. Instead, he says, "It's a shame we didn't find out what Wendy wanted to tell you."

Then he starts talking to the captain again. And then he finally remembers to let me go.

In the meantime, there's nothing I can do for Wendy – but Logan is still bleeding. "Let me see your arm."

Logan makes a dismissive gesture. "It's through and through. Just a flesh wound."

I insist on taking a look. He's right. The bone in the arm is intact, and the bullet hole doesn't look that bad. Logan uncurls the fingers of his other hand. He's holding a piece of plastic. "This is what our subject shot me with. It's a plastic bullet, shot from a plastic gun. Which explains how they got a weapon through security. But it still doesn't explain what happened to Flint. There wasn't any plastic inside the wound that killed him. So why use a different weapon?"

I think about it, but nothing obvious comes to me. "Maybe Flint's murder was an impulse, and the weapon was handy at the moment."

Logan takes another look at his arm. "I seriously doubt that. Whoever did this acted meticulously when they figured out that Wendy knew something."

"Come on, let's go find you a doctor." I put a hand on his good arm and lead him towards the door. He's still bleeding and needs to get proper treatment – and I don't even have anything on me to improvise a bandage. I may have once been a physical therapist, but it's been a long time since I've had call to practice any sort of medicine. I try not to look back at the water, but I can't help it. "If Flint's killer threw Wendy overboard, then I'm not sure why we're still okay."

"Speak for yourself," Logan quips. Because even if there's not likely to be lasting injury, flesh wounds still hurt terribly, and blood loss can be dangerous. He adds, "But I know what you mean. My guess is this killer only wanted to off Flint, and probably won't hurt anyone else unless cornered."

"That's not a comforting thought. Considering we're trying to catch this person." I notice the bag with the boutique logo on it caught half under one of the lifeboats. I pick it up by the handles. "This is what Wendy wanted to show us."

"Well?" Logan asks. His curiosity is stronger than his pain response right now.

I open the bag and pull out a piece of tubing, maybe four inches in diameter. It's attached to a heavy metal box. I exchange looks with Logan. Obviously, he doesn't know what it is either. I put it back in the bag and hold the door open for Logan to go back inside the ship.

He asks me, "So what was the murder in Autumn's first book?"

I try to think back. I don't re-read books. There are so many to get through, it seems a waste to go back to one I already know. Which means it's been a long time since I read any of

Autumn's work – especially the first one. "The first one was called Discordant Melody." By the time we get to the elevator to go down to the ship's infirmary, one of the ship's staff who happened to be re-stocking a coffee station has given Logan an oversized cloth napkin to wrap around his arm – and I've remembered what happened in Autumn's book. "There was a lounge singer who got overdosed with laughing gas. But that doesn't make any sense. Flint was stabbed. Or shot." I circle my hands in a *you know what I mean* gesture.

"I doubt we're going to figure out which," Logan says. "Whatever the murder weapon is, it probably went overboard soon after the crime."

"Really?" I ask. The elevator doors open onto a hall that isn't nearly as lavish as everything upstairs. "Why keep the tee-shirt if the weapon went overboard while we were still under way?"

Logan's mouth drops open and he starts to say something, stops himself, then says, "I decided the weapon was gone before the dog found that shirt. You're right. The murder weapon could well be on board."

We're standing there in the hall, steps away from getting Logan bandaged up. But I have one more thing to ask. "Imogen is the only one who knew that Wendy was in the hallway outside mine and Autumn's room. Doesn't that mean she's the killer?"

"Not necessarily," Logan says. "Someone could have seen Wendy discover whatever that gadget is, or could have been following her towards your room and ducked out of the way when Imogen came by. Or possibly, Wendy could have told someone about the meetup."

It doesn't take long for the ship's doctor to get Logan bandaged up. You don't stitch up gunshot wounds, since that just invites infection, and nothing is severely damaged, so it's mainly a matter of swabbing him off and giving him a tetanus shot and an antibiotic – plus some over the counter pain meds, since he refuses anything stronger.

When the doctor tries to talk him into it, he says, "There's a killer loose on board this ship, and I have people to protect."

That's hard to argue with, with Flint's body somewhere down here on this deck.

We head back to the elevator. Getting shot seems to have put Logan into super protective mode. He says, "I think we should all move into Drake's suite. It's a much better option from a security standpoint."

"There's five of us," I protest. "That would hardly be fair to Drake."

"You and Autumn can take one room, Drake and his mother the other, and I'm fine on the sofa. Which is actually the best spot for maintaining security for everyone."

"Okay," I say, "but you have to pitch that idea to Drake."

Logan looks at me like I'm just not getting it. "If he cares about Autumn as much as he seems to, he'll want to see her protected. After what just happened to Wendy, anyone who the killer suspects of knowing anything is at risk."

"I'm surprised you aren't inviting Arlo to room with all of us too."

Logan seriously considers this. "If he doesn't feel secure, I'm sure we can get a roll-away for the common area."

I really don't see Arlo going for that.

But once we find him, Drake doesn't have a problem with it, so Autumn and I go back to our room to get our things. When we get there, there's another slip of paper under the door. Panic bounces into my chest, but this time the note is on official Sunset Cruise stationary, written by a member of the ship's staff. It is a request for me to call Carmen at my shop.

"Oh, wow," I say. "What could have gone wrong now?"

Autumn says, "The only way you're going to find out is to call."

I sigh and take my phone out again. "Might as well get it over with." I make the call. When Carmen answers, she sounds busy, but not upset.

I ask, "I got your message. What's going on?"

It has to have been important, for her to want me to call at these rates.

"What do you want me to say to the reporter who is on her way here? Are you really involved in another murder investigation?" Despite her words, Carmen's tone says she isn't surprised.

I sit down on my bed, trying to think of what I can actually say without compromising the investigation. "So I take it the news story broke?"

"Yes. Tiff called and told me to turn on the news. Since I don't have standard TV, I had to stream it, and by the time I figured out what was going on, we already had curiosity seekers hanging out again."

"Not that they've ever really gone away," I say.

Carmen laughs into the phone. "Thank goodness. They're what allows us to keep trying new things and expanding."

She does have a point. The background noise tells me the shop is packed. "I'm sorry you and Miles are there alone."

Carmen says, "Tiff came in to help out too, along with Sonya." Sonya is another friend of mine, who owns a yarn shop on Galveston. Neither of them actually works for Greetings and Felicitations, though both are in the shop often enough to know our procedures.

It's really sweet that I have so many friends now, and that they're willing to pitch in and help without even being asked. After everything else that's happened over the last two days, this comforting thought actually brings moisture to my eyes.

I tell Carmen, "Pay them as vendors, out of the petty cash."

"I can try," she says, "but I doubt they'll take it. They just want to help out."

"Then pay them with coffee drinks and your best baked goods," I say.

"Now that might work." Carmen sounds happy. "But about the reporter."

"Tell her I'm on board the cruise, and that you can neither confirm or deny anything else," I say. "Which is the truth."

Carmen says, "Maybe I can spin it into a positive review for the shop. I was testing a recipe this morning for chocolate empanadas. I put our Ecuador chocolate in the dough, and then I simmered down fresh pineapple, spearmint, pineapple mint and hibiscus flowers to make a filling."

So yes, the press has indeed descended to bring murder and death to my little chocolate shop. Again. Carmen has responded by making mint-pineapple-filled chocolate empanadas. And I can't think of a better response.

I ask Carmen, "Can you put Tiff on?"

When Carmen passes the phone over to Tiff, I ask, "You know anybody who can find out the contents of a will?"

After all, Tiff, despite being a relative newcomer to Galveston, seems to have connections everywhere.

"I can try. Hold on. Let me get something to write down the details." Once she's written down Flint's name and info, she asks, "Any other information you need while I'm at it?"

I hate to ask so many favors right on top of each other – but if Tiff is offering. "Apparently Flint had a new girlfriend, but the details of her story didn't add up. At all. If you can find out anything about her it would be helpful."

After I give her Lupe's name and details too, Tiff asks, "How did you get involved this time?"

"Ash, of all people, asked me for help. He says somebody is trying to frame him."

There's silence on the phone. Eventually, Tiff says, "So you're hanging up your shingle as an amateur PI."

"Of course not! I'm just helping someone out."

"Felicity," Tiff says. "Once is a happenstance, twice is a coincidence. But investigating three murders? Three is starting to be a habit."

I consider this. "It's not my fault I'm a murder magnet."

Tiff says, "I thought you said Ash was wrong when he called you that."

I tell her, "It's better than thinking I'm psychologically attracted to getting involved in murder cases."

"Whatever you need to tell yourself," Tiff says. "Look, promise me you're still going to take time for that massage. You need to relax."

"I'll try to make the time," I say.

Chapter Fifteen

Autumn and I get settled in to our new room and then meet in the living room to regroup. Charlene is sitting on the loveseat, reading one of Aarti's books. Drake is looking out the suite's generous window. Logan is trying to find somewhere out of the way to stash his stuff.

As he moves his suitcase over to the area between the wet bar and the wall, Logan says, "At least this isn't likely to be for long. The FBI should be here by the end of the day, and surely they'll make some decisions that will help get this ship back to shore, and anyone who isn't a suspect on their way home. After all, this was only supposed to be a three-day cruise, so we may not have supplies for much longer than that."

"Surely there's emergency supplies," Drake protests.

"Maybe," Logan says. "I've been on plenty of boats before, but this is my first time on a cruise ship."

Autumn scrunches her nose. "The emergency stuff would probably be canned food meant to last like fifty years."

That's possible. And it's not an appealing thought. There are so many reasons we need to solve this case, fast. I tell Autumn, "Logan and I are going back up to the boutique where I found Flint. That device Wendy found has to connect to something."

There's a knock in the cabin door. Logan goes to answer it. It's Liam.

Liam approaches me and says, "Mrs. Koerber, you are certainly a difficult woman to track down. It is unusual for people to change rooms like this."

I gesture around. "You have to admit this is a highly unusual situation. Besides, these are much nicer digs."

"Granted." Liam holds out a box, which has my logo on it. "I just wanted to let you know that this box of chocolates was returned as being defective."

I groan. That's about all I need, on top of everything else. "What's wrong with it?"

"I believe the chocolate inside wasn't tempered correctly or has lost its temper."

"Just replace it," I tell him. "I don't have the brain space to deal with it right now." After all, despite my determination to provide only the best quality chocolate, there's a lot more serious things going on than one defective box of chocolate. And after the amount of money I've been spending on communications, the cost of one box of chocolate is negligible.

"Very good. I'm on my way up to the boutique now. With Wendy – missing – I'm going to have to take her shift there this afternoon." He looks upset at the thought of what might have happened to her. And if the divers haven't found her by now – either dead or alive – it is hard to speculate on exactly what might have happened.

Liam is still high on my suspect list, so it isn't going to be exactly comfortable looking around the boutique with him there, but we are running out of time if we want to figure this all out before someone else takes over the investigation and potentially locks the space down.

In an attempt to make it at least slightly less awkward, Logan and I wait a while before heading up to the boutique.

He goes over to his suitcase and takes out clean clothes. "It'll also be a bit less awkward if I'm wearing something that isn't stained with my own blood."

While Logan is busy changing, I get a text from Tiff. *I found out about the will. He never changed it after the divorce, so Clove inherits most of it. Though there is something for Imogen. She gets the title to a boat called Santiago's Dream and ten thousand dollars. Apparently, the boat name is a reference to*

Hemmingway – that story about the marlin fisherman and the sharks.

Why does so much of this keep coming back to sharks? And why would Flint have left Imogen anything? He wasn't particularly generous, and he didn't have a strong connection to her. Maybe it could be guilt, over whatever had happened to her father. Maybe Flint really did kill the guy.

Thanks for the info, I text Tiff.

Those dots pop up under the text, like she's still typing. It resolves into a longer text, and then images that start popping up, one after another. The text says, *I checked around and found out Lupe and her young daughter moved from Section 8 housing into a luxury condo about six months ago. Another agent at my firm handled the sale, and she says Lupe provided a large cash down payment that she described as an inheritance, though my friend at the law office said he couldn't find any evidence of such a windfall. Wherever that money came from, she didn't report it.*

I examine the pictures. There is an image of the building that Lupe's condo is in. The structure is tall, and I vaguely recognize it. I think it is located somewhere on the south end of Galveston, in a nice part of town.

Then there's a pic of Lupe with a group of couples at an event – and she's leaning back against Flint, while Flint's other hand is resting lightly on Lupe's daughter's shoulder. They all look very cozy together. So she wasn't lying about being in a relationship with him. Then there's a photo from a university newspaper showing Lupe with several other students, doing a drone photography project for a marketing class. So yeah, she really did go back to school. Which means a lot of what she said checks out. But even so, that leaves even more questions than I'd had before.

"Remember," Logan says once we're heading up to the Promenade deck, "we're just casually shopping for something I forgot to pack. I'm half convinced that Liam killed Flint and shot me. We don't want to give him any reason to believe we're on to him."

"And Wendy." We're both silent for a moment. Flint had been dislikable and possibly criminal, but Wendy had simply been in the wrong place at the wrong time. Finally, I ask, "But when would he have killed Flint?"

We step out of the elevator. Logan says, "We have to be missing something."

We walk down the promenade, past all the shops with the glittering jewelry and swanky handbags. They're still beautiful, but I feel a lot more subdued seeing it this time around. I gesture at the Hawaiian shirt Logan had changed into. I ask, "How many of those did you pack?"

Logan says, "Four. I believe in being prepared."

Prepared. For relaxing. But yeah, that sounds just like Logan.

I stop for a moment when we reach the far end of the walk. I need to relax a bit, if we're going to look casual. I study the ice sculpture. It is a duplicate of the one that was out here yesterday, only it's earlier in the day, so it is a lot less melted. The crisp lines on the whale make it look even more wise and melancholy. Or maybe that's just my mood.

I tell Logan, "The ocean has always felt like part of me."

Logan grins. "People are roughly 60% water."

"I'm serious." I gesture at the sculpture. "There's something about this image that speaks to me. It's not a logo anymore, once it's been done like this in ice. It's a moment of the ocean, captured with the sun–" I stop talking as I look at the sun's rays and an idea dances at the edge of my mind. There's something about that shape. And then it hits me.

"What?" Logan asks.

I tilt my head, trying to make sure it makes sense before I say it out loud. I gesture at the sun's rays. "Yesterday, there was a sculpture just like this one – only a lot more melted. So the sun's rays were blunted, almost sagging. But look at them now. You're looking for something thin and pointed that would make a wound similar to a fencing foil. There's your shape."

Logan considers this. And for a moment, it looks like he agrees with me. But then he frowns and says, "It doesn't match up with the time of death. For the ice to have been usable as a weapon, Flint would have had to be killed hours before you found him, which wasn't the case."

"You're right," I say. But there's still something, nagging at my brain. I picture yesterday's sculpture. It was definitely too fragile to easily stab someone with. "But I almost think that yesterday, one of those rays on the left was missing."

"Must have melted off," Logan says, but he sounds troubled.

"None of this is matching up," I say. "Wendy seemed to think Flint was gassed, when he was clearly stabbed. Flint was stabbed, but you got shot. The people with the opportunity didn't have the motive, and Ash – who had motive and opportunity – well, I'm not sure he would have had the upper body strength."

Logan says, "He may be thin, but he's wiry. Don't underestimate him." Logan gestures at his bandaged arm with his good hand. "Besides, we haven't ruled out the idea that Flint might have been shot. From the angle of entry, it could have been Ash. Though none of the people we're looking at are exceptionally short or tall, so it could have been any one of them."

"There has to be a way to start narrowing all of this down," I say.

We go into the boutique. Liam is stocking a shelf with fancy shampoos.

Ash is in the facial care section of the space, with Craig, who I continue thinking of as Bow Tie Guy, though today Craig is sporting skinny jeans and a band tee. He certainly looks the part to be Ash's friend.

Ash walks over to us. "Felicity! Any news?"

There's such a hopeful look in his eyes. I feel horrible crushing that hope.

"Sorry, Ash. We haven't figured anything out that make sense yet." I pat his arm. If someone had told me a week ago that I'd be comforting Ash Diaz, I'd have laughed. But this has been one strange cruise. "How are you holding up?"

Ash gestures at his chin. "When I get stressed, I start breaking out, like I was still a teenager. I woke up this morning with a pimple the size of Mount Vesuvius."

Which explains what he's doing looking at high-end skin care. Even if the pimple in question is hardly noticeable. I tell him, "It's not as bad as you think. I wouldn't have even seen it, if you hadn't said something."

"Thanks for trying to make me feel better." Ash's tone says he doesn't believe me. "Nobody else in my family has half as many skin problems as I do. Maybe the adult acne is a Brewster thing. Maybe I'll never grow out of it."

I wince at the vehemence in the way he says Brewster. It's possible that he's having a harder time with having to re-evaluate his place in his family than he is with being a murder suspect. I make a sympathetic noise. "I hope everything's okay with you and your mom."

Ash's expression brightens. "Yeah, it is. We had this great talk. She said she'd been looking for the right moment for years to talk to me about being adopted, but she was always too afraid that I'd feel rejected."

"So you're okay with it?" I ask.

His face gets serious. "I think I may need to journal about it a bit, really sort out how I feel. But Mom reassured me that to her, I'm the same person, no matter what my genetics are. I'm a Diaz, not a Brewster. I'm not built on mashed potatoes, but mofongo." His expression slips into an affectionate smile. "She's always coming up with pithy things like that to say. I always assumed I got my love of words from her, and from my grandpa."

"You probably did," I tell him.

"Yeah," Craig says. "My psych class last semester, we learned how values form when you're a little kid, and how kids learn language. Affection, trust and words. That's where it is."

Ash's smile gets broader. "I've been thinking back on how I was raised. While my parents never told me I was adopted, they always taught me that family was what you make of it. They had friends that they treated like family – like Clove, who was basically an extra aunt growing up."

"Which makes Flint your honorary uncle," I say.

Ash tilts his head from side to side. "I guess so." He runs a hand through his hair. "Which means I had that much less reason to kill him."

Logan makes a low grumbling noise. "I don't suppose you have one of those tee-shirts Liam is so fond of handing out? The ones with the cartoon sharks."

"Don't answer that, man," Craig says. "You weren't at the event this morning. It's entrapment."

Ash squints at Craig. "It's not entrapment because I haven't done anything wrong." He looks back at Logan. "Those tee-shirts were a flop. Liam told me that on the first two cruises, they sold exactly one of that design. So he has a couple of boxes in his office, and he gave me one yesterday." Ash hesitates. "But I don't still have it. My cabin got tossed while I was locked in the spa, and some things went missing – including that tee-shirt. Which I thought was weird, since the other things that were taken at least had monetary value."

"And I suppose you reported this?" Logan asks.

Craig says, "Of course he did! It must have happened before the security cameras got turned on, because the security staff said there was no sign of anyone entering Ash's cabin after that."

I ask Ash, "Do you have a stateroom to yourself?"

Most people share staterooms on cruises, since almost all cruise lines charge a significant surcharge for people traveling alone, to make up the second fare they won't get. I can't see the cruise line offering an entire LARP group individual cabins, especially if they are being discounted or comped because the group is providing entertainment.

Ash says, "Our group has an odd number. Imogen wanted to room with her friend because they had a project they were working on. So I wound up with my own digs."

"Who assigned the cabins?" Logan asks.

"I did," Craig says. "But most of the group gave me requests for who they wanted to room with. I just paired up the extras."

Logan asks Ash, "You didn't want a roommate?"

Ash says, "Not specifically. I'm a very light sleeper."

I say, "Imogen said she got into your room while you were missing yesterday. She didn't say it looked trashed."

"Well, she didn't take my stuff," Ash protests.

"That's not what I'm suggesting. I'm just saying the theft has to have happened after Imogen let herself in." Unless Imogen herself was the burglar. But why would she want to frame her own fiancé for murder? Even if she *had* killed Flint, that wouldn't make any sense.

Logan takes a different tack, asking Craig, "How do you know that the cameras weren't on?"

Craig says, "Ash told me. Liam told him."

Ash says, "Liam was really embarrassed, because if those cameras had been on, they would probably have picked up the murder, or at least me going into the spa and not coming back out."

Craig says, "I can't believe those cameras were off that whole first cruise. Imagine what I'd have been able to get away with if I had known."

Ash puts a hand on Craig's arm to stop him talking. Ash says, "He's talking about pranks. Craig is not only our LARP group's leader, but our resident prankster." He tells Craig, "They're going to think you were talking about theft or something worse."

"Nah," Craig says. "If you want sugar in all the salt shakers, I'm your guy."

Since I don't know much about Craig at all, I ask, "What do you do when you're not LARPing or switching out salt shakers?"

"I'm a handyman for an apartment complex, down in Kemah. It's paying my way towards my electrical engineering degree."

Logan circles the conversation back and asks, "You've cruised on this ship before?"

Craig grins. "I was on the maiden voyage. That was when I originally pitched Liam about having the whole group on board to host a LARP."

Logan asks, "Did Liam behave any differently than he did when you came aboard yesterday?"

Craig says, "Yeah. He seemed a lot less nervous yesterday. I think he's started getting used to the job and schmoozing with everyone."

We've been speaking softly, and Liam is on the other side of the boutique, but he says loudly, "I can hear you guys talking about me."

Logan calls back, "Then is what he's saying accurate?"

Liam walks over to us and says, "More or less. This isn't my first job where I've had to schmooze. But on that first cruise, I didn't realize how much the captain was going to be relying on me to be his face in front of the passengers. I've been on other cruises, and those captains have always hosted evenings where they talk about what it is like handling a ship for a living and sharing stories of crazy things that people do at sea. But this guy – he was supposed to be at the opening reception for the maiden voyage, and at the last minute, he tells me he's too busy, and that I need to come up with an opening speech. So yeah, I was nervous, because I was giving the speech off the top of my head. And he's cancelled almost every social engagement the cruise line has scheduled. I can't decide if he's agoraphobic, or just a cranky old man."

Well, that at least explains why I haven't met the elusive captain yet, though he has given a number of announcements over the loudspeakers. From his accent, I believe he's Italian, and now I have a picture in my head of this cantankerous guy who used to run the Italian restaurant around the corner from my grandfather. The two of them liked to drink coffee together between the lunch and dinner crowds. I almost laugh out loud at the idea of the cranky chef driving this boat.

But Liam's face is serious, so I manage to hold in the chuckle.

Liam looks at Logan. "I know you think I'm a suspect, even though I don't have a single reason for wanting to kill Flint. I hardly knew the guy growing up, since he never hung out when we came to visit Ash's side of the family. I only invited him to speak because he was one of the biggest names I had any connection with, which gave me a reasonable expectation he'd show up. He didn't even recognize me at first."

Logan makes a noncommittal noise. Then he says, "From what I understand, you're a fluent liar. And we only have your word that you didn't have a motive."

Liam looks at me, his knitted eyebrows disapproving of me sharing my thoughts about his lying with Logan. "Word certainly does have a way of getting around."

Logan says, "Does that really surprise you?"

"Look," Liam says. "Maybe you'll find me less suspicious if I help you out. You know what I overhead two of the security staff discussing? They said they didn't think Flint was killed where the body was discovered. Because, duh, why would he walk into an awkward corner like that just to get murdered? They ran a black light over this whole area, and found traces where blood had been cleaned up in an alcove opposite the boutique, the one just opposite the ice sculpture."

Logan doesn't look surprised. He's been working with Arlo, and probably knew that already. "Thank you for sharing that information."

Ash says, "Whoever killed Flint must have nerves of titanium. Dragging a dead body through an open area of the ship, not knowing that the cameras weren't even on."

Logan says, "Let's not forget, without leaving a trail of blood."

Both Ash and Craig shudder. Craig says, "I don't even like the thought of blood. Ask Ash what happened when that one guy busted open his knee in the middle of one of our events."

"He fainted," Ash says.

That gets a chuckle from Logan, who says, "No shame in that. We all have our weaknesses."

"Oh, and what's yours?" Craig asks.

After all, Logan flies and dives, handles getting shot without freaking out, and looks like he was chiseled by a talented sculptor.

"I freeze up during written exams," Logan says.

Which gets him a chuckle from Craig. I guess that makes them even?

I follow Logan around as he examines the floorboards and all the vents in the room. We wind up over by the display of my chocolate. I find myself straightening the boxes, moving the dangling tags so the silhouette shapes of Knightley are all facing the same direction.

Craig asks, "Is that your chocolate?"

I hold up one of the boxes so he can see the details. "This is it. I didn't see you at my demo. I'd be happy to open up one of these so you can have a sample."

"Please don't bother," Craig says.

"Oh, okay," I say, trying to hide the fact that I'm a bit hurt by the dismissal.

"I'm sorry," Craig says. "I didn't mean it like that. I just didn't want you to open your product for nothing. I'm allergic to chocolate."

"That must be tough," Logan says. He's actually become something of a chocolate connoisseur since he became part of Greetings and Felicitations.

"Craig is allergic to everything," Ash says. "We have to have gluten free pizza when the LARP group goes out after events. Can you imagine my palate, dealing with gluten free crust?"

"I really can't," I tell him. I feel like I'm getting to know Ash on a whole different level.

Ash says, "If you're giving out chocolate samples, I'd love to have one of those caramel pecan truffles you do – the boozy kind."

"Nice try," I say, putting the box back on the shelf. "But these are cubes of solid chocolate."

Chapter Sixteen

"Well, that was a bust," I tell Logan as we make our way back up the promenade.

Behind us, Ash comes running out of the boutique and rushes after us down the hall. "Felicity, wait!"

The other cruise passengers strolling in this area all turn to look at us. Ash pulls me over to the side, outside the glass window of the duty-free shop.

Logan stays where he is, starts to cross his arms over his chest, then winces and drops his injured arm back down to his side. "I'll pretend I can't hear anything from over here."

"Thanks," Ash replies, and I can't tell whether or not he's being sarcastic. Ash leans in close, drops his voice to almost a whisper. "I saw something, but I really don't want to make Clove look bad in front of the cops. Because I don't think she would have hurt Flint. Violence isn't in her. She's always been so kind to me and my family. So maybe this can stay just between us?"

I say, "You should tell whatever you know to the cops."

Ash says, "You're the one I trust. Listen, yesterday, when I was on my way to the spa, I saw Flint and Clove sitting together at a little table near some of those floor to ceiling windows. They looked all cozy, and I thought, maybe after all this time, they were trying to reconcile."

I whisper back, "That is weird, after everything that happened between them. But hardly suspicious."

"That's not the suspicious part." Ash takes out his replacement phone and flips through his photo gallery. He must have taken three hundred photos since we got on board this ship. He stops at a picture of a woman looking intently through a window, a deep frown on her lips. She's sitting on one of those upright deck chairs, watching something happening inside the room. It's Lupe, Flint's girlfriend. Ash holds up the phone for me to get a good look. "This woman was staring at Flint and Clove, looking like she wanted to take them apart. I don't know who she is, but I think she might be the killer."

"Did she see you watching her?" I ask.

"I don't think so." Ash looks at me earnestly. "I'm not sure how this woman could have managed to break into my room, or lure me down to the spa. But I don't know of anyone else would have had a reason to."

I ask Ash, as gently as I can, "Did Imogen tell you what she told us about her father and Flint?" When Ash shakes his head *no, she hasn't*, I say, "It was a very sad story. But it gives her motive."

"I know my fiancé," Ash says. "She may be a lot of things, but she's not capable of coldblooded murder. What happened to Flint was all very calculated. And that's just not her."

I want Ash to be right. I want him and his fiancé to have a happy ending out of all of this. The last murder I'd gotten involved with had broken up Arlo and Patsy. And Arlo's still not entirely over it. It's a shame how far the echoes of a crime can go, damaging futures and destroying lives of people who haven't done anything wrong.

"Forward me that picture." I gesture at Ash's phone. "No promises, but I'll see what I can do."

Ash sends me the image. He says, "Now, if you don't mind, I'm going to try and enjoy whatever freedom I have left, with my friends. Arlo still seems to think that I'll probably be arrested when the FBI gets here."

I ask Ash, "So your LARP group – you're all friends? You haven't written any exposés about any of them? Or tried to psychoanalyze anybody?"

Ash shakes his head. "When I'm with my friends – or with Imogen – I turn off the reporter hat and just try to be in the moment. Any group is going to have minor squabbles, but the LARP club is just for fun." He shakes his phone. "I'm telling you. This is the killer."

I gesture at the phone. "I read your exposé on Flint. There was such an urgent tone to the piece. It wasn't like your other writing."

Ash says, "Clove was missing. I thought, if Flint had hurt her in some way, I could bring his misdeeds to light. But then she came home, and there were consequences I hadn't intended. It's the only piece I've ever regretted writing."

Ash and I tell each other to be careful. Then he heads back towards the boutique.

Logan steps over to me. "He tell you something interesting?"

"He has a theory," I say. "It ties into some of the things we've been looking into."

Logan's phone lights up. He looks down at it. "Arlo's convinced that if that tee-shirt is still on board, the murder weapon might still be here somewhere. The captain agreed, and security is organizing searches of everyone's rooms, starting with everyone who had motive to want Flint gone."

"He'd better hurry, if the FBI is on the way."

Logan looks at his phone again. "While he's doing that, we might as well try to answer a few other questions."

"I know what's at the top of my list. There's a lot about Lupe that still doesn't add up. The question is, how do we track her down on a ship this size?"

"I suggest checking out the place where we saw her last," Logan says.

"She's not a lost dog, Logan," I say.

"I know, Fee," Logan says. "But if people are alone and depressed, they're likely to look for routine. Or at least a familiar face. Lupe may well be hanging out at the same bar again today."

I don't have a better idea, so we make our way to the bar. Lupe isn't there.

It's the same bartender, though, and she recognizes us and waves us over. "Back for more egg creams?"

"I wouldn't object," Logan says.

While she starts making Logan's drink, I ask, "Have you seen the woman we were talking with last night?"

"Yeah," she says. "She was here about an hour ago."

I feel my shoulders slump. Thanks for the info." I turn to Logan. "Now what do we do?"

"You have more questions for her, huh?" The bartender's eyes are filled with curiosity. My guess is she's watched too much NCIS. "She said something about getting some sun now that the storm has cleared. She's probably up on the top deck. The pool up there is nice." She hands Logan his egg cream. "Just return the glass at the bar up there."

"Thanks," Logan says. He takes a sip of the drink. "Still the best egg cream I've ever had."

As we turn to leave, someone at one of the tables calls out to us. I turn, and Aarti Andrews is waving us over. When we get to her table, she says, "I heard you were trying to verify Clove's whereabouts last night."

"We were," Logan says.

"I was one of the writers in the group she was barconning with."

"Barconning?" I ask. I'm not sure I'm going to want to know what that word means.

"You know," Aarti says. "Networking by hanging out at the bar instead of participating in the formal events."

"Oh, right," I say. "Makes sense."

Aarti picks a cherry out of what looks like a Shirley Temple. "Clove was here with us all night."

"Thanks for the information," I say, though it's hard to sound enthusiastic, because she's telling us something we already knew.

"We were barconning earlier yesterday afternoon, too. Right after the opening party. Tucker's agent was here for that part. He mentioned that he'd seen the announcement on Publisher's Marketplace about Flint's new series. When he told us the title of it, Clove went ballistic." Aarti pops the cherry into her mouth. "I just thought you should know."

"Why was she so upset?" I ask. Maybe Clove resented Flint's success. That could be enough to make someone snap and kill their ex.

"I don't know." Aarti scrunches up her nose. "In a book, people's motivations are clear and all laid out, but in real life, who knows why people do things half the time? Clove didn't seem to care about the money amount Flint got for the deal. Just the title. She was with us when Flint was killed, so she couldn't have done it. But she was mad enough she looked like she wanted to."

We thank Aarti for the information, then leave the bar. Once we're far enough away, Logan asks, "Do you really think a person would kill someone for stealing a book title?"

"I doubt it." We pass a uniformed staff member in the hallway, wheeling a room service cart. He watches us, his eyes wary. He probably heard us talking about murder.

We make our way up to the top of the ship. And sure enough, there's Lupe in a tasteful black one piece, sipping a Mai Tai in a lounge chair by the pool. She looks the picture of perfect serenity, until we get closer, and I can see her eyes are red from crying, and her face looks rough and chapped.

She sits up when she sees us coming. "I don't guess you're here to catch some rays?"

"Not exactly," I say.

"What happened to your arm?" She gestures towards the gauze wrapping Logan's injury.

Logan says, "I had a little run in with a bullet."

Lupe's eyes go wide. "This ship is getting too dangerous." She gulps down the rest of her Mai Tai.

I sit down awkwardly in the lounge chair next to hers. It's too low to the ground, and it almost tips over as I settle into it.

"We wanted to clear up a few things," I tell her. I take out my phone and show her the picture Ash sent. "In this photo, you don't look happy seeing Flint and Clove together. Exactly how unhappy were you?"

Lupe frowns at me. "Not unhappy enough to kill Flint, if that's what you're suggesting."

Logan, still standing behind me, says, "Jealousy is always a strong motive. There's been a number of times when I've seen people cry over having killed someone they loved."

I wince. It seems really harsh, Logan telling her that while the evidence of tears is still on her cheeks. But Lupe doesn't seem to take it badly.

Lupe runs both hands over her face. "Yes, I was jealous about seeing Flint and Clove together. But if I was going to kill one of them, don't you think it would have been Clove? After all, with Flint still alive, I could hold onto the relationship."

She does have a point.

But Logan says, "If you thought the relationship was ending anyway, Flint might have been the one you were mad at."

"Honestly," Lupe says, "I don't think my Flint was going anywhere. We truly were in love."

"Was it love on your part, or was it convenance?" Logan asks. "How did you go from Section 8 housing to a fancy condo? It was with Flint's money, wasn't it?"

Lupe closes her eyes and takes a deep breath. Then she looks at me and says, "See? I had no reason to kill Flint. He didn't ever change his will, so Clove is still the one that inherits. With Flint dead, no one is going to pay for my school, or for my daughter's soccer uniforms. I needed him more alive."

"Yes," I say. "We've seen the will."

"Or maybe it was blackmail," Logan suggests. "We know your whole little meet-cute where Flint takes you out for pie is a fabrication. Flint didn't like sweets."

Lupe laughs, softly. "Actually, that part is true. Only, I was the one who suggested the place we met. And Flint really was a customer at the dry-cleaning place for years. He and Clove used to come in together, before they divorced, and after she left, Flint was a very sad man for a very long time. I think that's when I fell in love with him."

"But that was years ago," I say. "From what I understand, your relationship with Flint started maybe six months ago."

"That's when I blackmailed him," Lupe admits.

I look at Logan. "You were right."

Lupe says, "You have to understand, my daughter was being bullied mercilessly by these two girls who lived in our building. It was already not a great place to stay, and Vanessa's father was petitioning to get custody, to get her out of the situation. A mother will do anything for her little girl."

"So what exactly did you do?" I prompt.

Lupe sucks in her bottom lip and studies Logan. She knows he used to be a cop. And so far, she hasn't said anything specific enough to incriminate herself. I can see in her eyes the moment she decides to tell us the truth. "Flint brought in a suit he hadn't worn in years, to be dry-cleaned. It was in with a whole stack of items. He'd lost weight and finally got back into the smaller size. But that suit – I found a bullet casing and another man's ID in the breast pocket. So I did a little digging of my own. Edmund Foster was a fisherman, who had moved to Texas from England, in pursuit of the kingfish and the marlin. He was also an aspiring writer, and a great admirer of Hemmingway. With these two shared loves, he and Flint became fast friends. That day they went out on Edmund's boat to shoot at sharks with pistols wasn't the first time they'd gone fishing together. But Flint brought the boat back alone. In all the interviews, he claimed that there was a tragic accident, and Edmond got swept overboard. But if that were true, Edmond's wallet would have gone over with him. I've seen enough television to know that you remove an ID when you don't want a body to be identified, and you remove a shell casing when you don't want it to be matched to anything."

"That's true," Logan says.

"When I confronted him about it, and demanded enough money to take my daughter somewhere better to live, he was angry, of course. I was worried I'd made a mistake, that I might wind up dead too, but he gave me the money. We met up at the pie shop, and I gave him back the ID and the casing. I promised him that would be the end of it. Only, we genuinely hit it off."

"That seems unlikely," Logan says.

Lupe shrugs. "What is it they say? About how truth can be stranger than fiction? The killer and the blackmailer, falling in love. Eventually, he told me the whole story, about what really happened to Edmund. It was so tragic."

She lapses into silence, looks like she's about to be caught up in her grief again.

"Well?" I prompt. "What happened?"

"Edmund tried to kill him. They had been drinking, and Edmund was angry that Flint had gotten him caught up in an investment scheme that wasn't going to pan out. They both had pistols, and when it got heated, Edmund took a shot at Flint. He missed and Flint shot back."

"Do you have any proof that that's really what happened?" Logan asks. "I mean, with that explanation, there's a good case for self-defense. He could have just explained that he was attacked when he talked to the cops."

"But then he would have had to explain about the investment scheme. It wasn't exactly legal, and Edmund wasn't the only one Flint had gotten wrapped up in it." Lupe leans forward in her chair. "You've seen the will. Flint was loaded. But he was a mid-list author, so you know that much money wasn't coming in from his books. He'd get people involved in one plan to make cash or another. Somehow, he always held onto the money while other people lost it."

After that, there doesn't seem much else to ask.

"I'm sorry for your loss," Logan says. He holds out a hand to help me up from the awkward chair. "We'll let you enjoy the rest of the sunshine."

"Am I going to be in trouble?" Lupe asks.

"Maybe," Logan says. "I'd be thinking about what to say to the FBI when they get here, if I were you. Since the original crime was in their jurisdiction too."

Lupe says, "If it helps, I have information that should help to prove Clove killed Flint."

"Oh?" I turn back to look at her.

Lupe says, "Flint just signed a new book contract. He told me not to say anything to anyone. The books feature characters that he and Clove designed together, back before they split up. Flint said that a lot of work had gone into it, and it was a shame for all of the effort to go to waste, just because he wasn't with Clove. She has to have found out about it." Lupe looks up at us, intent meaning in her eyes. "You talk about motive."

It at least explains why Clove went ballistic when she found out about the series deal. There's a lot of emotion tied up in what Flint did, taking their jointly designed characters and going solo, and it does give Clove a motive. Which is something to think about – even if I still think Imogen probably did it.

Chapter Seventeen

We head back inside the ship. Once we're out of earshot, I say, "I really don't think Lupe killed Flint."

"Agreed," Logan says. "But it brings up a lot of questions about Clove, doesn't it? She was married to Flint when Foster went overboard on that boat. How much of this murder story did she know? And did she have any dealings with Edmund?"

"She didn't seem to know who Imogen was when we were at that first party," I point out. "So it's possible she didn't know Flint's friends very well. But she figured out Imogen's history, and her motive for killing Flint, by the time Ash was getting accused. She must be quite resourceful."

"Or that she's a good liar." Logan opens the door for me with his good arm. The sudden burst of air conditioning as we go through it gives me a chill.

"But she has an alibi for when Flint died." I try to think. "What about the other writers on the flier? Did they have any connection to Flint?"

Logan says, "Arlo checked on that, and apparently they all have alibis."

"You two seem to be working closely together on this one," I say.

Logan says, "He needs the backup, and I don't want to have to spend another night with a murderer on the loose on a boat full of my friends. I'm not about to let my personal feelings get in the way of doing the right thing."

I assume those personal feelings have to do with me, since otherwise he and Arlo have become friends. But I'm not ready to talk about the relationship thing again. Instead I say,

"Everybody seems to have these rock-solid alibis, or only short periods of time when they were unaccounted for. But it would take time to lure Flint to that alcove, and even more time to clean up the blood. Time to move the body, and to change out of the bloody tee-shirt. Time to hide or get rid of the murder weapon."

Logan pushes the button for the elevator. "Are you one hundred percent sure that Ash didn't do this? It's really the only thing that makes sense."

"Unless we're wrong about the time of death," I say. I keep thinking back about that missing ice ray.

"I touched Flint's body myself. He had barely begun to cool."

"Then maybe there was a way to cut down on the time it took to commit the murder," I insist. "Something. I just know Ash didn't kill anybody."

"I'm starting to give credence to your hunches on things like that," Logan says. "So we keep digging for the truth. Which means we need to talk to Clove."

"At least she should be easier to find." I pull up the schedule for the mystery conference events. "It looks like she's signing books in the lounge off the indoor pool."

"That's the place where they have the roast beef sandwiches, right?"

"Maybe?" Cruise ships have little places to get food pretty much any time of day, and I haven't even begun to discover all of them. I realize suddenly that with the events this morning, and all the running around we've been doing, we missed lunch. "I wouldn't be opposed to one of those."

It takes us a bit to find the lounge, which is down a narrow hall. Clove is sitting at a table with four people left in line to get their books signed. There's nobody in line at the stand on the other side of the room handing out food and beverages. Logan heads over and orders a sandwich.

"Make it two," I say.

"You heard the lady," Logan tells the guy.

We take our sandwiches over to a seating area to wait for Clove's line to clear. In the meantime, I unwrap the paper and take a bite out of my sandwich. The beef is flavorful, and it's on a ciabatta roll, which is toasted. There is mustard slathered across the bread, and crisp lettuce. Rather enjoyable, overall.

Logan finishes his sandwich in about three bites. I'm still working on mine when the last person gets their book signed, and Clove gestures us over to her table.

She asks, "Are you here for a book?" There are stacks of different titles covering the entire table. She is quite the prolific writer.

"Yeah," Logan says. "If I've never read any of your work, where should I start?"

"That depends." Clove taps the cover of a book called *The Bridge and the Candle.* "This is the first book Flint and I wrote together. We were newlyweds and in love with writing. If you like plot twists – we brainstormed the ones in that book for weeks." She sounds nostalgic, and her lips curve into a soft smile. "But if you want my favorite solo outing, it's this new series. The first one is *The Weaver's Chair*. My character is a female P.I. who gets involved with a kidnapping case in New Mexico and realizes that the kidnapping is only part of something bigger and more sinister. I've been living in New Mexico for the past couple of years, so it's a personal story to me."

Logan picks up *The Weaver's Chair*. "I'll take this one."

Clove signs it, adding a personal message that I can't see, since she's a leftie and her hand covers the page.

"We were also wondering if we could ask a few questions about Flint," I tell her.

"It's not like I'm busy down here." Clove gestures at the empty lounge surrounding her table. "Shoot."

Logan says, "We have witnesses who saw you and Flint together yesterday. Were you attempting to reconcile?"

"Flint was. I was just curious what his plan was this time."

"What do you mean?" I ask.

Clove flips the Sharpie over in her hand. "It wasn't the first time he'd tried to win me over. Either romantically, or as a writing partner. He kept saying that writing wasn't fun by yourself. That the best part was bouncing ideas, and 3 a.m. editing sessions."

"Would you ever have considered working with him again?" I ask.

She hesitates. "I mean, I miss it sometimes. But I couldn't trust Flint. He had lied about so much, even about his history before we got together."

"And you found out about it all when Ash's exposé broke?" I say.

"Exactly." Clove drops the Sharpie on the table. "Flint spent seven years in jail for embezzling from a finance company he worked for. He'd only been out for about a year when we got together. I didn't know a thing about it until Ash pointed out that mishandling money had become a habit for Flint. I think that's a big omission when you're getting ready to marry someone, don't you?"

"I'd have been angry," Logan agrees.

"I was as much hurt as angry. But it wasn't just that he'd hidden his past. There were other things that didn't add up, a few times that he would disappear and refuse to explain where he had gone." She looks sadly at that first book they'd written together. "You just can't be with someone you can't trust."

She obviously still loved Flint, though. Just look at her.

On impulse I ask, "Were any of these disappearances around the time of the accident on Edmund Foster's boat?"

"What an odd question." But Clove takes the time to consider it. "Actually, yes. There was a night about two weeks later when he said he had to go run an errand. He wouldn't say what it was, and he was gone for more than six hours. The next day, when I was doing the laundry, I found a set of car keys that weren't his in the pocket of his jeans. He said they belonged to a

friend who had been too drunk to drive, and not to worry, he
would return them."

"Do you remember what day this was?" Logan asks.

"This was years ago, Mr. Hanlon. I'm doing good to
remember that much."

"I read Ash's piece on Flint," I say. "And I asked him
why he wrote it. He says it was because he was concerned about
you, because you'd been missing for a significant number of days.
But he didn't ever write a follow-up explaining where you'd been
all that time."

"It was three weeks, actually," Clove says.

"I got a look at the missing person's report," Logan says.
Which is news to me. It must have been something he and Arlo
had requested together. "Flint's the one who filed it. From the
tone of the report, he was worried about you. According to him,
you stormed out of the cabin the two of you were sharing after
you read the new chapter he wrote."

Clove shakes her head. "I was in the office, but I wasn't
reading the chapter. Flint had locked one of the drawers on our
desk. There was no reason for him to do that – there were just the
two of us on that little writer's retreat, and we were in the middle
of nowhere."

"So you picked the lock on the drawer," Logan says. I've
seen Logan pick a lock or two myself, so it's not really a surprise
his mind goes there.

Clove nods. "Flint and I had been talking about having a
baby, which meant getting a bigger place, with a yard. We'd been
budgeting and saving, and we had just gotten an advance that
should have been enough for a down-payment on the kind of
house we'd been dreaming of. That *I'd* been dreaming of, at any
rate."

"Flint wasn't really on board?" I ask.

Clove flips over one of the books on the table, showing us
the author photo on the back. In it, Clove and Flint pose together,
leaning back-to-back. "Who knows? Maybe he thought he was

helping. When I opened that drawer, I found a thumb drive with financial data on it. Flint had sunk every penny we had – including the advance for the book I was writing with him that very weekend – into an investment scheme. I was angry. I wanted to punish Flint. And I had just finished reading *Gone Girl*."

My mouth starts to slide open in shock. I snap it shut. I study Clove for a moment, then I say, "That's a really creepy book to want to emulate in real life."

"I agree," Clove says. "But I had heard it was inspired by Agatha Christie's real-life disappearance, and I had done a bit of research on Christie's life before I picked up *Gone Girl*. Christie wanted her husband to feel consequences for his actions. And that's how I felt, too. So I packed my clothes and went to stay with my twin sister in Florida. I left my phone in the cabin and took a Greyhound bus. I made sure that if I went out, people thought I *was* my twin. Pepper kept telling Flint that she hadn't heard from me. And when I got over being upset, I went home."

"Where you got more bad news about Flint, from Ash's exposé," I say. Which must have been such a difficult and public way to learn the truth.

Clove makes a wavering gesture with her hand. "Not right away. I didn't realize that Ash even had a blog. He was really shy about it then. It was almost a year later when I stumbled over the article, while I was putting together a marketing package for the second book in our series. When I confronted him about it, Flint had explanations for everything, all easy and pat, like he'd rehearsed it all a million times. He wanted to work things out, and I really tried – but in the end we divorced."

Logan gestures with the book in his hand, which has a colorful the loom on the cover. "So you went your separate ways, and you managed to start writing stories that were more meaningful and personal. If you've moved on, why were you so upset about Flint using characters you had created in the past? You didn't need them anymore, so why did you even care?"

"So you heard about that." Clove's body language draws back and in, like we've finally hit a sensitive spot. "It was a promise he made. Detective Cody was my creation, and the character was basically my grandfather. My grandpa helped raise me, and we were very close. Flint never would have been able to get the nuances right."

"I can see why that might have been upsetting," I say.

Clove looks down at the picture of Flint again. "Yesterday, when Flint asked to meet, I was planning to give him a good piece of my mind, and demand he change the characters. But Flint told me he got the book contract hoping I would come back to co-write it with him. He said it was the one big important story we had left to write together, because these characters were important to us, and our story of our own intertwined lives needed the closure."

"That sounds powerful," I say. It has to at least be a more positive note for their last conversation.

Clove says, "Flint could be a poet, and he was charming when he wanted to be. I told him no, that I still didn't feel like I could trust him, and that it would be too complicated, now that he's seeing someone else. He wasn't happy, but he accepted it. He even asked me to beta read the manuscript of the first book, to make sure he got the characters right. It was so sweet, I almost changed my mind, right there."

"So when you and Flint parted yesterday, there was no remaining animosity?" Logan asks.

"A little, maybe. He still shouldn't have sold the book." Clove smiles at someone heading towards us through the narrow hall, possibly another reader wanting a signed book. "But I assure you, he was very much alive. I saw Flint's new girlfriend watching us. And she didn't look happy. The way Lupe looked at me – maybe you should check if she has an alibi."

The potential reader approaches Clove's table, so we thank Clove and step out of the way. Logan heads over to get another roast beef sandwich. He takes it, still wrapped, with him as we head back up the hall.

"I'm surprised that you bought a book," I say, trying to take it out of his hand to get a better look at the cover.

He holds it up, showing the signed page. "I'm getting tired of you making jokes about how I don't read. Besides, Clove's work looks interesting."

"Is that all?" I ask. "It feels like maybe you were trying to get her to give something away."

Logan points at Clove's slanted handwriting. "Chances are, she didn't kill Flint. The entry wound would have been at a weird angle for someone who is left-handed."

"Are you really going to read that, then?"

"I will." He takes in my skeptical look. "I promise."

But I'm focused on the inscription. Clove has written, *To Logan and Felicity! You two make such a lovely couple. XOXO.* And then she's scrawled her signature.

Logan has to have seen me reading that, and I can feel heat in my face broadcasting my embarrassment for him to see, but he has the good grace not to say anything about it.

Chapter Eighteen

When we get back to the central atrium, where we had the welcome party, Logan says that he wants to go talk to the captain again. Which means that, at least for the time being, I'm on my own. I sit down next to the water feature, just listening to the water spilling down the wall into the small pool near the floor. I've gotten used to being on a boat again, and the gentle rocking, now that the storm has passed, is actually relaxing. I've missed this. I need to be able to enjoy normal things again, without having everything I used to love remind me of what I've lost. I have a feeling it's still going to take a long time for me to get there. But this trip has been a big step. I need to thank Bea. After all, Satchmo had helped me get over the worst of my nervousness.

Liam comes up to me. "Felicity, we need to talk."

Yikes. Nothing good ever came after those words. "About what?" I ask, standing up.

"We have had three other people return boxes of your chocolates. I've looked at all three boxes. They're nothing like the samples you provided when we booked you."

Dismay sinks through me. As if I didn't have enough going wrong right now. "I don't know what could have happened. Let me send Logan a message and see if he has any ideas, since he's the one who brought the stock aboard."

While I type and wait for an answer, I try to think back. The offer to do the cruise had come in with short notice, which had given us all of two weeks to get everything prepared. I usually like to finish all the chocolate I have processed myself. It's part of the art of chocolate making, forming the final bars or making big blocks of bulk chocolate, testing the final snap. But we had needed to get these special boxes completed, with new molds and the cocoa butter decorations. Miles had 3-D printed the molds at the university he attends. He had designed them himself, off of a sketch I had made. Once we had a hard positive version of each mold, I was able to use the vacuum former at the shop to create a flexible version for filling. It's the newest toy I bought for the shop. Customers can bring in items, and I can use the machine to make a custom chocolate sculpture out of it. We can also use it to make standard shapes, such as the plastic trays we're using as dividers in the boxes.

Since the boxes celebrate the cruise, the molds are cubes, with sea-creature shapes that pop up as 3-D elements out of the top.

I'd been resistant to growing the company, and letting my employees take over creative aspects of the business. But really, both Carmen's recipe testing and Miles's graphic design skills are really paying off. Miles has been talking about setting up a Tik Tok account for the shop. If he's able to commit to the time it takes to create and edit video content for it, I'm all for the idea. I have a hard enough time keeping up with the Instagram account, and I'd had to plan content ahead, so that it could auto-post while we were on the boat where – in theory – we were supposed to be incommunicado.

By the time the molds were made, we'd been even shorter on time, so everyone had pitched in. It had to be done in stages. When you are working with molded chocolate, everything is upside down, and you have to think of artistic elements from the outside in. We had hand painted the various sea creatures with colored cocoa butter, letting each color dry before adding the next, and then filled the molds with chocolate. Each sea creature serves as a label, with all the cubes of that design filled with a chocolate I had created from a different origin. The octopus-topped squares are made of my Peru chocolate – in honor of Clive the octopus, who had belonged to my former employee Mateo – because Mateo had spent time in Peru. The sea turtles denote squares made from beans grown in Hawaii, since the turtles are such a part of the islands. And so forth.

It had been a massive amount of work, and I'd had to let go of complete control just to get it done. But I'd trained my employees how to use the tempering machine – which automates the tempering process. We'd all had a hand in creating the chocolate in the boxes, but each sea creature mold had been filled separately, by a different person. Even if one origin of chocolate had been improperly tempered, it should have only affected one chocolate in each box – not entire boxes.

The only way entire boxes of chocolate could have been ruined is if they had been mishandled, either by one of my employees, or by staff aboard the ship, and somehow a few of the boxes had gotten above 94 degrees. Maybe they had stored excess stock in the spa, too close to some kind of heating element. Wendy, who was the main person handling stock in the boutique, is no longer here to ask. Thinking about Wendy tugs at my heart. I still feel responsible for what happened to her – though logically I know it wasn't my fault.

In response to my question about what could possibly have gone wrong with the chocolate, Logan replies with a series of question marks and a gif of a cat shrugging. Underneath, he's typing. When the dots resolve, it says, *Let me know when you're free to go up and check the boxes. When I wrap this meeting with the captain, I can meet you there. We're talking about what happens if this isn't resolved in the time allotted for the cruise and people start demanding to go home.*

Well, Logan certainly has his hands full at the moment.

I tell Liam, "All of the boxes we brought aboard were processed in the same way as the samples. Do you know if they were stored in the same area?"

Liam starts to respond, but then his attention is caught by something behind me. I turn to follow his gaze. Arlo is striding purposefully towards us.

Arlo tells Liam, "Mr. Bosch, as you know, under the captain's orders, we have had a number of cabins searched by security."

Liam gives Arlo a puzzled look. "Yes, I know. I helped you coordinate it with him." Liam hesitates. "Why are you being so formal all of a sudden?"

Arlo says, "One of the cabins on the list was yours."

"I know that too." Liam's tone is starting to sound exasperated, but he stops and really considers the serious expression on Arlo's face. "Wait. Are you saying you found something in my cabin? If it's the murder weapon, I can assure you, I wasn't the one who put it there."

"No," Arlo says. "Nothing like that. But I'd like you to come with me to your cabin to explain."

Liam looks at me, panic in his eyes. "Felicity, come with me. Ash trusts you to help."

"I'm not sure what I can do," I protest, but Arlo gives me a slight nod. I'm surprised. Is Arlo actually making an exception to his rule about not allowing civilians inside his investigations? Is his judgement clouded by that kiss we shared earlier? Or does the fact that Liam asked for my help made a difference? Puzzled, I say, "But I can come along for moral support."

I follow Arlo and Liam down to a lower deck. When we get to Liam's cabin, the door is propped open. It's a tiny space. If I thought the room that Autumn and I had been assigned was small – you couldn't have put two beds in here if you tried. One of the security guys is standing right in the middle of the room, holding a plastic bag. In the bag, there's a silver pen. For a moment, I don't get the significance of it.

But then – what if that's the same pen that Autumn and Flint had fallen out over? That Flint had spent years convinced that Autumn had stolen? But how would Liam have wound up with it? Clove was his aunt's best friend, so conceivably he could have been in the right place to take it. But why? I suck in a breath. If Liam was the one who stole the pen, he must have been closer to all of this than I had realized. Close enough to have killed Flint? I know Logan has suspected Liam for a while now.

It still doesn't make sense. What would have been his motive? It couldn't have had anything to do with the boat "accident" – which seems to have given everyone else their motives. Liam didn't know Imogen and her family.

Arlo gestures to the evidence bag. "Can you tell me about this pen?"

Liam squints at the pen in the security guard's hand. "It's mine. I've had that thing forever."

"How did you get that particular pen?" I ask. My voice squeaks on the word *pen*.

Liam squints at me, like I've gone a little off mentally. He says, "When I was a teenager, I got a metal detector as a gift. I was bored one day when Clove was watching me and Ash, so I used it out in the back yard and found a fancy pen half-buried in the dirt. I figured nobody wanted it, so I kept it."

Arlo says, "Well if you wanted definitive proof that Autumn didn't steal anything, you can't do much better than this."

I say, "Yeah, and then he went home, so nobody from Flint's group ever saw him with the pen."

But I realize – that's why Arlo wanted me to come. Because he wanted me to see firsthand that he is looking out for my best friend, trying to make sure Autumn doesn't get swept up in this when the Feds arrive. It's sweet, really. I find myself giving him a soft little smile.

And the look he gives me in return – it is full of sparks that leave me smoldering. Arlo and I'd had something, once upon a time. And there's something about your first love that never goes away. It's just – the timing is terrible. Arlo had been taken when I'd started falling for Logan. And I'd said some things to Logan that I'm not sure I'm ready to take back.

I look away, down at the floor, where Liam has a shoe rack lined up with sneakers and flip-flops and two pair of dress shoes. This tiny room seems to be a semi-permanent home for him. Don't get me wrong. I like boats – and I've entirely gotten over how trepidatious I'd been at first about coming back onto one – but I don't think I'd like to live on one.

Liam asks, "What are you two talking about? Why would anyone have cared?"

Arlo asks, "You never wondered why the pen you found had the inscription of a famous author on it?"

Liam says, "Cove and Flint were both writers. There were a lot of writers around in their lives. If you throw a pen into the back yard, wouldn't that mean you didn't like the writer who gave it to you?" He shrugs. "I was a teenager. Teenagers don't often think."

"But why did you keep that pen all these years?" I ask.

Liam blinks at me, like I'm a bit dim. "It's a Mont Blanc. That was personally engraved by John le Carré. It's probably one of the coolest things I own."

"Because you wanted to be a writer too?" the security guy asks.

"No," Liam says. "When I was a kid, I thought I wanted to be a spy. But when I grew up – turns out I just like spy movies. Danger isn't really my thing."

"Except for the fast cars," Arlo points out. "I had a look at those unpaid speeding tickets, and some of those show you were being truly dangerous."

See, that's the thing about Liam. I can't ever tell when he's lying. Did he find that pen abandoned like he claims? Or did he take it from inside the house? There's probably no way we'll ever know for sure.

Arlo asks, "Why didn't you step forward, after the fight Clove and Autumn had this morning, in which Clove accused Autumn of having stolen this very pen. It is such a unique item. You had to have realized that it is the same one."

Liam's mouth drops open. He stares at Arlo for a full ten seconds before he says, "That's what the row during the panel was about? Someone told me it was because Autumn sent Clove dead flowers. I assumed that whatever the problem was, it was between the two of them."

"Then you did know it was Flint's pen?" Arlo asks. "Not Clove's?"

Liam hesitates. "I – I always assumed it was his. Flint was much more the spy novel type than Clove."

"Right," Arlo says – though he sounds skeptical.

I'm beginning to wonder if Liam is guilty – or if he's a pathological liar. I need to ask Ash if Liam has always had problems telling the truth. But first, I am supposed to meet my aunt and uncle for afternoon tea.

I stop in at the suite and change clothes. That's the fun thing about cruises – you have reasons to wear so many different clothes. I packed a summery A-line dress that feels afternoon tea worthy. It's black and white, with oversized flowers and a thick black belt. I add the string of pearls my grandmother had given me at my wedding. These carry so many bittersweet memories, but I'd rather wear them than leave them locked away. I finish the look with strappy black sandals.

A little before 4 o'clock, I go into the library. The space is much larger than expected. With other cruise ships I've been on, there was just a table or two for reading, and a few cases of paperback novels. But this library is shaped like a clover, with bookcases that line all of the walls. There are little curved seating areas and small marble-topped tables that echo the curves, and the open area in the middle is crowded with extra chairs and card tables. There are maybe forty people here for afternoon tea. Half of us are dressed for the occasion, but there are just as many in tees and shorts. Aunt Naomi and Uncle Greg have scored a spot on a curved maroon sofa. Naomi pats the velvet cushion beside her, where she has obviously been saving me a spot. She's wearing a pale pink dress, and Greg has on a dress shirt and tie.

I make my way over. The sofa is more comfortable than it looks, and the table in front of it has been set with three dessert

place settings with empty teacups and filled water glasses.
There's a feeling of elegance and anticipation.

"You look gorgeous," Aunt Naomi says. "Hoping you run
into a special someone, huh?"

I make a noncommittal noise in response. She means
Logan. And logically, I should be tied to Logan, trying to make
one relationship work, instead of rekindling these feelings for
Arlo. I mean, what am I thinking? But – why can't I stop my
heart from thinking it?

At precisely four o'clock, waitstaff wheel in three tea
carts and start offering attendees a selection of four different teas.

A few minutes after that, a couple of the LARPers come
in, looking for a spot, but all the seats are taken.

Aunt Naomi waves at the group. "Craig! Over here."
She asks the tea sommelier, "Surely you can set a place for one
more."

The girl nods and produces another teacup and dessert
plate from a shelf under the cart. "We'll find places for all of
them." She places the plate on the table to the right of mine.

There technically is room for four on the sofa, so we all
scoot over to make a fourth place. Craig is slight but solidly built,
and wears a cologne that somehow reminds me of the sea. I feel
uncomfortable sitting so close to a virtual stranger. His leg is
practically touching mine, but it would be rude to ask to rearrange
the seating.

After we all have tea in our cups, and towers of macarons
have appeared on the table, I ask Aunt Naomi, "How do you
know Craig?"

She gestures at him with her teacup. "He's helping with
the electrical wiring for the hotel renovation. His girlfriend is one
of the contractors."

"Guilty as charged," Craig says. He takes a purple
macaron from the tower.

"Pace yourself," Uncle Greg warns. "I read the menu. We
have four courses of desserts coming."

Aunt Naomi says, "And I plan to enjoy every bite of it." She takes a blue macaron. I can't help wonder, what flavor is blue? It has a dark filling, like maybe a caramel.

Craig says, "I'm also going to come back and take some drone footage when the renovation is complete. It should really impress potential buyers when you guys get ready to put together the real estate listing."

Aunt Naomi says, "You should see some of the drone footage Craig has done for his LARP group's page."

"Oh?" I try to sound only politely interested, but honestly, Craig has probably captured footage of some of the main suspects in this case. I wonder if Logan and Arlo already know the LARP group has a website? Knowing them, they probably already looked at it.

I ask Craig, "How did you get into LARPing?"

He finishes chewing a macaron – already his third – and then says, "I was in theater club in high school, and after we graduated some friends and I wanted a way to keep in touch. So we started the LARP group just for us, and when the whole concept took off, we opened it up to the public."

I ask, "Were Ash and Imogen part of the original group?"

Craig says, "Imogen was. She and I have gone to the same schools since elementary school." He picks up a fourth macaron. I take one from the tower too, to be polite. Craig adds, "You should have seen her as a kid. She still had a British accent, and a huge gap between her front teeth. Until the braces, of course."

I take a bite out of the macaron. It has a delightful strawberry jam and a light bite to the crust. Just about perfect. I take a moment to savor it. Then I ask, "But what about Ash? How did he wind up joining the group?"

Craig says, "Imogen started dating him. Ash was already into online RPGs and puzzle-based games. And he had the whole Mensa thing, you know?"

Mensa? Ash? I have to stifle a laugh. But yeah, somehow, I can see how that fits everything else I know about him.

I ask, "What about Liam? Did he ever show up at an event or anything?"

"Nah." Craig pauses as the first course of our desserts – the Victoria sponge – arrives. Once the server has moved on to the next table, Craig says, "I never met Liam until I took that first cruise. And that was only by chance. My mom had gotten a discounted ticket, and then at the last minute, she couldn't use it. I'd just gotten out of a relationship that wasn't working, so I needed something to cheer me up. And it all worked out."

Aunt Naomi says, "That must have been what, two months ago? So you and Julie met after the cruise?"

I wince. I wonder if Julie knows she's a rebound relationship?

I stay for the rest of the tea, and I really enjoy the conversation. Uncle Greg is a funny guy, and he tells a string of jokes about two guys fishing that make me laugh a lot more than they have any right to.

But once the desserts are gone, and we've all applauded a mini-lecture on the history of tea, I head back to the suite, take out my tablet and sit on the sofa in the shared area. Watching video is going to pull a ton of data, but at this point, I don't even care about the cost. I want to see this LARP group.

The first video is of a science-fiction themed event, where Craig's LARPers have entered as a team against several other groups, each with a themed set of costumes. Craig's group are all dressed up as robots, with silver makeup and knee and elbow pads for joints. Watching Ash running around like that cracks me up. It should make excellent emotional blackmail footage. Only – Ash willingly put this on the Internet. So obviously he doesn't care. Which is kind of a shame, since he'd embarrassed me so many times.

Imogen is the star of the video, which zooms in on her face more than once, catching her laughing, then later yelling a fierce battle cry as the robots storm a building that has been decorated to look like a mad scientist's lab. I think she must be leading the team, because she gets all the hero shots. And, knowing that her friend recorded it, you can see the affection in the camera angles. But yeah, there's no trace of Liam, or of an argument between anyone on the team, or anything that might relate to events currently taking place on this boat.

I shut off the tablet. I'm running out of time to help save Ash – and I feel like I'm no closer to the solution than where I started.

Autumn comes into the suite. "Felicity, your data bill when we get off this boat is going to be enormous."

"I'll just ask my rich friend to pay it for me," I tease. But from the almost-hurt look on Autumn's face, she's not sure if I'm being serious. I hold out a hand. "Kidding. I promise, nothing will change between us."

"I can pay it," she says, "Since most of what you're doing is to make sure I don't get suspected of murder."

"Technically, it's so Ash doesn't get framed, since he's the one that asks for my help. Proving your innocence too is just a side effect of figuring out who really killed Flint."

"Either way, I'll take it."

"I do have news for you," I tell her, as I set the tablet aside. "That pen Flint accused you of stealing? Liam has it. He claims to have found it in the backyard around the time Flint lost it. But I'm not 100% convinced he didn't actually steal it."

Autumn's mouth drops open. "Liam? Really?"

I expect that she's going to be mad at Liam for causing the misunderstanding, but she looks more bemused.

"You're not mad?"

"No," Autumn says. "But I suspect Clove and I may owe each other a number of apologies. Would you be willing to come with me to talk to her about it? Given the questions Arlo has been asking me, I don't think it's a good idea for me to approach her without witnesses."

"I'm pretty sure he realizes you didn't do it," I say. I feel my lips curving upwards, thinking about how far he'd gone out of his way to make sure I know that.

"I am too." She takes another look at herself in the mirror of the built-in with all the cubby holes. She purses her lips and applies another coat of lipstick. "But before he turns over the case to the Feds, he has to cover all his bases."

Chapter Nineteen

Autumn knows exactly where to find Clove: exercising. She gets me to change into workout-appropriate clothes, so that we can fit in. We bring tote bags too, with bottled water and hand towels, which feels like a bit much just to try and make things less awkward when Clove sees us coming, but if it's what Autumn needs, I'm game. As we make our way to the fitness center, Autumn says, "If there's a Zumba class, Clove is going to be there. Any kind of cardio dance is her thing."

I wonder if it has always been completely true that I've been Autumn's best friend. I'm realizing now that I could have been a better friend to her along the way. And that there had been more dynamics to her life that I have ever suspected. I should have paid more attention to what was going on with Autumn in the years when I was away from Texas.

"You and Clove must have been close at one point," I say.

Autumn says, "A bit. The whole critique group hung out a lot. But Clove and Emilia – Ash's mom – were inseparable. They were always nice enough, but anywhere you went with them, it was clear you were always tagging along."

"Including Zumba class?" I tease. Autumn likes to dance, but gyms were never her thing.

"Oh, girl, heck no," Autumn says, and we both laugh. Then she adds, "When we went to Zumba class, *they* were tagging along with *me*."

Surprised, I ask, "Do you still Zumba?"

"Nah," Autumn says. "Classes are no fun alone. I gave it up, along with the writing."

"We could go sometime," I say.

I feel bad about having been jealous yesterday of Autumn having another friend on board. It's just – I'd had colleagues and acquaintances in Seattle, and Kevin and I'd had a lot of couple friends. But after Kevin's death, it had been awkward for those couples, and I realized I'd never made a network of close girlfriends over my whole married life. I'd just started rebuilding my friends network when I returned to Galveston, reconnecting more closely with Autumn and making friends with Tiff and Sandra and Sonya. And building a sense of community through the employees and customers of my small business, in a way I'd never felt connected to my patients as a physical therapist.

Autumn stops in the middle of the hall. "Felicity, you know your health would not allow you to do Zumba."

I have had some experimental treatments for my asthma that have improved my health a great deal, but she's right: high impact cardio is definitely still against my doctor's orders. Still. "I could shuffle around on the back row. I don't have to be good at it to have fun. It's not a competition, is it?"

"Not *technically*," Autumn says.

She gestures at the glass wall of the fitness center, where the class is in progress. I have to say, Clove is really good at Zumba, holding the rhythm of a choreographed routine that seems to be combining salsa steps with belly dancing arm movements. Clove's in the middle of the front row, and the boat has started rocking a bit more heavily, but it doesn't seem to affect her balance. She's wearing a purple and teal geometric-print leotard and looks like she walked out of a workout video from the 1980s.

We wait for the class to end. Clove sees us through the glass wall, makes eye contact with Autumn, then glances away again. She tries to avoid us as she leaves the room, hiding being a group of giggling teenagers, but Autumn bocks her way.

Clove says, "Look, I don't want any trouble. Flint's gone. Let's just agree to avoid each other."

"Girl, I'm sorry," Autumn says.

Clove freezes, looking somehow fragile as she studies Autumn's face. "What?"

Autumn says, "I'm sorry for what happened on the panel today. And I'm sorry about letting Flint's pettiness come between us all those years ago."

Autumn explains about finding out that Liam had Flint's missing pen all along. The two of them move over to the side, opposite the treadmills. I can't quite hear what they're saying, but their voices are intent, both faces going through hurt and anger, to regret – to hope. And then Autumn and Clove reach out and hug each other. Good for them. I don't think Autumn needs a witness anymore. And I'm more convinced than ever that Clove didn't have anything to do with the murder.

I'm debating whether or not I should leave, when Arlo comes into the room, dressed to work out in a form-fitting black tee-shirt and grey basketball shorts.

I ask, "Shouldn't you be focusing on your investigation?"

Arlo gestures over at the line of treadmills. "I do my best thinking when I'm running. Besides, the FBI team has been delayed. They're not going to be here until tomorrow morning."

Arlo gets onto one of the treadmills. I take the water and hand towel out of my bag and get onto the machine next to his. He sets his for a brisk running pace. I set mine for a moderate walk. The thudding rhythm of his feet makes me feel like I should go faster, but that's the beauty of a treadmill – I don't have to go fast to keep up.

Arlo asks, "Have you thought any more about what I said?"

I feel a blush spread across my face and arms. I glance over at Clove and Autumn, but they're engrossed in their own conversation. I say, "About that kiss, you mean?"

Arlo bites at his bottom lip, unconsciously bringing attention to how kissable it is, as he sighs out a breath. He's jogging without even breathing heavily. "Well that too. But I was talking about getting training if you're going to keep getting involved with investigations. I think what happened to Logan kind of drives home the point."

"You mean him getting shot." And yes, I do feel guilty about that. "I know. If I hadn't been too ambivalent about what we're doing to tell you, you might have come too and been in a position to capture the killer."

"That's a possibility," Arlo says. "Or something could have gone even more seriously wrong. Feeling bad about might-have-been won't change the fact that Logan took a bullet in the arm."

I say, "I feel more responsible about Wendy. If I hadn't met up with her, maybe the killer would have decided whatever information she had was worthless. She might still be on this boat."

I can't bring myself to say she's dead, because the divers never actually found her.

"Now don't say that," Arlo says. "If Wendy knew something important about Flint's death, the killer would have seen her as a threat no matter what she did with the information. Her death is not on you. In any way."

"Thanks?" I'm not sure what the proper response to that actually is. "But I don't want to become the kind of person who actually needs training. Kevin hated–" My voice breaks, and I have to start again. "Kevin hated violence, and I do too. That's one thing about me that I don't think is going to change."

Arlo looks at me levelly. "And yet you're willing to get serious about either me or Logan? Are you sure this is something you should be pursuing? We both deal in danger, Lis, and if that's a dealbreaker, I'd prefer to know now."

I swallow. My throat suddenly feels dry and I fumble as I open that bottle of water. "I thought it was, when I first met Logan. I told myself – told him, actually – that I wasn't interested, because of that. But these days danger seems to find me, no matter what I do. And I'm not sure what I want my life to look like anymore." I gesture down to the bruise forming on my knee. "Obviously, I'm not going to be good at handling danger myself."

"To be fair, you did get jumped from behind. Logan says the person who shot him was hiding in the lifeboat and jumped out at you. Presumably, they were intending to eavesdrop on your conversation with Wendy and just jumped the gun before getting any real information. Which tells me that we're looking for someone impulsive, who lets their emotions get the better of them." Arlo looks thoughtful. "But does that fit any of the suspects?"

I think he's talking to himself. He's told me often enough that the police can't discuss their cases with civilians. Still, I answer him. "Not really. I think I just don't know most of them well enough to figure out how they would react in any given situation."

Arlo gets this embarrassed look, and I think he realized he's gotten into discussing-the-case territory without meaning to. He says, "I'm sorry. We shouldn't be talking about this."

I tell him, "I need to find out what is going on with my merchandise, anyway. Logan is going to meet me at the boutique to check all the boxes of chocolate. We need to know how many of them had bloom, or outright melted. So that maybe we can track down where things went wrong."

"Give me a few minutes here, before you go," Arlo says. "This is nice. I'd like to do something normal with you for just a little while."

"Okay," I say. I walk for a few minutes, while Arlo runs, and I have to admit, it is comfortable.

Arlo says, "I spent some time in Arizona. It was impossible to run outdoors there. It was so hot and the heat was so dry, you'd start to melt into the pavement. I started taking trips up into the mountains, where it was cooler, to do some hiking. You would love those mountains, the way the light filters through the trees at sunrise."

"That sounds gorgeous." I can picture myself there, with him – on a quiet adventure. The thought feels as comfortable as Arlo's kiss had earlier. And I'm not sure what to do with that feeling. I try to distract myself, and I wind up right back considering the case. "Can I just ask one thing? What was that hose that Wendy brought for me to look at? The box that was attached to it didn't look like anything I'd ever seen before."

Arlo looks at me, without missing a beat on his treadmill. At first, I think he's going to tell me again that he can't share information. But then the hardness goes out of his jaw, and he says, "I've never seen anything like it before either. It looks like something someone cobbled together from scratch. But best guess is still that it's a device for remotely controlling the flow of some gas through the tube it was attached to."

"Which still doesn't make any sense." I see what Arlo means, about movement getting thoughts flowing. "Unless maybe Flint was exposed to some kind of gas before he was stabbed."

Arlo sighs. "Maybe we should talk about, I don't know, pancakes or something?"

I look over at his machine and laugh. He's still running, without being out of breath. The fact that he wants a high carb breakfast for dinner when he finishes his workout just seems a bit ironic. "You run so you can afford the carbs?"

"Partially," Arlo says. "But I enjoy it, especially alongside the ocean. You do have to be careful where you run on the island, though." By the island, he means Galveston. "Drivers aren't always careful. You wouldn't believe how many close calls we get reported by joggers and cyclists, especially in the crowded area of the seawall."

I know the spot he's talking about. It's near Stewart Beach, the first beach you see if you take the ferry across from the Bolivar Peninsula. Then there's a whole strip of restaurants that are popular with the tourists, and some cheesy beach shops that have signs in the window that say things like, *Fifteen Tee-Shirts for Twenty Bucks*. I remember what Autumn said, about the hit and run that had caused her to stop writing. When she'd first told me about it, hadn't she said that it had happened along the seawall? Probably in the same area Arlo is talking about? "Sometimes more than just a close call, huh?"

Arlo grunts in assent. From the look on his face, that isn't something he wants to talk about. He really has seen some things he'd rather forget. "It's the most senseless thing the police get called in to handle. Most of the time people are drinking and driving, or just being stupid with their friends in the car or they're on their phone."

But what about when it isn't just that? What about when it's murder? Things start coming together in my head. I gasp, and nearly fall off the back of the treadmill.

"Lis, are you okay?" Arlo hits the emergency stop on his machine and jumps onto the side rails as the belt comes to an abrupt halt. "Where's your inhaler?"

I recover my balance and turn my treadmill off less abruptly. "It's not that. I just realized something. Which I probably should have put together sooner."

"Are you going to share?" Arlo asks.

"In a minute." I want to get this straight in my head first. Autumn and Clove come rushing over. Seeing them together like that makes it all the more obvious. Autumn said she suspected Flint might have been involved in causing a hit and run. Clove had said Flint had gone out one night with no explanation and come back with a strange set of car keys. Those keys could prove that Flint really *had* been involved in a hit and run. If he still had them. And if I was even right. Could the hit and run have had something to do with the boat accident? It's a lot of *ifs* to voice to a couple of mystery writers and a cop.

But now they're all staring at me, so I have to say something. After I assure Autumn that I am not having an asthma attack over the mere thought of exercise, I ask her, "The hit and run that mirrored what had happened in your book. That had to have happened the same year as the boat accident, right?"

Autumn gives me a horrified look. "Why would you bring that up in front of another writer? I told you that in confidence."

"I'm sorry." I glance at Clove. She looks puzzled, but like she's working out what I'm talking about. I say, "I wouldn't bring it up if it wasn't important."

Autumn doesn't look convinced.

I ask her more urgently, "Could the two events be connected?"

"I've always thought they might be." Autumn looks over at Clove. "Did you know Nathale Daye? She wrote the *Night in a Forgotten Land* books. She was friends with Edmund Foster, and they did those events together about history in mysteries?"

Clove shakes her head. "Edmund was Flint's friend, not mine. I only even met him a couple of times before that accident on the boat. It was all so tragic."

I don't correct her use of the word accident, even though I believe what Lupe said, about Flint confessing to having shot Edmund. Though the reason Flint gave her still seems flimsy.

Autumn says, "Nathale was supposed to go with them on the boat that day, but at the last minute she changed her mind. Said she had a headache, and she was prone to migraines, so I didn't think anything of it. But then two weeks later, she's dead in a hit and run. It wasn't until months later that I started thinking – what if she had seen something? An argument at the dock, anything. It was exactly what had happened to the first act victim in *Write Me a Melody*. She'd seen too much, but there was nothing to connect her to the killer. My bad guy steals a car and after hitting the character, drives it into the bay, obliterating any leftover DNA evidence. The police chalk it up to teenagers gone joyriding, since they can't find anyone who had a reason for killing her. He gets away with the murder – until at the end, the cops finally nab him for a tangentially related crime."

Arlo asks, "And you've been holding onto those suspicions for all these years? Why didn't you ever approach the cops?"

She takes a deep drink from her water bottle. "I just figured it was too much mystery writer brain, making me jump to conclusions that would never happen in real life. I mean, I knew Flint had seen the outline for my book. I had the sarcastic critique notes to prove it. I'm not sure what had been going on, but he'd turned cantankerous towards me, even before the incident with the pen."

Clove says, "He'd turned that way towards everyone. Around the time you're talking about, I found some anti-anxiety pills in his bedside table, but he didn't want to tell me what was going on. Instead, he got mad at me for snooping."

"Exactly," Autumn says. "Behavior like that. But while Flint may have been a jerk, it's hard seeing him as a murderer. And without proof?" She shrugs. "It was easier just to step away from the whole thing, than to be branded as that writer who lost the ability to distinguish fiction from reality."

Clove turns to me, where I'm still standing backwards on the treadmill, holding onto the railing. She says, "That night Flint went out and came back with someone else's keys. You asked me about that because you think he was capable of running someone down? Someone that he was friends with?"

"I don't know what Flint was or wasn't capable of," I say as gently as I can. "I never met him before a couple of days ago. I just think you have some facts, and Autumn has some facts and putting them together will help make a clearer picture."

Arlo says, "Though I don't see how you hope to prove what happened in a hit and run after all this time."

Clove says, "If it was two weeks after the boat accident, it could have been the same night. And I'm not sure he ever did return those keys." She lapses into silence, obviously thinking over the possibilities. Finally, she says, "Flint always kept a safety deposit box. He'd had it before we got married, and I don't think he ever realized I knew about it. If there's anything he kept, but he didn't want anyone to find, it would be in there. I can't imagine he ever would have gotten rid of that box. If I'm the heir to the will that means I have the right to get someone to open it, right?"

"If you have reason to suspect it may contain evidence pertinent to an ongoing murder investigation?" Arlo says. "I'm sure we can manage it. Either Galveston PD or the FBI."

"What do you think will be in there?" Autumn asks. "It's not like he would have kept the keys that proved he stole a car with the intent to hit someone with it."

I shudder. Because even if the story Flint told Lupe was true, and he killed Edmund on the boat out of self-defense, running down a witness two weeks later qualified as cold-blooded murder.

Chapter Twenty

I meet Logan outside the boutique. He's studying the ice sculpture, which is busy slowly melting away. When he sees me, he smiles. "Hey."

"What are you thinking?" I ask.

He gestures at the ice sculpture. "Security has been searching the ship for half the day, and the divers were out looking for Wendy just as long. They never found a murder weapon. So either the killer did find time to toss it overboard before the ship stopped, or–" He gestures at the sculpture. "Maybe we're missing something. Could someone have broken one of the ice rays off earlier when it was still sharp and kept it frozen somewhere?"

"That's possible." I look over at the alcove where Flint actually died, which has been roped off with caution tape. "Maybe the device Wendy found was used to give Flint some kind of gas before he was attacked. And the killer needed a way to move the body quickly, and a tarp or something to keep from leaving a trail of blood all the way from here to the boutique. What if the killer had all of those supplies on a cart? Either like something from room service, or maybe a luggage cart? If they could access that, they could have grabbed one of the ice buckets for chilling champagne."

"That all sounds rather elaborate," Logan points out. "It feels like we're overthinking things here."

I shrug. "The killer managed to bring a plastic gun onto a cruise ship. And we haven't found that either."

"Actually, we did," Logan says. "Well, security did. Two decks below where we were attacked. But it was broken into pieces, and stomped on. I think the gun got damaged in the swinging-through-the-window maneuver, so the killer abandoned it."

"That's a relief, right?" I say. "This person isn't armed anymore."

Logan gestures at the ice sculpture. "Not necessarily."

And there we are, right back where this conversation started.

"Come on," I tell Logan. "Whatever's wrong with the chocolate isn't going to fix itself, just because we procrastinate looking at it."

"Whatever you say, boss," Logan says playfully. He's invested in the craft chocolate company, so I'm not his boss. But he seems to like saying that whenever I'm showing him how to do something new with the chocolate processing equipment, or explaining something about how to coax nuances of flavor out of cacao beans.

We go into the boutique. There are a couple of customers in line, and Liam is behind the counter checking them out. One guy has a box of Greetings and Felicitations chocolates. The customer ahead of him picks up her bag and breezes past us into the promenade. The guy puts the box of my chocolate onto the counter, and I see Liam wince.

My heart sinks, but Liam sells the box. Maybe that means the problem was limited to only those few boxes he'd mentioned. Liam helps the last few customers, then he turns to us.

"I see you're still selling the boxes," I say, gesturing over to the Greetings and Felicitations display. "I assume you figured out what the problem was?"

"Nope." Liam gestures at the resister on the counter. "We just can't afford not to. If it turns out the chocolate was mishandled once it was in stock on the ship, the cruise line will have to eat the loss." He laughs a little as he realizes what he just said. "No pun intended. Most people buy high-scale food items as souvenirs or gifts, rather than to eat while on the boat, and by the time an item goes through all that luggage and handling, it's a lot less clear who's at fault if something got melted, so most people won't even bother to complain."

I can't believe how unethical Liam's business model is. His – or this cruise line's. It's hard to tell which, since I've not figured out how much authority Liam actually has. I can't even think of an appropriate reply. Instead, I just stand there dumfounded.

Logan is more in control. He says, "I'd rather pull the product than ruin the shop's reputation. Greetings and Felicitations is all about providing a gourmet experience, while teaching people about the global nature of chocolate."

I nod enthusiastically, and I find myself beaming at him. Logan and I share the same values and direction for the business – and I'm incredibly fortunate to have that, especially since we only became business partners because he bailed me out of a financial crunch.

"I'll run that past the head of sales," Liam says. "But we need to know how much of the product is actually damaged. And when and how. If it seems likely that the problem is a manufacturing error, you'll wind up owing us for all the returns."

I clear my throat, which has suddenly gone dry. "We are careful, with all of our processes." I explain how each chocolate in a given box is from a different batch, made with beans roasted to different specifications.

Logan says, "We should get started checking the boxes. They're sealed, inside the plastic trays, so it shouldn't hurt anything if we untie and then re-tie the ribbons."

There's a knock on the glass door, and we all turn to see a guy in a track suit, his face red from too much sun and possibly running across the ship. He frowns at us, but when we don't move towards the door, he turns, goes into the Spa and goes through to the open area between the spa and the boutique.

Liam says, "We're closed for a quick inventory."

The guy holds up a bag with the boutique's logo. "All I need is to make a quick return," he says. "That girl who was working in here yesterday checked me out. It's under my cabin number. Nick Hathaway, in 1704."

Liam takes the bag over to the counter and takes out a box of my chocolate. The ribbon is still attached to the bottom part of the box and flops onto the counter with a *thwack*, which probably sounds louder in my ears than it does in reality. Liam peers at the box, looking genuinely puzzled. "Why do you want to return it?"

I can't help making a tiny, indignant noise. Liam knows full well why this customer is unhappy. But he's managed to look both mystified and sympathetic. Honestly, it feels like he has a harder time *not* lying.

The guy gestures at the box. It's the largest special collection set on offer. "It's all melted. My wife took one look at it and started crying."

"That seems like quite a reaction," Logan says.

Nick says, "We've had some problems. It's hard not to, with three teenagers in the house. This was supposed to be a romantic getaway to bring back the good times, and then there's a murder – and I'm afraid these chocolates were just the last straw. She's not going to see that I'm really trying here, you know?"

I get an awful feeling in the pit of my stomach. I feel like I've singlehandedly ruined this guy's marriage. I know that isn't logical, but after all, I'd been the one to find the body, too. I step over to the counter and ask, "Can I take a look?"

Liam lifts the lid. I brace myself.

The box is supposed to be filled with cubes, each with a different 3-D sea creature on the top. But inside this box, there's a puddled mess where each of the chocolate cubes has melted down to fill the bottom of each plastic compartment. It set up again – but it had solidified improperly, leaving the surface looking gray and crumbly, with starburst shapes on the surface, surrounded by streaks of white. Some of the sea creatures are partly intact, but they look monstrous, drowning in the chocolate, or melted into multiple pieces.

I look over at Logan, and the panic in his eyes matches exactly how I feel. I ask him, "Did you leave the boxes in the sun while you were waiting to get on the boat?"

He shakes his head. "I would never do that. You've drilled into me how easily chocolate loses its temper in Texas, especially in the summer." He takes a deep breath, lets it out slowly. Then he moves over to the display. "Maybe it's not all of them."

"So about my refund?" Nick asks.

"Of course." Liam starts to process the transaction. "I will have some complimentary chocolate covered strawberries sent to your cabin, along with champagne."

Logan takes out a business card. "And when we get back to port, Greetings and Felicitations and Ridley Puddle Jumping will give you an hour-long sightseeing flight with a correct box of chocolates."

"That's generous of you." Nick takes the card. "Thanks! You may just have saved my marriage."

Logan asks, "If you don't mind my asking, when exactly did you buy these chocolates?"

Nick says, "It wasn't long after this store opened last night."

Which means that whatever happened to the chocolate likely happened before the murder. But I'm not sure how that helps us figure out anything.

After Nick leaves, I tell Logan, "That really is generous of you. But it's also a great idea. You should offer flights with chocolate as a regular option on your website."

Logan says, "It would be a way to tie my business interests together and cross-advertise." Logan moves over to the display and opens a second box of our chocolates.

It's just as much of a mess as the first. He grimaces. "We can work on that once we've sorted out this problem. One way or another." Because, yes, it would be a financial hit if we wind up out the cost of materials for this order, and we would probably have to cancel one of our two upcoming sourcing trips – but it wouldn't be enough to sink the company. Logan looks thoughtful. Finally, he says, "I can guarantee you the chocolate was fine when it left the shop. And we now know that whatever went wrong happened before the boutique opened. Which only leaves a limited window."

Renato, the guy who staffs the desk at the spa comes into the boutique. "I couldn't help but overhear. Wendy comped two boxes of those chocolates for the spa staff when they first came on board. They looked fine then."

That raises my hopes that yes, we will be reimbursed. If we can prove what happened. I say, "The box that was in the basket for winning the LARP was fine too."

I want to ask Renato which of the chocolate cubes he liked the most, but he's already turned around and headed back to the spa.

Liam tells me, "If this damage to your product turns out to be this ship's fault, we will of course reimburse you completely."

Though that still won't repair the damage to my business's reputation, or give us the sales we had hoped for with this trip. After all, one of the main reasons for doing the demos on board this boat was to advertise my chocolates to a group of people who would be walking past the boxes every day. Of course, given Flint's murder, and my connection to it, we've probably made up some of the difference with the sales Carmen is getting back home.

Logan says, "We need to go through all of the boxes, and see how many are damaged. We may be able to re-build the display, and if not, we may be able to figure out where things went wrong."

Liam says, "It's going to take you a while to sort through all of those. I need to go announce a shuffleboard competition. I'll be back. If anyone wants to buy something from the boutique, have someone from the spa pop in here to check them out."

I look longingly through the opening between the two spaces, to where the kitten is playing at the desk. Renato, who is supposed to be working behind said desk, is dangling the belt of one of the spa robes for the kitten to pounce on. It certainly seems more serene in there than in here dealing with all this melted chocolate. I tell Liam, "My friend Tiff said I was stressed out and should get a massage. And that was before we discovered all this ruined product."

"Done," Liam says. He walks over to the spa side, and says, "Renato, can we get Mrs. Koerber in for a massage, facial and pedicure package?"

Renato folds the robe belt on the counter and goes around to the computer. "We have an opening at 7 tomorrow morning."

"Perfect," Liam says. He turns back to me. "The cruise line will comp the massage, for all the trouble you've been through on this trip. Just pay the tip."

"Wait," I protest, leaving my spot on the floor to join Liam in the spa area. "I wasn't asking for preferential treatment." And honestly, I didn't really plan to make time for a massage. I had just been wish talking.

There's a hissing noise as a diffuser on a timer releases more of that soothing lavender-based scent into the air.

"Too late," Liam says. "You're already in the computer. I promise you, it will be worth getting up early for. The green juice smoothie alone will get your day going right."

I am not about to mention that Tiff said I should go for the hot stone massage.

Renato asks, "Should I put you down for the Swedish massage? Or the hot stones or the shiatsu? I can combine any of those with aromatherapy."

"Hot stones and aromatherapy?" I say, warming to the idea. "If you're sure it's not too much trouble."

The kitten starts climbing the leg of my yoga pants. I ask Renato, "What did you name the little guy?"

"Sebastian," Renato says. "I'm petitioning the captain to let me keep him aboard even after this cruise is over, as a mascot. The spa staff has gotten fond of him."

I can see why." I detach Sebastian from my clothing and try to hold him in my arms. After a second, he stops squirming and starts licking my arm. "I hope the captain okays it."

"Check this out, Fee," Logan calls from the other room. "Arlo just sent me this with strict instructions that I was not to share it with you."

"At some point he's going to stop trusting you," I say. But I hand the kitten back to Renato and head over to Logan's side of the display to see what he's received.

Logan tilts his phone towards me, showing me a picture of the contents of Flint's safety deposit box. Go figure. He kept the keys. Logan taps the image, enlarging it to show where one of the keys is sticking out. He says softly, "They haven't verified it for sure, but there's a pretty good chance this key is the match for the vehicle that struck Nathale Daye."

"Why would he have kept those?" I ask.

Logan closes the image. He glances over to make sure no one is coming back into this space from the spa. Even more softly, he says, "Any number of reasons. It could have been a trophy, if Flint was actually proud of killing those people. Or it could have been something like the tale-tell heart, where it's always there, symbolizing his guilt. Maybe it was to remind himself what he'd done, so that he wouldn't be tempted to do it again."

Each of those possibilities paints a very different picture of Flint.

"Whatever the reason," I say, "Autumn is going to be relieved that she wasn't being paranoid all those years ago."

I hear a noise and look up. Liam is peeling the Temporarily Closed sign off the glass door. Which makes me feel like he's abandoning us, even though he said he's coming back.

I untie the ribbon on one of the boxes from the very top of the display. The damage isn't as bad as to the ones on the bottom shelf, but everything still looks a bit smudgy. I wouldn't sell it, since it isn't up to my usual standards – though I don't think Liam would have any problems with the idea.

I look at a few boxes, and overall, it seems like the top tier sustained a lot less damage. I show Logan the small stack of undamaged boxes I'm making. It looks truly pathetic, compared to the giant display. "I think these ones are salvageable."

"None of these are," Logan says. "Maybe we can melt all this chocolate back down and Carmen can use it for baking or something."

"That's true." After all, chocolate doesn't have to be tempered if it's going into a batter. I move closer to Logan. "I love that you're able to find a silver lining in all of this."

Logan looks like he wants to reach out to me, maybe even kiss me again. But he holds back – probably because of this thing with Arlo. And that's probably for the best. I'm not the kind of girl who kisses two different people in one day. Logan clears his throat and turns his focus back to the display. "It's weird. If this display got filled off the dolly, then the boxes that were on the top are now on the bottom. So maybe the dolly got left near the windows? And somehow the sun reflected onto it and melted the top boxes, despite the air conditioning in here?"

"I guess?" I'm used to Logan supplying solid theories, and right now, it feels like he's spitballing. I say, "I think we're overcomplicating all of this again. Is there any way the base of the display itself could have gotten hot?"

"I don't see how," Logan says. "Nothing is venting into the room in this area. And that base is one solid piece."

But he keeps looking at it, then around it. And I bet he's thinking the same thing that I am: We've been basing the time of Flint's death on the idea that his body hadn't had time to cool. But what if somehow Flint's body had been *kept* warm. It would mean that all those people we've assumed had alibis could easily have committed the murder. And that that ice ray could actually have been the murder weapon.

"You know," I tell Logan. "We have most of the boxes off of that thing already. If we finish emptying it, it would be easier to move it out into the room."

Logan takes out his phone. "It would be even easier if we get Arlo up here to help us out."

I continue sorting through the boxes as Logan takes them off the display, stacking the good ones on the counter. I ask Renato for the dolly we brought aboard. It takes a while and several phone calls, but he gets someone to bring the dolly to the boutique. I start stacking the boxes of damaged chocolate onto it. Arlo comes in to help, and the work starts going faster. Some of the chocolate completely melted, and some of it just has spots of bloom or smears of cocoa butter. But the amount of work it all represents makes me physically sick to my stomach.

When all the boxes are moved, there are twenty-three good ones. Twenty-three. Out of 500. And we haven't even looked at the ones stored for inventory.

Liam comes back. He takes one look at my face and says, "That bad, huh?"

I try to remind myself that it's just chocolate. That it isn't nearly as important as the loss of a man's life. Even if we're pretty sure that Flint was also a murderer, he was still a fellow human being. This really is like *Murder on the Orient Express*. Just like the bad guy who was killed in Christie's novel, Flint had been responsible for a crime that he wasn't prosecuted for, and that crime had changed the lives of a number of people currently trapped on board a non-moving vessel.

This difference: Flint was only stabbed once. Which means that only one of the people Flint had hurt had been prepared to kill him.

Arlo and Logan enlist Liam and Renato to help them move the display out into the center of the room. We all examine it. On the back, there is a long slit in the base, about an inch tall, running at least six feet.

"Is that normal?" I ask.

"No," Renato says. "These displays are meant to be able to be re-arranged, so the base should be the same on all sides, in case we wanted to put it out on the promenade, or in the center of this room."

Arlo kneels down close to the slit and shines his phone's flashlight inside the piece. I lean over, trying to get a better look. There are crimson splotches on the slit, and inside the base.

"There's dried blood on here," Arlo says. He squints and leans down closer. "And in the back, there's a crumpled-up shopping bag."

"Weird," Logan says. "I was hoping to find a radiating heater or something. But there's nothing like that."

"Then why cut a slit in this thing?" I ask.

Logan shrugs. "Who knows? But if there's blood inside, it has to relate somehow to the murder."

Arlo says, "What it means is that we're looking for a killer who is a more elaborate planner than we could have imagined. Somebody smart and organized."

"Oh." I sound profoundly disappointed. Because I can't help think of what Craig said about Ash and the whole Mensa thing. I still don't believe Ash killed anyone – especially since I'm no longer sure we have the right time of death. But with a few bloodstains and a shopping bag – I can't imagine we're going to be able to convince the FBI.

Logan turns towards Renato. "Speaking of re-arranging things. Our chocolate was special ordered for this cruise. Obviously, something else would have been on this display when the ship sailed before."

Renato taps his cheek, looking thoughtful. Then he says, "Yeah, that's where all those ceramic whales and lighthouses were."

I see where Logan's headed with this, but I don't say anything, because I don't want Arlo to remember that I probably shouldn't be part of this conversation.

Arlo says, "So whoever killed Flint wouldn't necessarily have known that what was on this display could be damaged by heat."

"Wait a minute," Renato protests. "You're making it sound like this murder was set up before the ship even sailed."

Arlo says, "Wasn't it?"

Renato replies, "I don't believe any of the people I work with are capable of murder."

"Nor do they have a motive for hating Flint." Logan looks significantly at Liam. "Except possibly one."

Chapter Twenty-One

By the time we have dinner, my stomach's rumbling. Tonight, the dining room has gone all out with Texas-themed choices. There's a barbecue plate, Tex-Mex options – even a giant bowl of chili. I've learned on trips before that cruise lines tend to go for bland versions of anything that's supposed to be spicy to avoid tummy upset among passengers who might be on the borderline of seasickness. So there's no way I'm going to waste a dinner like this on inevitably disappointing chili.

Instead, I go for the brisket plate. The menu says the barbecue has been supplied by a popular restaurant, one known for low and slow brisket with flavorful burnt ends.

Like most cruises, this one has assigned seats for dinner. Which means that Logan, Autumn and I are at a table with five strangers. There's a single elderly woman, a Miss Cage, who says she breeds parrots in Houston. There's also a family with two children. They're the Shaws, from Oklahoma City.

I haven't seen many kids on board. I'm guessing that has something to do with the theme of the cruise. But obviously, not everyone has been participating in the mystery-theme events, since there's seating for 700 at this dinner service. There are a lot of empty seats, though the cruise is supposed to be full. That's only to be expected, with two specialty restaurants taking bookings for sushi or Italian fare, people opting for room service like my aunt and uncle did last night, and people eating on the go at the casual spots. Last night, we'd opted for that because of the LARP.

The little girl, who's maybe six years old, keeps sneaking looks at Autumn and then looking down at the table.

Finally, Autumn asks, "What is it, sweetie?"

The girl points at the necklace Autumn is wearing. It's an elaborate piece, with three strands of pearls supporting a walnut-sized faux emerald. The emerald is surrounded by swathes of small pearls and gold beads, and there's a thumb sized opalescent teardrop dangle. The girl whispers, "Are you a princess?"

"Of course not," Autumn says overdramatically. Then she winks.

The girl giggles and hides her face in her hands, convinced she's met a secret princess.

Her brother, who's closer to ten, rolls his eyes and puts a toy car on the table.

Mr. Shaw says, "Anton, don't roll your eyes at Amy."

"Sorry," Anton mutters.

Our table isn't far from an arched staircase leading up onto that balcony overlooking the entire dining room.

A bit farther out into the center of the room, the whole LARP group has taken over three tables. They aren't fully in costume, but many of them have props that are little nods to the mystery genre. One of the guys has an oversized detective's notebook, and Imogen has an oversized spyglass.

Tonight, Ash is the one wearing the Sherlock Holmes deerstalker. I don't think it is the same one Imogen had yesterday. His is a darker color. Ash sees me checking out his group and waves.

Logan leans towards me and says, "It still doesn't make sense. We went over every inch of that space. There wasn't a vent on that whole side of the room. So even if the tubing Wendy found could have been used to transfer heat, there's no way it would have been close enough to affect Flint's corpse. The piece wasn't long enough."

At the word *corpse*, Miss Cage's eyebrows go up.

Mrs. Shaw clears her throat meaningfully. "We've been trying very hard to protect our children from the effects of this M-

U-R-D-E-R on what was meant to be a happy vacation. We would very much appreciate your cooperation."

"Patricia," Mr. Shaw says, in a warning tone. "Don't make a big deal."

Anton pipes up, "I'm eleven, mom. I can spell murder." He leans forward against the table and asks Logan, "Are you a policeman?"

"Not exactly," Logan says.

Amy's eyes go wide. She asks Autumn, "Are you a princess policewoman?"

"No," Autumn says. "That's more her thing." She points at me. "But if we are still here for dinner tomorrow, I'll wear my tiara."

Autumn really did bring a tiara. She also brought one for me. Not that I have any intention of wearing it.

Logan asks, "If you're avoiding talking M-U-R-D-E-R, then why did you bring your family on a mystery cruise?"

Mrs. Shaw says, "This was the only cruise sailing on the days Herb had vacation time."

Ash comes over to our table. He looks more anxious than when he was sitting with his friends. He asks, "Have you made any progress in figuring out who really killed Flint?"

Mrs. Shaw makes a noise that sounds practically apocalyptic.

I give her a careful look, then I get up from the table. I gesture for Ash to follow me over to the empty area under the staircase. There, I tell him, "Yes and no. It feels like every question we answer about this whole thing brings up three more."

"What can I do to help?" Ash asks. "I am a reporter. I'm good at digging up answers."

I wince, imagining Arlo's response to that. "You can't. You're a suspect. That would just make the guys coming to take over the case look at you even more seriously."

I know first-hand. I've been a suspect in a murder investigation before. Arlo had given me the same advice. I'd ignored it. But I don't think Ash will.

Ash takes off his glasses and polishes the lenses. "Then what am I supposed to do? I've been trying to act like this isn't bothering me, that if I know I'm innocent, I won't go to jail. But every time I turn around, it feels more like I'm being framed."

I feel sympathetic for Ash's predicament, but there's not a lot I can do to reassure him. We have no proof that Flint's time of death was altered. We have no other solid suspects to present.

"Maybe there are a few questions you can answer."

Ash's expression brightens. "Okay, shoot."

I say, "I know Liam's your cousin. But – has he always been a pathological liar?"

Ash half chokes-half laughs. He puts his glasses back on. "You've met him, right?"

"I know Liam's lied to me several times. He's gotten caught in those lies and just changed his story." I give Ash a few moments to absorb that. "I'm pretty sure he lied to me about finding Flint's priceless pen in the back yard."

Ash grins. "I knew you were a good judge of people."

"Not always," I admit. "I've been taken in by a murderer or two in the past."

Those aren't comfortable memories. I tend to always look for the best in people, and realizing you're wrong, that someone you thought was a nice person had actually killed someone – it's hard to take. Yet, I don't want to become jaded. That would be giving up too much of who I am.

"That's the price of being an optimist," Ash says.

"I think Liam took Flint's pen, knowing full well it was one of Flint's most prized possessions."

"Liam might have done that, as a prank. He never really liked Flint." Ash leans back against the wall. "But if he did, he didn't tell me."

"Do you think Liam might have wanted Flint dead?"

"Probably not," Ash says, but his tone makes it more of a question. "I mean, he had a reason to hate Flint. But I doubt it was serious enough to want to kill over."

"What was it?" I ask.

Ash says, "He and Flint got into a fistfight one time. You'll have to ask Liam the details. He never wanted to talk to me about it."

I try to fit that in with what I already know. It's a far cry to go from punching someone to murdering them. And that still doesn't prove that Liam took the pen. There's only one more thing I can think to ask. "Did Liam have a metal detector back when you were teenagers?"

"A metal detector?" Ash repeats. "No. He would have thought that was too geeky. Why?"

"Just another lie," I say.

"I feel like I should talk to him," Ash says.

"No!" I take a deep breath and slow down. "If Liam is the one framing you, confronting him about his lies could be dangerous."

"It's not him," Ash says vehemently. "Liam's family. He would never do that."

Given everything that Ash has recently learned about his family, I can see how adamantly he needs to believe that. "Okay. But be careful. No matter how you look at it, someone on this boat has it in for you. The way they've been working to frame you – it's probable that it's someone you know."

Which is most of our suspects. The only one that doesn't seem to have some connection to Ash is Lupe.

Ash's face goes a little pale. "That's not a comfortable thought."

"Good. You need to be careful, not comfortable."

"What else did you want to ask me about?" Ash asks. He looks so vulnerable.

I need to be delicate here. Careful to keep my voice neutral, I ask, "What can you tell me about Imogen?"

"Why?" Ash looks guarded now.

I shrug, trying to make it look casual. "I just don't know much about her, or how she fits into all of this. What drew you to her?"

"Imogen's smart, and she has a great sense of humor. After we'd been on a couple of dates, I looked up her work. She's amazing."

"What does she do?" I ask.

"She's a game designer. A lot of it is video games, but she's also written role playing game modules for major companies, which is why it is so cool that she's one of the main writers for our group's LARP scenarios. Without good writing, those things can easily go from fun to lame, you know?"

"I can see that." I'd played the game last night and enjoyed it – right up until I'd found Flint's body. "Are any of the members of your group particularly bad writers?"

Ash winces. "I don't really want to say. Is it important?"

"Probably not." I had been more curious than anything.

"Craig," Ash says. "And Lucy. But at least they're trying. Half the group doesn't even try to design anything. Jim, Min and Reagan don't even do their own costumes. They pay Lucy or Avery."

I nod along, though I haven't even met half of the people he's talking about. I'm pretty sure none of them have a connection to Flint. Just in case, I ask, "Does anyone else in the LARP group know Flint or Clove?"

"Not that I know of," Ash says.

I need to direct the conversation back to Imogen. "So the game modules Imogen designs. Is that freelance? Or is there a company she works for?"

"Pretty much everything she does is freelance." Ash glances over at his table, where Imogen is pretending to peer through the spyglass at the bread roll on her plate. "Lately, she's been designing elaborate locked room puzzles for that new place in Houston – Let Me Out! Maybe you've heard of it? It's gotten a lot of good press."

"Imogen builds sets for a local escape room?" I look over at Imogen again, and she's still playing with the spyglass. But somehow the expression on her face looks a lot more ominous.

"Yeah," Ash says. "I'm going to have my bachelor party there. Imogen is designing a special puzzle just for me and my friends."

If there is even still a bachelor party. We're looking at a murder here that was centered on an elaborate puzzle, not, as Ash still believes, a simple stabbing. Ash doesn't realize it, but he practically just told me his fiancé did it.

There's the click and whine of a sound system coming on somewhere in the room. Liam's voice comes over it, and I can hear him actually speaking from somewhere above me at the same time. Which means he's on the balcony at the top of the staircase. Ash and I both back away until we can see him up there.

Liam says, "I want to thank everyone for your patience with our itinerary change. And to apologize for the inconvenience, Sunset Cruises would like to offer each and every passenger half off a future booking." There's a smattering of applause across the dining room. Though there are some disappointed grumbles too, probably folks who were hoping the cruise line would offer them a replacement trip for free. But this is a small cruise line, and a new venture. It would probably sink Sunset to have to let a whole boatload of folks sail for free. Liam continues, "It's almost time for us to raffle off our mystery-related prizes. Staff will be circulating here in a moment, in case you need to buy any additional tickets before you miss out. You do have to be present to win, so if you forgot your tickets in your cabin, now's the time to go get them."

I get back to my chair. My dinner arrived while I was talking to Ash. There's a piece missing from my pile of brisket. I can see the outline in the sauce on the plate. Autumn and Logan are talking to each other, across my chair. Which one of them wasn't able to resist sampling my barbecue? Not that I'd begrudge either of them. I feel comfortable around them both. So I don't let on that I noticed. I enjoy my brisket, rich and flavorful, with a smoky edge to the barbecue sauce. The scalloped potatoes that came with it are creamy too.

We make small talk with the Shaws and learn far more than we probably need to know about parrots from Miss Cage. In the middle of that quiet moment, there's a commotion at Ash's table. The LARPer sitting to the right of Craig – Shaggy from the night before – becomes violently ill.

I feel my own stomach roil in response. I'm glad I'm done eating, but there's the instant worry: if someone gets ill at the dining table, is it because of contaminated food? Or could there be a stomach bug, about to become an outbreak? Instantly, there's tension in the air, even though Craig offers to take his roommate down to the infirmary, and a maintenance guy shows up almost immediately to take care of the mess.

Without acknowledging the incident, Liam starts announcing raffle winners. I take out the single ticket he'd given me and place it in front of me on the table. The number ends in 667. It's not going to be hard to remember.

Several members of the cruise ship's staff are ferrying down the items from Liam's stack at the top of the stairs, and handing them one by one to the people who won them. I don't usually enter this kind of thing, so it is interesting to watch how excited people are getting over a couple of paperback books, or a jigsaw puzzle.

Autumn has all her tickets laid out in a grid. One of the numbers gets called for a bookstore gift card. Autumn slides the ticket across the table towards Amy. "Tell them you won."

That gets us the first smile of the night from Mrs. Shaw.

It is clear that Liam is building up to the big prize: the signed copy of Agatha Christie's *Murder on the Orient Express*. Every time he mentions it, Autumn does this mini-clap thing. It's obvious that a mystery writer would enjoy reading mysteries, but

I never realized exactly how much Autumn admires Christie. I really hope she wins.

I try to scoot my ticket over into Autumn's grid, but she won't let me.

We've ordered and received our desserts by the time Liam finally gets to *The Orient Express*. Spontaneous applause breaks out across the dining room. Apparently, Autumn isn't the only one who's hoping to win the book.

Liam makes a *quiet, quiet* gesture with his hands. "And now what you've all been waiting for."

Logan leans over and whispers, "He might be a killer, but he certainly knows how to work a room. He's good at his job."

I whisper back, "I found out Imogen designs escape rooms. Liam is probably in the clear."

Logan looks skeptical. "Agree to disagree."

Mrs. Shaw clears her throat meaningfully again.

Right. No murder talk at the dinner table.

Liam is reading out the number. He finishes with "-6, 6, 7."

I ask Autumn, "What was the first part he called?"

Autumn looks down at my ticket, and her eyes go wide. "Felicity, you won!"

"Really?" I squint at the ticket. Liam re-reads the number. I jump up from my seat, before he decides to move on to another number. "It's me! I won!"

One of the members of the staff comes down the stairs with the book. She says, "Hold onto this one."

"Thanks!" I turn back to the table, where Autumn is stacking her tickets.

Autumn had 54 entries. I just had the one ticket. But instead of looking disappointed, she still seems excited. Maybe she's expecting me to give her the book. And honestly, I don't mind.

"Here," I say. "You're the one who loves mystery writing."

A look I can't quite understand crosses Autumn's face. It's wistful, and maybe hopeful? Is it possible she's considering starting writing again? I don't want to say anything that would pressure her, either way.

Autumn holds her hand out, but it's palm down. She's refusing to take the book. "You won it. And in a way, it reminds me of this case. I'll just go see it at your shop, along with the others."

She's referring to the books I kept, after solving those other murders. But this is different. There's no way I'm going to be the one to solve this one.

Still – I can see why people might want to see it on display. "Okay."

Bea makes her way over to me through the dispersing crowd. "Congratulations! I don't suppose I could take just a peek. Christie has always been my favorite author."

"Mine too," Autumn says. "Her Poirot books are the reason I started writing mysteries in the first place."

"Mine as well," Tucker McDougal says, walking over to us. He's dressed much as he had been for the panel he had been on with Clove and Autumn, in a neat button-up shirt and slacks.

I'm just a regular reader, standing between these three superfans. I tell Bea, "You can hold the book if you want."

"Really?" Bea takes it and opens it up to the title page, to see the inscription.

It says, *Never give up hope!* And then there's Christie's signature.

I'm not sure who she intended that message for, but it feels appropriate at the moment, for all of us. From the expressions on their faces, Bea and Autumn seem to feel the same way.

Liam makes his way down the stairs carefully, since he's carrying a box with the leftover supplies from the raffle. Satchmo trots over to him. Liam puts the box on the floor, then gives Satchmo a bone-shaped treat.

Logan says, "See? He's trying to condition the dog to trust him. Maybe he's still up to something?"

I give Logan a look that means, *yeah, right.* "Or maybe Satchmo's just adorable, and Liam has access to treats in case there's a service dog on the ship. I've done basically the same thing, except I've been feeding him off my plate."

Bea hands me the book back. "Thanks for that. This cruise has certainly been a memorable experience."

She calls for Satchmo, and they head out of the room.

Logan steps over to talk to Liam. Even though I haven't gotten a chance to tell him what Ash said about Liam and Flint having a fistfight, I figure now is as good a time as any to ask Liam about his motive.

Liam smiles when he sees us walking towards him. He gestures at the book in my hand. "I didn't rig the drawing, I promise."

"At least that I believe," I say. "But I had a word with Ash. He says you never had a metal detector."

Logan makes a small surprised noise. He gives me a disappointed look. I guess he doesn't like walking into situations without all the available information. I'll keep that in mind in the future.

Assuming we ever have reason to question someone together again.

Logan asks, "Then how exactly did you find that pen, again?"

Liam looks uncomfortable. I wish there was time to brief Logan before asking the real questions, but there's no turning back now.

I say, "Ash also says you had a fistfight with Flint when you were a teenager. Which means you also had motive for this murder."

Logan makes another noise, this one happier. After all, he's pretty sure Liam committed the murder. Me turning up a motive for it has to be a good thing.

"Wait. I don't want this to affect my job." Liam looks around, but it doesn't seem like any of the stragglers still in the dining room were paying any attention. He leads us into the same quiet spot by the stairs where I'd had the conversation with Ash. He says quickly, as though he needs to get this story out all at once, "Flint was delusional. He thought he'd actually fallen into a spy novel. He accused me of stealing papers from his office that were vital to his mission, and then he hit me. A few years later, after the whole thing where Clove disappeared, he apologized. Said his doctor had put him on some bad meds and he'd been paranoid. He told me he'd give me whatever I wanted to make it up to me. I never wanted anything from him, though. Not until I took the job on this ship, and I knew him being here could be the key to drawing passengers for the event." Liam waves his hands in an exasperated circle. "But he's not here five minutes before he punches Ash. So I guess he never really changed."

"You must have been angry that he was ruining your event," Logan says. "Angry enough to kill him?"

"No!" Liam crosses his arms over his chest. "Do I look that stupid to you?" He takes in the look on Logan's face. "Don't answer that."

Chapter Twenty-Two

Logan and I catch up with Autumn, Drake and Charlene in that same bar where we first met Lupe. I know we could just as easily have gone back to the suite, since it's the same group we're rooming with, but I don't think any of us are ready to call it a night. I'd like to have Arlo here to complete the group, but I'm about to tell Autumn information that Arlo didn't want even me to have.

I glance around to make sure there's no one else in earshot. The bartender – a guy this time – is wiping down tables at the far end of the space. We seem to be the only ones here at the moment.

I say, "The cops found the keys to a stolen car in Flint's safe deposit box. It's the car from the hit and run that killed Nathale Daye."

The glass Autumn's holding floats back towards the table, as though the strength has gone out of her arm. "He really did it? He really killed her?"

Drake's eyes go wide, and he looks from Autumn to me and back. "Who killed who?"

Autumn has to go through it all again, telling her fiancé and her future mother-in-law about her falling out with Flint, the later incident on Edmond's boat, and the subsequent hit and run – and how that had haunted Autumn so much she had stopped writing, since she feared she'd written the hit and run that had inspired an actual crime. But that she'd convinced herself that it was all paranoid imaginings.

In the middle of Autumn's story, Drake puts his hand on top of hers. When she's done, he squeezes her hand and says, "Sometimes, all you need is for someone to believe you."

"Yeah," she says absently. Then more focused, "Yeah. It really does help."

Logan takes a sip of the decaf coffee he'd ordered. "There's no way to prove for sure that your manuscript was Flint's inspiration for running down Daye. Liam told us that during that same time period, Flint attacked him convinced that Liam was an enemy spy. Arlo pulled Flint's medical records for the time in question. He was on an anti-anxiety medication that was later recalled. Again, there's no way to prove it, but it sounds like the medication may have made Flint prone to delusions, and he could have been mixing in everything he was reading and writing with his own version of reality."

Autumn blinks, repeatedly. There are tears in her eyes, but she keeps her composure. "I spent all this time resenting Flint, and a little afraid of him. There were nine of us in that critique group, including Flint's wife. If any one of us had realized what was really going on – that Flint was suffering from and hiding a mental illness. Maybe we could have helped."

"There's no way you could have known," Charlene says.

"I just chalked it up to him being a jerk. He'd always been intentionally aspiring to be as hard-edged as Hemmingway. But his behavior got worse then." Autumn brings a hand to her mouth. "And I got mad and sent him dead flowers."

Drake says, "I wonder if he even remembered what he'd done, after his meds got fixed. Like, maybe he really believed he'd fallen into a Carré novel and been a spy when he killed those people?"

I say, "He told Lupe that he killed Edmund Foster out of self-defense, over an investment scheme. Maybe he told himself that so many times over the years that he convinced himself that it was true."

Knowing about Flint's mental illness tempers the hard edges of him, gives his death a hint of tragedy. I've been looking at finding out who killed Flint from the perspective of keeping Ash from getting blamed for it. I'd kind of forgotten Flint deserves justice in his own right. He might not have been a nice person, may even have been a villain, but no one deserves to wind up stuffed behind a shop display.

There's giggling as a group of twenty-somethings come into the bar. There are nine people in the group, mostly girls, and they're making the best of their vacation. Flint's death hasn't touched them. It hasn't affected the lives of most people on this ship.

One of the girls makes her way over to our table. She tells Autumn, "I just wanted to say, I love your writing."

"Thanks." Autumn looks instantly embarrassed.

"No, I'm serious. I was at the panel earlier, and afterwards, I downloaded the first Melody book. I meant to just read a few pages, but I got so caught up in it, I missed dinner. That ending – I didn't see it coming."

"That's very kind," Autumn says. "I wish it was a paper copy. I could sign it for you."

"How about the next best thing?" The girl takes a selfie with Autumn, promising to post it to social media once we get back to shore. She asks, "There's a rumor going around the ship that you're working on a new book. Is that true? I'd love to accidentally leak the news."

Autumn leans forward, steepling her hands on the table. "I'm sorry to say, that isn't true. You see, I promised myself that I would never writer another murder. For personal reasons."

"Oh," the girl looks disappointed. "I'm sorry. For whatever happened."

Autumn says, "Thank you. But – I think this trip has helped me find closure. I haven't written for so long – I assumed all you readers would have moved on, that I'd be a joke. But a lot of people were actually excited to see me at this event. A number of them have encouraged me to start writing again."

The girl says, "You really should."

"I–" Autumn starts blinking again, but I think there's a whole different emotion behind it. "I'll try."

It's hours later. Through the magic of practical furniture, the ship's staff managed to split the large bed that had been in Autumn's and my room of the suite into two beds, with a lot more space between them than we'd had in our original room. Autumn is asleep, and a moment ago, so was I. But I can feel the presence of someone else in the room, a breathing rhythm that isn't Autumn's. The intruder is over at our closet, easing open the door.

I gasp, the noise soft in the darkness – but the intruder freezes.

I lie quietly, trying to pretend I'm still asleep, and after a long, long time, the intruder starts moving again. Much better to just let this person take whatever they came for than to risk anyone in this suite getting hurt.

Eventually, the intruder leaves the room. I hear the door to our room swinging shut, and then Logan's deep voice rumbling, "Just stop right there. Let's see what you came for."

I don't understand. If Logan was awake out there, why would he let someone dangerous come into the room with me and Autumn? Maybe he had been too far from the door when the intruder came in, had wanted to avoid starting a fight in the same small room with us.

There's the sound of a brief scuffle, then the light comes on in the main room. Somehow, Autumn has been able to sleep through it all. I get out of bed and crack the door open. Logan is alone in the room, bending over to pick an object up off the floor.

Logan turns and sees me in the doorway. His face goes crimson. "I'm sorry. I never should have let that happen. I dozed off."

I move into the main room and softly shut Autumn's door. "You were right about us needing security."

Logan gestures to the door. "The guy got away. He ducked my punch and practically crawled out the door."

"Could you tell who it was?"

"No. He didn't say anything. But it was definitely a guy, fairly tall." Logan rubs at his cheek. "He chunked this at me."

He holds out the object he picked up off the floor. It's the copy of *Murder on the Orient Express*.

I take the book from him. "At least now we know Flint's killer is a guy. That narrows the suspect list down pretty far."

"Not necessarily," Logan says. "A lot of people on this ship are Christie fans. It is just as likely whoever broke in is a thief unrelated to the killer." He rubs at his cheek again, and I see there's a bruise forming. "Still. If this guy wanted the book so bad, he was quick to throw it away. It's a good thing we've turned over all the evidence we found to Arlo."

That evidence just amounts to the piece of tubing Wendy gave us. Which means – assuming it was what the thief was after – it must be the key to solving this murder.

Chapter Twenty-Three
Saturday

The next morning, I crawl out of bed when my alarm goes off. I have one clear thought in mind: coffee.

It had taken me forever to get to sleep last night after the break-in. I would have just turned my alarm off and slept in if I hadn't had the massage appointment at the spa.

I manage to secure a cup of French roast from one of the food stations open even at this hour, and I make my way to the promenade. The shops are all closed, making this a quiet space, with only a few people walking around. Even from half way down the promenade, I recognize Arlo, who is standing in the hallway near the morning's brand-new ice sculpture, almost in the same position Logan had been before. He has a tablet computer cradled in one arm, stacked on top of a folder filled with papers, and a backpack slung over that same shoulder.

"Hey, Lis," he says as I approach. "I wish that coffee was for me."

"It wasn't." I hold the cup out to him. "But I can get another one. And it looks like you need it more than I do."

"Thanks." He takes the cup and drinks deeply from it. We both take our coffee black. "I'm waiting for the FBI. Once I show them the scene, and hand over the evidence, this whole mess is their problem."

"You don't honestly feel relieved," I say, surprised.

"No. Of course not. A case with this kind of puzzle doesn't come along very often. But they have jurisdiction, and there's not much I can do about that."

Two women get off the elevator at the far end of the promenade and start heading purposefully this way. They're wearing identical dark skirt suits, and there's not the least hint of cruise atmosphere about them. I hadn't expected that the FBI guys would be girls. They're both brunettes, though one of them has mass of curly hair, and the other one has her hair slicked back into a chignon at the base of her neck.

When they get to where we are, Arlo offers them a broad smile and holds out the tablet. "Special Agent Wendt. Special Agent Cargill. I'm Detective Romero. It's good to put faces with the voices on the phone."

Wendt – the one with the curly hair – takes the tablet and the folder. "Thank you for your assistance, Detective Romero. We've reviewed the reports, and I must say you are very thorough. Now that we're here, you can go back to enjoying your cruise. Just point us in the direction of Ash Diaz, a.k.a. Ashley Brewster."

I wince. They really are going to arrest Ash. I give Arlo a pleading look, but seriously, what is he going to do?

He ignores me, that's what. He pulls the backpack off his shoulder. "Here are the exhibits I was talking about. The piece we pulled out of the display base is the most interesting."

Cargill studies me for a moment, then asks, "Why are you here?"

I gesture at the spa behind me, "I just came up for a massage appointment and stopped to talk to Arlo – I mean Detective Romero."

Wendt takes the backpack and unzips it, peering inside. "I think everything was pretty clear from the reports. Maybe you should hit the spa with your friend, Detective. You look a little tired. Rejuvenating facials can do wonders for the bags under your eyes."

"Maybe I will do that," Arlo says. "You can probably find Ash in the dining room. He was there for breakfast yesterday. If not, he's scheduled for a workshop on investigative blogging in two hours, in the ballroom."

Arlo offers me his arm, and I take it. We walk together into the spa. I glance back. Special Agents Wendt and Cargill are examining the alcove where Flint died. But it looks like they're just confirming everything looks the same as in the photographs they've already reviewed.

"Did you have to make such a good case against Ash?" I ask, once we're inside the spa.

"It's where all the evidence points," Arlo says. "A lot of it is circumstantial, but the motives are the kind of things a jury will believe. I told them Logan's theory about someone faking the time of death, but I couldn't explain how, so I don't think they took that seriously."

That was actually my theory first, not Logan's, but I'm not going to quibble.

"You did say it was a puzzle." I approach the desk to check in for my appointment.

There's a girl behind the desk, instead of Renato. She looks up all my information. Then she turns to Arlo. "Are you checking in for an appointment too?"

"No, but I'd like to make one, if there's an opening." He runs a hand across his chin. "It was suggested I need a facial."

I choke back a laugh. I didn't think his comment to Wendt had been serious.

"At this hour, we can take you as a walk-in," the girl says.

A few minutes later, Arlo is in the room across from me, and presumably he's getting just as much skin peeling gel slathered on his face as I have on mine. When the esthetician tells me I have to leave the gel on for a while and then leaves the room, I can't help myself.

I walk across the hall. I ask Arlo, who is also sitting by himself, "Since this isn't your case anymore, can you tell me what you found in the base of the display?"

Arlo considers this. "I've been dying to talk about it. I got one of the deckhands to cut a hole in that base, so I could get the bag out of it. I had tried a wire coat hanger first, to try and pull it out, but there was something inside the bag, so it wouldn't fit through the slit."

"What was it?" I ask.

"There was a little robot, all tangled up inside a sheet of reflective mylar. In theory, the mylar could have been like an emergency blanket, to try to keep Flint's body warm. But there's three problems: it wouldn't have been enough insulation to make it look like Flint's death was only minutes old. And it wouldn't have melted the chocolate on the display. And here's the really hard one: if there had been a blanket over Flint, someone would have had to come back and remove it. Wendy would have seen them."

"Could the robot have removed it?" I ask. "There had to be a reason for it being there."

"I thought of that," Arlo says. "But there was nothing about the robot that could have grabbed onto the mylar. It was just inside the balled-up piece."

I'm stumped. Without thinking, I touch my face. My finger comes away tacky with the gel. Which gets me thinking. "What if there was an adhesive? Maybe something like eyelash glue, that is meant to peel off without much residue? Or a magnet, inside the mylar?"

"A magnet just might be possible." Arlo starts to get up, then abandons the idea. "I wish I hadn't turned it over already. I doubt they'd be happy if I asked to examine it again."

"It feels like we're so close to figuring this out." Frustration roils inside me. "But we're at a dead end. And Ash is out of time."

Arlo takes my hand. "I'm sorry, Lis. Some cases you just can't solve. If the clues aren't there – whatever happens to Ash is not your fault."

"That's hard to accept," I say.

Arlo smiles sadly. "I wish I had something else to offer you. You're just going to have to try to enjoy your massage, and whatever that green drink is they were talking about. Unless you have any new ideas?"

"I don't." On some level, I had assumed that since I had been able to solve both of the murders that had happened at my shop, I would be able to solve this one too. The disappointment that I've failed is profound.

My esthetician comes back. She makes a tutting noise. "Mrs. Koerber, you are not supposed to leave the treatment room."

She takes me back across the hall and starts peeling off all those dead skin cells. There's soothing music playing, and an herbal aroma in the air. I try to let it soothe me. I had warned Ash that I'm not a detective. I hope he got to enjoy breakfast. Because he's probably getting his next meal in jail. I try to think what I'm going to say to him when I get to see him. I feel rotten for getting his hopes up, for nothing.

The esthetician tells me to close my eyes. The room suddenly smells of lavender. She keeps applying and then removing creams and gels, and I try to relax. The soft background music is soothing, and I feel some of the guilt over how little I'd actually been able to help Ash ebb away. After a long time, she stops applying things. After a minute, I sense her hands moving near my face, and the scent of peppermint fills the room. She has me inhale several times. I've heard that peppermint is good for increasing alertness while reducing stress. I think it can feel it working.

She has me keep my eyes closed for a few moments longer, then tells me, "You're ready for Helga."

My massage therapist is seriously named Helga? That feels somehow – stereotypical.

But Helga turns out to be petite and cheerful. She even jokes that she always has to lower the massage table to work, since she's not quite five feet tall.

There are several portable massage tables folded up and leaned against the far wall. They have wheels for easy transport. Helga catches me looking at them, instead of listening to her explaining how the massage she's planning to administer works. She says by way of explanation, "Some clients prefer to be massaged in the privacy of their staterooms."

"Yeah, I get that," I say, though I'm not really paying attention – because I've noticed a dark stain on one of the wheels. I move over to the table, and examine it more closely. There are several other dark spots on the underside of the table and down the same leg as the stained wheel. I kneel down and ask Helga, "Does this look like blood to you?"

"What?" Helga asks. She giggles, sounding nervous. "Let me, uh, find Renato." Then she leaves the room. Apparently, handling my unusual behavior is above her pay grade.

When Logan and I had been brainstorming about how this murder might have been committed, I'd thought maybe the killer had used a luggage cart. But wouldn't a massage table work just as well?

There's a faint spot on the floor near the wheel. And another one about six feet away. I follow the direction, and it leads to a little smudge in the hall, like the killer had realized they had been leaving a blood trail and tried to clean it up, but hastily, missing spots.

I search for more spots, and I find one near the sauna. I go inside – grateful that it is a clothes-on co-ed space – and study the room. Why on earth would a murderer bring a body into a sauna? That might raise the body's temperature temporarily – but not enough for that body to then melt chocolate. In theory, the killer could have stashed the body behind the display and then used the massage table to carry supplies to – something. I study the sauna's main heating element, since all of this seems to come back to heat.

The element is up on a platform. I walk around it, looking at the base on all sides. On the back, there's a gap. I lean down and look into the gap, and inside there are two fist-sized metal spiders. "Yikes!" I stumble back.

Arlo had said he'd found a robot tangled up with the mylar near the body. These robots *have* to be related. I kneel down and pull one out of the space – and the end of a length of the same tubing Wendy had found comes out with it. The spidery legs have flexible round feet on the end of them, something like a gecko's toes. I peer into the space. The tubing starts at the heating element, then disappears into the room's floor. It comes back up through another hole, about eight inches away from the first one, and winds up coiled into the space – and the end portion is connected to the spiders.

It would be incredibly elaborate, but someone could have run this tubing in the space between decks, to a crack in the floor in the boutique. With enough heat coming through, it wouldn't even have to be a big crack. With a sheet of Mylar for insulation, Flint's body could have been held at temperature until just before Wendy opened the boutique.

I carefully place the metal spider on the floor near where I found it.

"Arlo!" I call. I race to the room where he had gotten his facial. The woman who had given it to him is cleaning up, but Arlo isn't there.

The esthetician tells me, "He's hydrating in the relaxation room."

She gives me directions to a room deeper inside the spa, and I run over there. I find Arlo holding a cup of cucumber water, his eyes closed. "Arlo!"

He jolts, spilling some of the water on himself. "Geesh, Lis. Calm down."

I tug at his arm, pulling him up out of his chair. "I figured it out! You have to show them. Before they take Ash."

Arlo puts his water cup down. He places his hands on my upper arms. "I will. But first you have to slow down and tell me what you figured out."

"Okay." I take a deep breath and lead him through to the sauna.

One look at those spider robots is all it takes for him to pull out his phone and try to get ahold of the Feds.

When they don't answer, he calls Logan. I hear his end of the call, where he explains what's going on and then says, "Hanlon, see if you can locate Ash. Felicity and I are going up to the top deck to try and catch them if they head for the helicopter."

Then he hangs up, and start taking pictures to show to the FBI gals.

I find myself grinning, despite the tension of the situation. "This is the first time you've asked me to go with you on an important mission."

"The first and the last," Arlo says. "If I thought it were dangerous, you wouldn't be going. I am still a cop and you're still a civilian. Even if the lines are a little blurred this time."

Still. It's nice not being shut out.

I notice a small plastic clamshell with a set of tools in it. There's a set of pointed pliers, a screwdriver, a utility knife. I take it out and start to give it to Arlo, but he's already heading out the door. Without thinking, I put the case in my pocket.

As we rush out of the spa, Arlo tells Helga, "Lock the sauna and don't let anyone use it, no matter what. Police business." She looks too overwhelmed not to listen. Arlo turns to me, "Don't overexert yourself, Lis. Even if that helicopter takes off, we can still try to talk the captain out of returning to shore."

Because if the passengers all get off of the boat, the odds of solving the crime go down exponentially.

To keep Arlo from freaking out, I contain myself to a brisk walk back up the promenade. Once we get to the end, the elevator ride to the top deck feels like the longest one of my life.

Eventually we reach the top, and make our way through the corridor and then out onto the deck. The helicopter pad is at the bow of the ship, and as we approach, I can see the blades of a solid black helicopter sitting in the spot.

Logan comes running through the door from the inside of the ship, and catches up to us on the open deck. The cheek he was rubbing at last night has developed quite a bruise. He gestures with his chin at Ash. "They took him out of his workshop. Right in front of his students. Half of them took out their phones to document the event."

When we get close enough to see the whole helicopter, we find Special Agents Wendt and Cargill standing at attention in front of it – with a pathetic-looking Ash standing in between them. All the color has gone out of his face, and he looks about two seconds away from tears.

Ash is wearing the same deerstalker hat he'd had on last night. But now it's paired with a dress shirt and tie. His hands are cuffed behind his back.

"Why are they all just standing there?" I ask.

Arlo says, "They must be waiting for the helicopter pilot."

When Cargill catches sight of the three of us rushing towards her prisoner, her hand goes to her gun. Arlo waves us to a stop.

"Wait here," Arlo says.

He steps closer, holding out his phone to show the pic of the heat setup. We're close enough to hear most of what he's saying, as he explains how fortunate it was that the Special Agents sent Arlo into the spa, where he and I uncovered these clues. I might be miffed about not getting the credit when I'd solved the puzzle if it wasn't for the fact that there are less doubts in a jury's mind if a law enforcement officer claims said credit.

Finally, Cargill waves me and Logan over. She has me recount what I had found and how. Then she asks if we have theories on who could have set all of these things up, if it wasn't Ash.

Logan gestures to the picture of the sauna base. "With this kind of access to the spa and the maintenance areas, it had to be a member of the staff. The only staff member we've identified with a motive is Liam."

"It wasn't Liam," Ash insists. "He wouldn't kill anybody. Someone could have gained access while the ship was docked, between cruises."

"That's possible." I hesitate. But I have to say what I think happened, even if it hurts Ash's feelings. "Someone like Imogen, who's capable of popping locks. And who designs escape rooms for a living."

"A cabin door isn't the same level as breaching security on an entire cruise line. Besides, she wouldn't have stabbed anybody."

I watch Cargill and Wendt's faces. Ash's protests are doing more to convince them that there are other viable suspects in this case than anything Logan and I could have said.

Wendt says, "I suppose neither of these people have an alibi in the revised timeline."

"Probably not," Arlo says. "We focused our inquires on the presumed time of death. But now that window is a lot wider and includes the hours between the organized party and the LARP event."

Wendt uncuffs Ash. "After we talk to all the other people in Detective Romero's very detailed file, we'll probably have more questions. Please make yourself available."

"My schedule is on the big bulletin board," Ash says. "I have a big gap, but you can find me hanging out near where my lectures will be this afternoon."

I feel bad that my theory about Imogen and Logan's about Liam are the main reasons Ash isn't going to jail. But he seems to be taking it well. He rubs at his wrists, but the color is already coming back into his face.

"Come along, Detective Romero," Wendt says. "I think we need to do a full debrief."

The two FBI agents stride away, heading for the door leading back inside the ship. There, they can take the elevator to some other deck, to start all over with what we've already done – interviewing all the possible suspects. Arlo goes along with them

– though it's unclear if they're planning to let him continue helping investigate the case.

Logan and I have just made the special agents' day a lot more complicated. At least they were nice about it.

Chapter Twenty-Four

Ash is so excited about being free, he hugs me. I'm too startled to even try to hug him back. He takes the deerstalker hat off of his own head and plops it onto mine, saying, "I knew you were the detective I needed."

"I keep telling you I'm not a detective."

"Okay, Koerber, whatever you say." Ash winks at me, like we're sharing a secret. "But I'm telling the truth in the piece I'm writing about all of this when I get home."

"Do you have to write about me again?" But I know it's pointless to protest. "Let me guess – you think I'll give you the biggest ratings you've ever had."

"With you getting me off a murder rap?" Ash says. "Can you imagine the clickthrough won't be huge?"

I tell him, "But I didn't even solve the murder this time. All I did was figure out how to show you weren't the most promising suspect. Honestly, I think you're still pretty high on their list."

"But I didn't do it." Ash looks back at the helicopter. It looks a lot less ominous now, without the two FBI agents framing it. "And now that the agents know that I'm not the only one who could have done it, they'll look at everyone else a lot harder."

"Fair enough," I tell him. "I hope I really have helped you out."

"Want to go with us to breakfast?" Logan asks Ash, which is really nice of him, since Ash has never been one of Logan's favorite people. Ash has been growing on me. I guess he's growing on Logan too.

Ash looks surprised and sounds a little disappointed when he says, "Can't. One of the members of the LARP group asked me for writing advice and I promised a one-on-one after the workshop was over. I need to grab a latte and head that way. I'm supposed critique a short story, and I absolutely cannot do that without coffee."

"I understand. I can't do much without coffee myself." And now that he's mentioned it, I find myself yawning. I haven't gotten enough sleep over the past couple of days. "I hope you can find some before you go to make that meet-up."

"I'm sure I can," Ash says.

A thought hits me, startling, and wakes me up. "The group member you're meeting. It's not Imogen, is it?"

Though if it is, he probably would have said meeting his fiancé. Who, I am still convinced is most likely the one who is framing him for murder.

"Of course not," Ash says. "She doesn't need my help with anything creative."

"That's a relief." I try to laugh. But now that the plan to frame Ash seems more likely to fail, it could make the killer desperate. If it is Imogen – she's a smart creative person. And that would put Ash in even more danger. None of the other LARPers are on my personal suspect list. So if Ash is meeting one of them, at least he won't be alone and therefore vulnerable.

"Koerber, you're getting weird," Ash says.

Then he heads for the door back inside, which just leaves me and Logan standing on the deck, looking at the helicopter.

"That hat looks cuter on you than it did on him." Logan pulls at the edge of one of the hat's flaps.

I take the hat off. I tell Logan, "Arlo said I should go to the police academy."

My tone is joking, but the look Logan gives me in return is serious. "If you're going to keep doing detective work, that's not a bad idea. Or at least get your PI license."

I let out an exasperated sigh. "I'm not looking to be a private eye. Yes, several things have happened that have gotten me involved with murder cases. No, I didn't seek any of them out. And I sincerely hope I never see another dead body again."

"You don't think you would miss it?" Logan gives me a rakish grin. "Not even a little?"

I give the question serious consideration. "Honestly, no. I like solving puzzles, and spending time with you. But I think we find ways to do that without asking people to bring us their problems. That's the reason I quit my physical therapy practice. I just couldn't deal with all the pain. Think about all the pain we've dredged up, digging into Flint's past."

"But sometimes you have to lance open the past, to allow people to heal from it." Logan moves a few strands of my hair that have blown upwards, smoothing them back into place. "I think that's why you went into physical therapy in the first place. Because you're good at helping people with their pain – whether you asked them to share it with you or not."

I'm not sure what to make of his words. I think maybe he meant it as a compliment. But I want to know for sure. "Are you saying I was weak for giving up the practice?"

"No!" He says it forcefully, then closes his eyes for a moment. "I love the chocolate shop, and I think that's what you were meant to do. But whether you're doing a physical therapy session or handing someone a cup of hot chocolate on a miserable day, I know you're going to show empathy and be a good listener. Which is what most people need. And what makes you good at getting information other people might miss."

His sincerity leaves moisture in my eyes. I blink it back. "I hope Ash is wrong. I don't want to be a murder magnet. Even if I have wound up helping people, it's all too sad."

"Then I hope he's wrong too."

Logan knows I'm not sure if I belong in his world – a place where getting shot is a thing that actually happens. Where people need bodyguards, and innocents can die. I've stepped farther into it than I would previously have imagined, by choosing to meet with Wendy. But I'd like to believe I have a choice, ultimately, about which world I belong in.

I tell Logan, "I want to take a few minutes to sit by the pool. I haven't gotten to do any of the normal cruise things since we got here. And at the moment, there doesn't seem to be any more clues to chase. Maybe I can brainstorm a few different ways to put the clues we already have together."

"I hear you." Logan gestures at the flip-flops he's wearing. "I was looking forward to the day on shore we were supposed to have in St. Thomas."

We walk over to the pool and I sit in one of the lounge chairs. I think this may be the same lounge chair I'd sat in when we questioned Lupe. Only, right now, I don't want to think about how many questions are still unanswered. I lean back in the lounge chair. What I need is to feel the waves rock me, now that I've made my peace with the ocean. Then when I have the clarity, I can think again. It is a truly gorgeous day, with puffy little clouds in the distance, and the azure pool looking so serene.

"You be careful out here," Logan says.

"I'm hardly alone," I tell him. There are easily a dozen people walking laps around the deck, and four of the other chairs are taken with people reading or sunbathing.

Logan looks around, and I can practically see him assessing threats. "Exactly."

And – that's part of the reason I'm not sure I want to belong in Logan's world. He never gets to relax, not completely. I suddenly feel a bit on edge.

Still, after he leaves, I shift the hat so that it is shielding my face a little, and I close my eyes, letting the rocking of the boat lull me. It's hard to believe I can feel this much peace while still on the boat with a killer. I start to review the suspects in my mind. I need to think beyond the two that Logan and I have settled on. After all, assumptions close the mind to possibilities that could lead to the truth. Clove, as a mystery writer, could have come up with a plan this elaborate. And Lupe works with machines all day. And–

Someone puts their hand on my shoulder, and I jerk to sitting up, instantly in a panic, even as Imogen says, "Felicity, are you awake?"

"Yes." I focus on Imogen, who is smiling down at me. She looks innocuous enough, but I have a hard time shaking my sense of panic. I can believe that she has it in her to kill Flint as an act of simmering revenge. But would she hurt someone just for being nosy? Yes, if she's the one who got rid of Wendy. I try to act casual. I don't know for sure she's the killer, and I don't seem to be in immediate danger. "What's going on?"

She straightens up and clasps her hands behind her back. "I just wanted to say thank you for helping Ash. You saved my wedding."

I hadn't even considered that. I'd been a lot more concerned about figuring out if Imogen is a murderer. She's still the suspect at the top of my list – even if I can't for the life of me figure out why she would have chosen to frame Ash, rather than Clove or one of the other people with a direct tie to her father's death.

Maybe I can get her talking, find the proof I need that my theory about her is right. Or find some way to eliminate her from the suspects list, if I'm wrong. So I ask, "Tell me about you and Ash. Obviously, there's a whole side to him that I've never gotten to see."

Imogen sits in the chair next to mine. She leans back, instantly relaxed. "Ash told me you two got off on the wrong foot. I hate that. I know he tends to barrel over people when he's working. But if you take the time to get to know him, he can be a really fun guy to be around. And if you're troubled, he is probably the best listener I've ever met. He's not like most guys, who want to step in with a solution before they've even heard half of why you're upset."

"It sounds like you're really in love," I say.

Imogen shows me the ring on her finger, tilting it so it glints in the sun. "I'm not the kind of person who would accept a marriage proposal if I wasn't. I know Ash isn't perfect. No one is. But he's supportive, and he has a good heart. I don't need perfect to be happy."

"Did you get to tell Ash about what happened between Flint and your father?"

"I finally did." Imogen drops her hand back to her side. "Last night. At first, he was really upset. Ash thought maybe I had sought him out to find someone who had a connection to Flint. He even asked me if I killed the old poopbrain."

"What happened after that?" I ask.

"I'm still engaged, aren't I?"

"Definitely." I swivel sideways in my chair, giving her my full attention. "Craig told me you brought Ash to visit the LARP group. How did you two meet?"

Imogen shakes her head. "Craig has it backwards – I met Ash the first time he came to the LARP group to check things out. Later, Ash told me that he'd only come to visit the group because he wanted to write a story about it."

"That sounds like Ash." I gesture at her ring. "And it was love at first sight?"

"It was like at first sight," Imogen says. "He was cute and smart. We went for coffee after the session was over, and he had good taste in beans. But I've always been reluctant to give away my heart, so it was a lot longer than that before there was any talk of love."

"Do you think that reluctance had to do with losing your dad so young?"

She purses her lips. "Maybe? I've never thought about it that way. You can ask Craig. I've always been somewhat reserved. That's why the LARP thing is so good for me. I love being the center of attention for a room full of people – like when I did theater. But it's different being creative one-on-one or in flux with other people."

"So you and Craig were close growing up?"

She nods. "Craig is a few years older than me. I was only three or four when Craig's dad left, and after that, he basically became part of my family. His mom was working all the time, and he lived next door. After my dad died, Craig was someone I could really talk to, because he had dealt with a lot of the same feelings."

"But you never dated Craig?"

"Eww!" Imogen slaps at my arm with the side of her hand. "That would be like dating my brother. And Craig wouldn't have wanted to date me either. I was in middle school when he was in high school and in high school when he started college. He had to quit for a while, to help out after his mom got sick, but he's back in school now."

That means that Craig is the only person on board who goes all the way back to Imogen's childhood. She thinks of him as a brother. But there are those drone videos Craig took, which showed clear affection for Imogen. I'm not so sure about him never having a crush on her. But if he's never said anything about it – who am I to cause trouble between them?

Imogen settles more comfortably into her chair, and uses the back of her right hand to screen her eyes from the sun. "Now this is what I had in mind when Craig pitched us all on going on a cruise."

Here in the sunlight, I can clearly see a raised scar that starts in the bottom third of her right hand and runs a few inches down into her wrist. It's an unmistakable scar from carpal tunnel surgery. As a physical therapist, I had seen countless copies of that same mark. I'd always preferred to see a patient *before* they'd had surgery. Sometimes, manual physical therapy techniques can prevent the need for surgery altogether.

"You seem a little young for carpal tunnel," I say. My tone is light, and I'm no longer so much on my guard.

"Cheerleading accident," Imogen says, not bothering to move her wrist. A lot of people try to hide scars, but she seems perfectly comfortable with it. Eyes still shaded, she holds up her other hand, which has a much smaller scar just at the base of the wrist. "There was a hairline fracture on my right wrist, and a lot of swelling on both. They said the bones shifted in my left forearm, and that the way my bones were formed left me with a predisposition for the condition anyway. So now I have some serious conversation starters. Why no, random stranger, I'm not depressed."

I love her sense of humor. But Imogen's scars are more than just conversation starters. They mean my strongest suspect for Flint's murder didn't do it after all. "Imogen," I ask, "Are you still experiencing weakness or tingling in your right hand?"

"Sometimes." She moves her hand so she can look at me. "The weakness can be unexpected, and I'll just drop something. But that doesn't happen very often, since the surgery."

Still. Not very often isn't never. Technically, Imogen has the body strength to have broken an ice ray off that sculpture and stabbed Flint with it, especially in the heat of rage and the need for revenge. But. This murder was meticulously planned. If Imogen has even occasional problems with hand strength, wouldn't she have chosen a different method for killing Flint? Just to make sure there was no chance of anything going wrong.

It is possible that Imogen could have factored that into a truly diabolical plan, expecting that the cops would eliminate her as a suspect because of her scars. Or that she'd intended to shoot Flint with the plastic gun, then been so enraged she'd broke off the ice and stabbed him with it. But somehow, I doubt it.

On one level, I'm relieved. Ash and Imogen get to have their wedding and their happily ever after. Which is great.

But the uneasiness inside me tells me how convinced I'd been the Imogen must be the killer. And one of the people I had thought didn't really seem to have it in them to be a murderer must have killed Flint.

There's barking coming from the doorway leading back inside the ship, and then Satchmo comes running across the deck towards me. He jumps up into the lounge chair, but the nylon strips it is made of seem to confuse his balance, so he winds up leaning heavily against me. I scratch him behind the ears, and he relaxes.

Bea walks over more slowly and with more decorum. "That dog has made more friends on this ship than I have."

Imogen says, "It's because you can't get away with just jumping into other people's laps."

We all laugh.

Then Bea says, "Felicity, can I borrow you for a minute?"

"Sure." I push Satchmo off the lounge chair, and then I get up myself. I follow Bea over to the railing on the opposite side of the deck. "What's up?"

"I was wondering if you had any contacts for potentially starting a therapy program in Galveston. Logan said something about how he'd love to see the program expanded, but he didn't have ideas where to start."

"I know I'd love to see Satchmo again." I look over at the dog, who is now trying to climb into the lounge chair with Imogen. "But I don't have any contacts here, either. We should definitely keep in touch once we're off this boat, and I can look into it."

"Is everything okay?" Bea asks. "You seem a bit distracted."

I gesture over at Imogen. "I just eliminated my most probable suspect for Flint's murder."

Bea looks incredulously at me. "You thought *she* did it?"

Of course, Bea doesn't know about Imogen's dad's death – or Flint's role in it. And that's not information I should share. And the conflicted feeling of wanting to share, so Bea can understand, while not feeling I have the right to share Imogen's personal business without serious reason – I think this gives me a small insight into how Arlo feels about all my questions about his cases. I just say, "Yeah, but now I'm pretty sure she didn't." I consider again all that went into planning the murder. I'd been so sure that Imogen's experience with escape room setups had given her the skill to have pulled it off that I hadn't really listened when Logan had said it had to be a member of the staff. After all, the only person who had staff access to various areas of the ship – even if he repeatedly claimed he didn't have the appropriate keys – was Liam. Only, of all the people who might have wanted to kill Flint, he has the weakest motive. No murdered parent. No stolen literary characters. Just the fact that Flint had punched him once, back when Liam was a teenager. I suppose it could be enough, in the right person holding a grudge over his formative years. "I guess I think it's Liam," I say miserably. Though I'm not quite ready to give up on my theory about Lupe and the dry-cleaning equipment, or Clove and her mystery writer's ability to plan a crime.

"You think what's me?" Liam says, coming up on my left side.

The wind is so noisy up here, I didn't even hear him walking up behind me. I flinch away from him, and then force a smile. "You know. The coolest employee on board this ship."

After all, I'm not about to tell a potential killer that I'm convinced he murdered someone.

Liam nods, like that's perfectly reasonable. "The special agent twins just cordoned off the spa. You were there this morning, right? I was wondering if you know what happened. People are starting to ask questions."

I tense. If Liam's the killer, of course he would want to know what's going on with the investigation.

I want to test his reaction, without making it sound like I know enough to be a threat – like Wendy was. My lips are dry. I lick at them before I say, "It sounds like something odd happened with the heating system in the sauna."

"Do you think they're afraid that it might not be safe?" Bea sounds concerned. "You know, I never considered what might happen if there is a fire on a cruise ship."

"We need to find Craig," Liam says, looking genuinely alarmed. "After all, he installed half the electronics on this boat." Then he takes a deep breath and more calmly tells Bea, "Cruise ships always have firefighters on board."

"What?" I freeze, mid-motion.

"We have firefighters," Liam says. "It's okay."

"No, not that." I hadn't even thought about what role Craig might play in all of this. He hadn't seemed close enough to either of the people Flint had killed to be seriously considered as a suspect. But he'd grown up with Imogen, had thought of her dad as his replacement father figure. And he wasn't part of the crew – so he had seemed unlikely to have access to the required spaces. "I thought Craig was the maintenance guy at an apartment complex."

"I think so, yes," Liam says. Satchmo comes over to him, and Liam slips the dog another treat. I feel silly for thinking that him doing that at dinner last night had been suspicious. "But he hires on for freelance projects. I mean, isn't he working for your aunt?"

"Well, yeah," I say. But I hadn't thought anything of it.

"Why didn't you mention this before?" Bea asks.

Liam gestures at me. "I thought you guys already knew. I mean, he was bragging about it the whole time he was aboard the inaugural cruise, to anyone who would listen. He even got the captain to let him give his friend a behind the scenes tour."

"I thought he came on that cruise alone," I say. "He told me he was lovelorn at the time, and that his mother had given him a last-minute ticket."

Liam splutters out, "What a little liar."

I refrain from pointing out that Liam has been the most frequent liar on the whole ship. But he must see the thought on my face, because he gives me a look that clearly says, *yeah, yeah, I know.*

Liam says, "Craig got a complimentary cabin on the inaugural cruise as a thank you for his work. He brought a friend of his from the LARP group. It was the same guy who was dressed as Shaggy during the event that first night on this cruise."

"You meant the one who came down with that stomach bug yesterday?" Bea asks.

"If you want to make sure nobody questions you staying out of your room as much as possible," I say, "there's no better way than giving your roommate a case of the tummy yucks – especially if it seems contagious. Craig could have been the one to break into the suite last night, and nobody would have missed him."

I look at Bea, and panic sparks between us. Because right now, no one is keeping track of Craig either. And since his plan to frame Ash seems about to fail – he may be planning something desperate.

Ash had said he was meeting a member of the LARP group to talk writing. He hadn't said who it was, but it doesn't take a Mensa member to figure out its Craig. Only – Ash didn't say where he was going to meet up. I pull out my phone. Ash is so addicted to social media – maybe his phone is on. But when I call him, it goes immediately to voice mail. On the off chance that he's receiving texts, I send him one saying, *You may be in danger. Where are you?*

There's no immediate reply. Which feels ominous. If Craig is planning something drastic – I can only hope we're not too late. I tell Liam, "Call security. Get them to locate Craig or Ash."

Please, please, let me be wrong. Let them not even be together. But I don't hesitate to text both Logan and Arlo, with a quick, half-coherent outline of why I think Craig is the killer, and how urgent it is to locate Ash. It is only after I hit send that I realize I've just created a text thread between me, Logan and Arlo. Eh. I'll worry about the implications of that later.

Liam makes his call, but after a moment, he gets this strange look on his face.

"What's wrong?" Bea asks.

Liam says, "I asked them to find Craig on the security cameras – only the whole camera system had a glitch and crashed."

We stand there for a moment, absorbing the implications of that. If Craig had programmed that system, he could easily have left himself a backdoor to crash it. But he only would have done that if he intended something drastic.

Suddenly, Satchmo is at my side, pawing at my yoga pants and then laying his muzzle against my calf. He must have realized that my blood pressure just shot through the roof.

"Satchmo," I say, realizing that he can do more than comfort me in that moment. I whip the deerstalker hat off my head, hoping that Ash had worn it long enough for his scent to be strong on it. I hold it out to Satchmo. "Seek."

Satchmo dutifully snuffles at the hat, then starts snuffling around the deck. We're not far from the helicopter pad where the FBI guys had brought Ash, so as he left, he should have passed by here. Still. Anxiety roils in my stomach. Can Satchmo sniff out Ash if he's not even on the same deck? And even if the beagle picks up a scent – we've all been all over this ship, going to different decks for meals and shopping and relaxation. Our scent paths are bound to be crisscrossed. Who's to say Satchmo will discover where Ash is going now instead of where he went yesterday?

Satchmo gives a little yip and heads confidently for the aft end of the deck. The anxiety in my stomach hardens into a lump. I haven't exactly had the best experiences with that part of this boat.

Bea and I follow the dog.

Liam says, "I'm going to stay here and contact some of the crew to see if anyone has seen Ash. Just in case." There's genuine worry in Liam's eyes for his cousin.

Satchmo looks back at us and whines, telling us to hurry up and stop hesitating.

"It's going to be okay," I tell Liam, even though I can't really promise that. But it is what he needs to hear. Then I race after the dog. Satchmo has already reached the steps, but with his little legs, the stairs are a bit of a challenge. He starts doing a hop-jump down them, stopping every couple of steps to make sure the scent is still there.

With my health condition, I'm not supposed to do much running. But I've been doing progressively better since my treatments. And at least, if we're starting at the very top of the ship, the only direction to go is down.

Chapter Twenty-Five

By the time Bea and I have followed Satchmo down seven flights of stairs, I'm wondering why Ash didn't just take the elevator. I'm also out of breath. But I'm doing better than I would have expected. The fact that I've been working on my health is starting to pay off.

Satchmo exits the stairwell, and I text the Logan and Arlo thread to tell them what floor we are on. The beagle waits for us to catch up, then heads down the corridor. He seems to know exactly where he's going. We wind up outside the library. The door to the space is closed, but I can hear voices coming from the other side

Satchmo alerts, staring straight at the door. When neither Bea or I move to open it, he makes a whining noise and starts gently pawing at the door.

There's a crash inside the library, and a few words of angry shouting. We can't wait for the guys to get here. Ash is obviously in trouble now.

I step up and gently turn the handle to the door. Bea moves to stop me, shaking her head. She whispers, "It's too dangerous."

I whisper back, "Ash is my friend."

Bea gives me a resigned look. "Okay." She crouches down next to Satchmo and says, "Sneak."

Instantly, Satchmo drops to his belly.

I crack open the door and peek through it. I don't see anyone in the main part of the room. But I hear Ash say, "Fine, Craig. Do what you have to, but I'm not drinking that, and I'm not writing that I never loved her."

It sounds like they're in one of the rounded alcoves.

Craig sounds cold when he says, "That's the most important part. Imogen needs to know that she was making a mistake in choosing you over me."

I move into the room, sticking to the wall as I go around to where I can peek at what's going on. Meanwhile, I listen to Ash protesting that he won't besmirch the memory of what he had with Imogen. And slick anxiety settles into my core – because Ash is talking about himself in the past tense.

When he comes into view, Ash is sitting in one of the elegant chairs. He's been tied to it, with sturdy cording around his torso and around his ankles. His hands are free, an there's a piece of thick paper on one of the marble tables, which has been placed where he can reach it. I think Craig is trying to force Ash to write a suicide note. Ash has a pen in his hand. It looks like he's already started.

A shadow moves across the floor which must be Craig pacing as he waits. A chill of dread runs down my spine and all the way up into my scalp.

Ash sees me, and his eyes go wide. He looks meaningfully at a spot near the arc of the alcove, and he shakes his head, warning me not to approach. He mouthes the word, *gun*.

I thought Craig's plastic gun had gotten smashed. He must have brought another one.

I look back, to the route of safe retreat. Bea is waiting outside, and she gestures me back to her. But I can't just leave Ash to whatever Craig has in mind for him.

Satchmo has followed me into the room, sneaking on his belly. Which gives me an idea.

I still have that tool kit in my pocket. The case is roughly the size of my phone. And I've seen Satchmo manage to carry a phone in his mouth. If I could get that utility knife to Ash, he could manage to free himself from the chair. But in order to do that, we would need to distract Craig.

I show Bea the case, and pantomime my plan. Bea doesn't look happy, and shakes her head no – right up until Craig says, "I'm giving you thirty seconds to drink the coffee and finish that letter. Or I'll finish it for you and make sure your body disappears – just like Wendy."

Bea winces, then she nods her agreement. There isn't time to wait for another plan. Whatever's in that coffee will likely mean the end for Ash.

I crouch down between a chair and an arched sofa in my part of the cloverleaf. I whisper to Satchmo, "Sneak." He's already doing it, but I want to make sure to reinforce the command. "Sneak."

Bea opens the door wider and says loudly, "Yoo-hoo! Is anyone in here? I'm very much in need of a book."

Craig comes around the corner, one hand behind his back. As he walks past me towards Bea, I can see there's a white plastic gun in his hand. If Bea seems too determined to explore the room, it doesn't look like he'll hesitate to shoot her.

I hold out the case, and whisper to Satchmo, "Pass the teacup." I point to Ash, and the beagle wriggles across the floor, actively sneaking. The dog takes a path that keeps him out of Craig's line of sight, looking up several times to keep track of what Craig is doing. I can't see from where I'm hiding if Satchmo has reached Ash.

Craig asks Bea, "Is there a particular book you're looking for?"

Bea shakes her head. "I was hoping the librarian would be here. I could use some recommendations. You're not a fan of romance novels, are you?"

Craig says, "Afraid not. Maybe you should come back later."

"I'll do that." Bea leaves. It's agonizing to watch her go, leaving me alone with a bound man and a killer. I feel a pang of déjà vu. This isn't the first time this has happened to me. Sadly.

The difference is that this time, the killer isn't pointing the gun at me. Maybe I can engineer a distraction that will give both me and Ash time to get out of here. If there's a way to get Craig to go into the other alcove then maybe–

"Okay, Felicity," Craig says, turning towards my hiding spot and pointing the gun at me. "You can come out now. I can see your shoes."

I hold my hands up as I slowly stand up. I don't hear anything from Ash. Maybe he's quietly freeing himself from the chair. Maybe he drank the coffee. I don't even want to think about that possibility.

Craig asks me, "What are you doing here?"

"I figured it out." I can't help the note of pride that sneaks into my voice. "I found the robots in the sauna, and I know how you used them to fake Flint's time of death."

Craig's eyebrows arch. "Why aren't you clever."

"Not as clever as you." I try to force a smile, but I can tell it looks half-hearted. Logan had said I know people, that I'm a good listener. Maybe I can use those skills to get Craig monologuing long enough for one of the guys to get here. "There's one thing I just don't get. You meticulously planned each aspect of the murder, and you even brought a gun." I gesture at the gun in Craig's hand as though the sight of the barrel pointed at me isn't turning my kidneys to water. "So why break the sun ray off the ice sculpture and stab him?"

"I originally intending to shoot Flint, but got so angry, I wound up stabbing him instead." Craig says it matter-of-factly. The ease of that confession – he doesn't intend for me to leave this room alive, to be able to share it with the FBI gals. The only reason I'm still alive right now is his ego. He's enjoying getting to tell his side of this to someone. A note of sadness comes into Craig's eyes, which is confusing. "Edmund Foster was the only father figure I've ever had in my life. Even before my actual father left, he wasn't much for bandaging scraped knees or giving fatherly advice. That boat accident? There's no way things happened the way Flint said they did. So I confronted Flint about it, here on the boat. I told him he could confess and let me record it, die with a clean conscience. But he refused. Said he hadn't done anything wrong. Begged for his life, begged for mercy. When he hadn't shown mercy to the people I cared about."

Ash peeks around the corner. Thank goodness, he's got himself out of the chair. He's crouched down, one hand holding Satchmo's collar. He's got the rope he'd been tied up with dangling from that same hand.

I need to keep Craig's attention focused on me, and to keep him talking so he doesn't decide to just shoot me and get it over with.

"But why frame Ash?" I ask. "I thought he was your friend."

"Have you met Ash?" Craig asks. "He's a member of my LARP group, but he's too annoying to ever be anyone's friend."

Ash's face goes pinched, then settles into a frown. It can't be easy to hear someone say that about you. It seems to upset Ash more than when Craig had been threatening to kill him.

"Ash is *my* friend," I say, and I find that it is true. Now. Especially because Ash is taking careful steps towards Craig, the rope now stretched between his hands, obviously intending to subdue Craig from behind. He must have told Satchmo to stay, because the dog is sitting, looking anxiously at me.

Craig rolls his eyes. "You think you want to be Ash's friend because you're naïve. Just like Imogen. Imogen and I grew up together. I was the one who was always there for her. And instead of me, she picks him? So you have to see that this is the only way. Flint's death to bring justice for Mr. Foster. And frame Ash for it, so that I can be there, ready to comfort Imogen once he's out of the picture."

"So the real reason you killed two people is to make Imogen realize she's always been in love with you?" This is like *My Best Friend's Wedding* – only gone horribly wrong. There's not going to be a moment where Craig realizes he needs to let

Imogen go and dance at her and Ash's wedding. But I have to try to reason with him.

He says, "She *has* always been in love with me. She just doesn't realize it."

"The relationship you said you just got out of when you took that first cruise – you were talking about Imogen, weren't you? Because on some level you realized you were never going to be with her after she got engaged to Ash."

Craig's face goes crimson. "I tried to move on. I found a girlfriend. And Julie's great – but she's not Imogen. And I can't break up with her, because how do I explain that Imogen hasn't realized she loves me yet? But I can't, you know, love her. Because I belong with Imogen."

"No, you don't," Ash says as he lunges at Craig and manages to get the rope around him, pinning Craig's arms to his sides. Craig jerks his elbow up, partly breaking the hold. The gun goes off, hitting the books on the shelf not far from my head. Geesh. Even half-subdued, Craig is still shooting at me. I dive behind the nearest chair, and Craig shifts in Ash's grasp to turn to aim again.

Satchmo growls and rushes Craig, sinking his teeth into the killer's shoe. Ash gets the rope tightened around Craig and wrenches the gun out of his hand and throws it across the room. Craig falls, heavily, and Ash lands on top of him.

"Kerber, you okay?" Ash asks as he secures Craig's arms to his sides.

"I'm all in one piece," I say. Past that, okay is relative. I'm trembling, and goosepimples have risen on my arms and legs. I manage to make it around and climb up to sit in the chair I had been hiding behind.

At that moment Arlo rushes through the door, Logan not far behind.

Now that he's been subdued, Craig seems like a totally different person, his gaze trained on the floor, his tied-up hands in his lap.

Logan asks, "Felicity believes you set all of this in motion before you even knew Flint would be on this ship. You really planned all this that far ahead?"

Without looking up, Craig nods. "I'd been looking for a place to confront Flint, and while I was working to get everything here working right, I realized the irony of killing him on a boat – after he'd killed Edmund on a boat. After I realized Liam was game for lining up Flint for a speaking event, I hacked into security and gave myself a back door into the cameras. I turned them off, never suspecting that no one would think to turn them on again. And once the cameras were off, I took my time rigging up the tubing from the sauna, and hiding it and the tarp in the AC ducts in between."

"But why did you break into the suite?" I ask.

"I didn't."

I knew it. There's still a thief somewhere on this ship that had been willing to risk a lot because they wanted the rare book. That's going to call for even more security, if I'm going to keep it on display.

Arlo asks Craig, "When you made your initial plan, the boutique hadn't had a chocolate display in that spot. Did you even realize what was on the display when you placed Flint's body behind it?"

Craig nods miserably. "I saw that the display had been changed when I brought Flint into the shop. By then, it was too late to change the plan. I gambled that I would be able to come back later that night and move the body before the melted chocolate was discovered, and that the two occurrences would never be connected."

He'd gambled – and lost.

Ash, who has been wandering around the library in a state of shock, huffs out a noise and walks out into the corridor. I follow, in case he needs to talk. Just as we are leaving, Special Agents Wendt and Cargill enter the library.

I hear Wendt ask Arlo, "Why didn't you notify us immediately when this incident occurred?"

Oh boy, do I not want to be part of that conversation. But since Arlo is giving them a killer who has confessed and is literally tied up with a bow, they probably won't make too big a deal over it.

Ash sits down on a bench next to a palm tree. I sit down next to him. "You okay?" I ask.

"Sort of." He gestures vaguely at the palm tree. Which doesn't make much sense. Maybe he's still reeling from finding out Craig secretly hated him. "I thought I was going to die. That's a harsh reality, you know?"

I do know. I'd been in that same position once before, and it had brought a moment of clarity to my life, changed the way I live it.

"What was in the coffee?" I ask.

"A massive overdose of sleeping pills. Craig thought it would help sell the suicide note." Ash reaches out and touches the palm tree. "I can't believe I just said that, all calm."

"Maybe you learned more about yourself on this trip than just that you're adopted."

"Maybe." He looks at me, and the focus comes back into his face. "How about you? I know your husband died on a boat, and now there's this murder on a boat, because of another death on a boat. That has to be bringing up some old feelings."

"That's true. But this whole thing has helped me disconnect my love of the ocean from the unfairness of Kevin's death."

Ash says, "Thus helping you to move on. Do you care to comment on your relationship with Detective Romero, and the kiss you two shared yesterday?"

Really? After all of this, and Ash is right back to focusing on what he's going to write in his blog. "Is anything with you ever off the record?"

"Generally, no. But you did save my life, so this one time, I'll give you a pass."

I glance in the direction of the library. "Off the record? It was a very good kiss. And Arlo – he really surprised me on this trip. I'm very confused right now, and I don't know the status of my relationship with Arlo – or with Logan."

"Interesting," Ash says. "I'm going to have to keep an eye on that development."

Great. I never should have opened up to him.

"Seriously, though, Koerber." Ash turns to squarely look at me. "Thank you. You risked your life for me. I don't have a ton of people in my life who would have been willing to do that."

"Don't worry," I tell him. "You'll be getting my bill – my phone bill."

Epilogue

It's been a week since I stepped off of that cruise ship and back onto dry land. And it has been a busy one, with the expected gawkers coming to look at the new book, and to ask me what it was like to look down the barrel of a gun – again.

Today, we're doing the demo, which had been scheduled for the last full day of the cruise. Since so many people who had been on the ship were actually Galveston locals, it makes sense to offer to let them stop by the shop and check out what they had missed. I had ordered a number of cacao pods for the event, and I saved one to cut open today, even though it's not going to be the freshest at this point. The pod looks like a red and yellow Nerf football, and several people have already expressed interest in learning more about it. We have the tabletop equipment all set up, so that we can let attendees participate in making a batch of chocolate, hands on.

Imogen comes in the front door. She is holding a lidded basket.

Logan is in the shop today, and he's wiping down the tables in our café area. He gestures at the basket. "Whatcha got there?"

Imogen says, "We want to do tea bag and honey jar favors for the wedding. I have samples of fourteen varieties of honey we're supposed choose from – only I can't tell much difference between them. I thought you guys might be able to help."

"Tea and honey," Logan says thoughtfully. He turns to me, "Fee, what happens if you try to sweeten chocolate with honey?"

Logan is still exploring flavor combinations, with the idea of creating his own bar for the shop – but he hasn't come up with anything he's happy with yet. Given the level of his perfectionism, he may never get there. But at least he seems to be enjoying the opportunity to experiment.

I tell him, "There are some delicious bars made with honey, from other chocolate makers. I've never tried working with it, personally."

Though I did do something new, for a special edition bar honoring Satchmo. I've incorporated brown sugar and coffee to create a rich, decadent limited-edition bar.

Autumn is at a table in the corner, with her laptop. She's spent a lot of time at that table over the past couple of days. She's refusing to give any details, but I think she's working on a new book. Drake keeps stopping by and bringing her gumbo or sandwiches. It's sweet. Their relationship not only survived the dive into Autumn's past – the shared experience seems to have strengthened it.

While Imogen is still setting out her honey jars for us to sample, Arlo comes in. He promised to be here, front and center for my demo. Arlo seems serious about that kiss. And Logan is still playing it cool. I'm going to have to make some decisions relatively soon, but today I'm just happy to have both of these guys in my life. I hope I can figure out what I want for my future without losing one – or both – of them as friends.

Arlo asks, "So how is that new glass case working out?"

We both turn to face it. All five books are neatly displayed, with the three volumes of *Emma* in the center and *The Invisible Man* and *Murder on the Orient Express* flanking them on either side.

I tell Arlo, "I got a bigger case since I had to replace it anyway."

The day after the cruise, we finally found out who had been trying to steal the Christie book from my room that night. Logan and I were in the back of Greetings and Felicitations, just getting everything set up for the shop's next big order, when out front there had been a huge crash. Tucker McDougal, the author of the Lost to the Dark books, had attempted to make a smash and grab to take off with the book – only Carmen had thrown a chocolate cupcake at his head and hit him in the eye. That had slowed him down long enough for Logan to take the book back.

Tucker admitted that he is a huge Christie fan and hadn't been able to resist – even though he's never done anything as stupid as that before.

We'd agreed not to press charges as long as he paid for the damages – but Tucker is banned from Felicitations for life.

I tell Arlo, "I also bought a safe to store the books in when they're not on display. This is getting to be a problem, you know."

Arlo laughs and says, "I'm sure you can handle it."

Then he moves to take his seat for the demo.

Tiff has brought Knightley up to the shop in his crate so I can introduce him to everyone. Miles is doing video of all of this. Who knows? Knightley at the chocolate shop could go viral.

I take my bunny up to the front of the room, so everyone can see him before we get started. I tell my audience, "This little guy is the main thing I have that bridges my old life in Seattle, with my new one here, in my hometown."

Knightley wiggles his little bunny nose and hops over to start chinning my shoe. A few people on the front row laugh. Arlo beams at me.

Ash, who has taken the seat next to Arlo, takes a picture. He turns the camera around to show me smiling, leaning down to pet the rabbit that is the logo of my company. "You can have that one for your Insta."

"That sounds perfect," I say. Then I look at the people who have come here, despite everything that happened on that cruise, to learn. I ask them, "Who's ready to make some chocolate?"

ACKNOWLEDGEMENTS

Special thanks to Jael Rattigan of French Broad Chocolates in South Carolina, who has consulted extensively on this series. And to Kevin Wenzel of Wiseman House Chocolates whose feedback on tempering was invaluable in this book. And to Sander Wolf of DallasChocolate.org, who put me in touch with so many experts in the chocolate field.

I'd also like to thank Kathryn McClatchy for sharing her knowledge of service and therapy dogs. Thanks to Stacie Jefferson for the valuable input, edits, encouragement and general love of dogs, with all the pics of Obie over the years. And Cassie Koerber for the insight and detailed proofread.

And of course, thanks to Jake. We just celebrated our 25th anniversary, as even after all that time, he's still supporting my art and being my biggest cheerleader. I love how he brings up references to my books in casual conversation, just like we were talking any other work of literature or film. He's also the one doing the practical side of our books: reading the manuscript umpteen times, and doing all the formatting things to make this thing happen. He always keeps me going, even when things are stressful.

And thanks to my agent, Jennie, for her input on this series, and her encouragement to keep moving forward.

And for this series especially, I'd like to thank both my family and Jake's. The Cajun side of both our families comes through in Felicity's family in the books. For this one, I especially want to thank my mom and dad. Like a certain character in this book, I'm also adopted. Which makes some of what that character is saying personal to me. My parents have always taught me that family is what you make it, and that love can bridge almost anything.

Thanks to James and Rachel Knowles for continuing to sharing their knowledge of bunny behavior (as well as videos of their ADORABLE bunny – Yuki pics will always make my day).

I'd also like to thank Cassie (again), Monica and Tessa, who are my support network in general. I don't know how I would have gotten through this year of social isolation without you three.

And lastly, thank you all, dear readers, for spending time in Felicity's world. I hope you enjoyed getting to know her. Her fourth adventure will be available for you soon.

Did Felicity's story make you hungry?

Visit the Bean to Bar Mysteries Bonus Recipes page on Amber's website to find out how to make some of the food mentioned in the book.

AMBER ROYER writes the CHOCOVERSE comic telenovela-style foodie-inspired space opera series (available from Angry Robot Books and Golden Tip Press). She is also co-author of the cookbook There are Herbs in My Chocolate, which combines culinary herbs and chocolate in over 60 sweet and savory recipes, and had a long-running column for Dave's Garden, where she covered gardening and crafting. She blogs about creative writing technique and all things chocolate related over at www.amberroyer.com. She also teaches creative writing in person in North Texas for both UT Arlington Continuing Education and Writing Workshops Dallas. If you are very nice to her, she might make you cupcakes.

www.amberroyer.com Instagram: amberroyerauthor

CPSIA information can be obtained
at www.ICGtesting.com
Printed in the USA
LVHW050321140222
711073LV00009B/360